girl
walking

backwards

st. martin's griffin ⚕
new york

girl
walking

backwards

bett williams

Permission to use the lyric from "Teeth" by Kristin Hersh is gratefully acknowledged by its author and Billy O'Donnell.

Design by Michaelann Zimmerman

Library of Congress Cataloging-in-Publication Data

William, Bett.
    Girl walking backwards / by Bett Williams. — 1st ed.
        p.   cm.
    ISBN 0-312-19456-0
    I. title.
    PS3573.l44747G57 1998
    813'.54—dc21   98-21574
                                                              CIP

10 9 8 7 6 5 4 3 2

Acknowledgments

For their support and help in making this book happen, I'd like to thank Oona Bender, Joanna Hurley, Anna Gallegos, Sarah Rutigliano, Barry Graham, L. B. Williams, Virginia Williams, and Michelle Falvey.

for oona

This hairdo's truly evil, I'm not sure it's mine.

—Kristin Hersh, "Teeth"

one

runaways are romantic. The girls are waiflike with dyed
ratty hair and baggy pants. They usually own a stray dog of the
mutt variety and drag it along by a rope, plopping down in front
of storefronts to beg for money from passersby. They're a mess. It
is likely they'll charm you, make you think you're their best friend
and savior only to end up using you and then they'll disappear.
That's why they're romantic. They're there and then they're gone.
Romance is always about people appearing in a flash out of nothing or people who are there and then suddenly are not. A magic
trick.

It was a fantasy I had for a long time. I find the girl behind
the Dumpster, half dead. I pull her into my arms and try to love
the life back into her. She starts crying. She lets her pain come out
all over me and I take it into my heart. A heroic thing, I guess, my
runaway fantasy. Of course, fantasies have no smell so there is no
body odor or stale cigarette aroma and in my imagination the
girls never call me "poseur" and ask for ten dollars like in real life.
They're always pretty, tough on the edges, and mysterious.

A therapist once told me the runaway girl was really me,

that I wanted to save myself. Whatever. So where do we go from there? If everything you dream is just you, where is the world in all of it?

if you wanted, you could do community service instead of Study Hall. It was written in small letters at the bottom of the weekly school newsletter that nobody read. They didn't really want us to know, more paperwork for them. I only saw it because I read everything—cereal boxes, random flyers found on sidewalks, any kind of magazine. Compulsive reading is a symptom of having no social life.

Other than hanging out with my boyfriend, my life had no real events, nothing that could be organized into any kind of plot. Despite schoolwork and volleyball, it seemed like I had more free time than anybody else I knew, time that loomed ominously, void of phone calls and over-the-top teen activities like sliding down hills on blocks of ice and stealing mascara from Wal-Mart. At sixteen, I was already looking through the classified ads for volunteer jobs. I considered working at a soup kitchen but my basic laziness prevented me from stopping by. Any kind of community service would have to involve some selfish interest on my part.

The runaway shelter was only a few blocks away from my house. The stucco building with the brown gravel roof had an air of mystery and heartbreak. I was always walking by it slowly, trying to see inside the dark one-way windows. No one ever came in or out. I always wanted to go inside but was too afraid, fearing it might be some sleazy back-door operation run by Scientologists. The newsletter gave me an excuse to drop in under the guise that I was looking for a volunteer job to get school credit.

Thinking about working there, my runaway fantasies took on a whole other dimension—holding a girl down on a cot while she convulsed and gagged from heroin withdrawal, her hand in mine as the memories of incestuous torment came flooding in on her again, stopping fights, spaghetti dinners followed by chores, the inevitable bonding. Moments of tenderness.

i skipped volleyball and went down to the shelter after school. I walked up the stairs into the building, nauseous with nerves. Inside, it looked like the place where my mom picked up Meals on Wheels during her brief interlude with volunteer work. The carpet was worn through and smelled like dog pee. The fresh paint and posters promoting safe sex didn't cover up the water stains on the walls. I went down the hallway and knocked on a hollow-core door. A man wearing an African mud-cloth jacket greeted me. He looked about thirty, with long blond curly hair.

"How are you doing today?" he asked. He looked familiar, like he might have been one of Mom's friends from her personal-growth workshops.

"Fine," I said.

He didn't say anything else. He looked at me with such an unflinching stare, all I could do was stare back at him like a frightened rabbit. I told him I was interested in helping teens with drug problems and kids who lived in abusive families. I was curious about their volunteer program and explained that I had some experience in counseling. His stare made me feel like I was required by him to speak from the very depths of my soul, like he could catch me in a lie if I wasn't careful. He gave me an application to fill out. I took it to the waiting room and answered the questions in pencil using a copy of *Psychology Today* magazine to support the page. Address—age—hobbies. I went back inside his office and handed it to him.

"Sit down," he said, looking at me from head to foot and

back up again, taking interior notes. "Why do you want to work with runaways?"

I said something about wanting to help people, knowing right off it was the wrong answer. His godlike persona was making me nervous.

"What year were you born?"

"Nineteen eighty-two."

I forgot that I had written down my age on the application as being eighteen instead of my real age, two years younger. My face flushed red. He looked down at the paper and was quiet for a long time. He took a deep breath.

"Why did you lie about your age?" he asked with a pained expression.

I was more embarrassed than I should have been. Lying has never been something that comes easy for me. My whole body hurt. He kept staring. I averted his gaze by looking up at the posters of Tibetan monks on his wall.

"I don't know. I wanted the job. I wasn't sure if it was okay to be only sixteen."

"Why did you feel the need to lie?"

"I don't know."

"Are you okay? You seem afraid."

"I'm a little nervous, I guess."

"Maybe you came here because you needed something?"

I started crying. I don't know why. It seemed like anything could open the floodgates. All it took was—*the counselor stare*. I got paranoid that he was going to call my mother and report that I was disturbed, that I came into the runaway shelter seeming to need some help. The number was on the application.

"Can I have my résumé? I want to check something."

"Why?"

"Can I just have it?"

His cheeks had a pink glow, like a German. He radiated health.

4

"I need to go."

"I'd like to invite you to stay and talk. It seems like a lot is going on for you right now. What's your home life like?"

"I really need to go."

"But it seems like you—"

"You don't know me."

I stood and took my application from his desk and walked out of the office, tears streaming down my face. My walk turned into a run. My lungs were bursting but I didn't stop until I got to a park where no one could find me. I wasn't sure if he had the right to arrest me or what. It was a runaway shelter. I'd acted like a psycho.

i ended up volunteering for Planned Parenthood because it was the only organization that really dealt with teenagers' right to privacy. They fight hard to make sure kids have access to abortions without having to get permission from their parents. I know firsthand what it's like have a parent find out about something they're not ready to know. It's a disaster. Parents need to be protected from the truth of their children's lives.

Planned Parenthood was suspiciously omitted from the list of community-service organizations registered with the high school. When I asked the secretary how I could get it signed up, I was sent to the Dean. The Dean asked me why I wanted to work for them. He, too, had counselor eyes, but this time I was on guard. I toughened up and said: "Teenagers dealing with those kinds of issues sometimes trust someone their own age better." Mention Planned Parenthood and any school official will break out in a sweat imagining hoards of pro-lifers picketing the school lawn, only to be pelted by condom-throwing teenagers.

The Dean, acting calm and cool, sent me to Mrs. Stanley, the Special Ed teacher who also took on the job of coordinating the community-service program. I walked all the way across campus to a metal building surrounded by dry weeds, annoyed by the fact that getting anything done in an institution means making pilgrimages to a series of ugly buildings and completing menial tasks with people who wish you weren't there.

Mrs. Stanley was sitting at her desk, wearing a skirt and jacket with bright floral patterns. Her hair was dyed midnight black, presumably in an effort to be punk. In fact, everything about Mrs. Stanley was about effort. When she spoke, she broke into a sweat. She had gigantic Popeye forearms which looked like they were pulling weight even when they were hanging limp on top of her desk. She was a church lady without a church. She wanted to do good.

"Why do you want to do that?" she said loudly when I presented her with my idea. She took a sip of coffee and fumbled through a stack of papers in a seeming panic. I told her about my interests in peer counseling in a mousy, barely audible voice. The air around her was singed with a cold coffee smell that contributed to an atmosphere of tension, like she could self-destruct at any moment.

"It's going to take some effort. Write me a proposal and tell me exactly what you are going to be doing, where exactly your efforts are going to be focused. Get it signed by the head of the organization, drop a copy by the Dean's office and one to me. Each copy needs to be signed by both parents."

It took me a solid week of office-hopping during Study Hall to get my proposal put through. It turned out that Planned Parenthood didn't even have a peer counseling program, only a peer education program run by an enthusiastic man named Don. Three people signed up and we had to meet in the evening every Tuesday and Thursday at his apartment on Johnson Street.

The night of the first training I arrived fifteen minutes early. I knocked and a tall stocky man with brown hair answered the door, wet from the shower. Music was blaring and something was cooking on the stove. I thought I was at the wrong house.

"You must be Skye," the man said. I blushed, not knowing why.

"Yes. Is this the seminar?"

"I don't do seminars," he grinned. "This is the peer counseling program if that's what you're looking for. I'm Don. Come on in and I'll get you a Coke. Make yourself at home. I was just making dinner. Are you hungry?"

"No. Thanks anyway."

I walked inside reluctantly, fully aware that I had made the wrong decision and was going ahead with it anyway. I tried to relax on his black leather couch while he brought me a Coke and went into his bathroom to take care of further hygiene issues. The smell of hair gel and deodorant wafted down the hall. I stared at his exercise equipment and extensive record collection while he talked to me from the bathroom.

"Have you ever rock-climbed?" he asked.

"No. I don't like heights."

"Rock-climbing is awesome. I should take the group out sometime. It's a great way to build trust."

One thing that wasn't building trust was the fact that I was alone in an apartment with a strange middle-aged man whose living room was filled with graphs of the human orgasm and diagrams of penises and vaginas propped up on easels. Above the fireplace was a signed photo of Glenn Frey from the Eagles—*Hey Don, what a summer, love Glenn.* The apartment smelled like athletic clothes and pot. He closed the bathroom door and I heard the deep, almost melodic sound of his peeing. My crotch contracted, like when I see blood. He came back out to the kitchen and wiped down the Formica counters with a sponge.

Don was a very casual guy. He wore shorts, a T-shirt, and the kind of sandals you can only get in serious sporting-goods stores. His legs, arms, and neck were covered in a thick mat of black hair. Unlike most adults, he didn't try to pretend like he was

7

my therapist or a big brother. In fact, he acted like we were on a date, asking me what I wanted to drink and offering up trivial bits of information to discuss. I couldn't tell if he was simply trying to treat me like an adult or if he was just acting like some adult version of a teenager. Whatever his position, it made me nervous. After a half an hour went by, I was beginning to think I'd made some treacherous mistake when two others arrived, knocking on the door.

Gabe was a frail and wan neo-hippie boy who smelled like baby food and had hair as thin and white as an angel's. Tracy was a brash, straight-A student type who began talking immediately about her older boyfriends. She dumped the one that was forty and was now dating a mere twenty-eight-year-old. I got the sense she might have dated Don. They had this way of ignoring each other as if they'd been there, done that. I wondered what kind of losers' club I'd signed up for.

We spent half the evening talking about music and movies. Don became animated when he described action sequences. He was like a little boy. He wanted to be our friend. Badly.

After stuffing ourselves with tortilla chips, salsa, and Coke, and after listening to a particularly worshipped Jimmy Page guitar solo on his stereo, he began the course. First item—the human orgasm.

"You already know most of the stuff, the sperm-and-egg stuff; everybody knows that stuff, we don't want to insult people's intelligence here. We'll tell them about sex, real sex. We'll tell them about diseases, how you get them, how you prevent them. But first we have to talk about what sex *is*."

He had this slack-jawed California way of wrapping his mouth around a word that made it impossible to take him seriously. He pronounced the word sex with two syllables. *Se-ax*.

Don was an expert in graphs, charts, and xeroxed copies. Over the course of the evening, it didn't take long for my stack of xeroxed diagrams of genitalia to grow thick. Genitals in different states of arousal, diseased genitals, genitals stuck together, genitals with devices stuck in them and over them. That's what Don called them anyway—genitals. Gabe, Tracy, and I held siege and told him that the word made us sick to our stomach and we would all be using the terms *willie* and *beaver* from now on and he would just have to get used to it.

"Sex is nothing to be ashamed of. We like doing it but we don't like talking about it," Don said, absentmindedly snapping a condom between his fingers.

When Don talked about sex, which was obviously his favorite thing to talk about, his attitude reeked of sportiness. I found myself staring at his thick thighs swelling out from underneath his shorts, thighs that had memories of football, tennis, golf, rock-climbing, and *se-ax*. It all mixed together forming some singular essence in his casual Californian thighs. I imagined his thighs smelled like Astroturf; his nuts, fresh tennis balls. He referred to testicles as *balls* and I realized I hated that. I don't want men to call them *testicles*, either. I don't want them to call them anything. I want men to ignore their balls, leave them unnamed, therefore invisible till absolutely necessary. I learned more about balls that night than I ever wanted to know, that and obscure Led Zeppelin trivia. (The band lived in Alistair Crowley's castle.) Men's balls move and contract involuntarily even in a nonaroused state. That settled it for me, an intimate relationship with a penis was out of the question. Speaking of penises, we spent much of the training session watching Don's. We could see the shape of the tip bulging under his red satin shorts. Gabe swore he saw the outline of a large vein. When the session ended we were all sure that Don was some kind of pervert. Gabe wasn't sure who Don was going to hit on first, him or me. Although he seemed like a pretty straight guy, Gabe was wary of athletic types after a bad experience with a junior-high softball coach, also a fan of the Eagles. We

9

stood out in the driveway and said a vow that we would look out for each other and report any hairy-hand episodes that might occur.

after only four training sessions, Don told us that we were ready to be peer educators. We made it through five classic Led Zeppelin albums and the six stages of human orgasm. What else was there to know? We had the xeroxes. We had bodies. Don wasn't all that into complex details anyway; he seemed to think that talking about sex was its own reward, that it had some magical power. Talking about sex healed the world.

"It's no big deal. You know it all. Right?"

We nodded, clueless.

I was chosen to go first. I would give a presentation to the fifth-period sophomore Health class. In one hour, we were to cover sexually transmitted diseases, HIV, contraception, and Don's favorite—human sexual response.

don met me in the hallway before class started. Even though he was weighed down with cumbersome charts and graphs, he managed to give me an elated hug.

"Are you ready?"

"As ready as I'll ever be. Can't *you* do the banana thing?"

"I want you to do it. Don't be embarrassed."

If I got caught masturbating in the school bathroom by my whole English class I'm sure Don would tell me not to be embarrassed. He flashed a boyish smile. I smiled back out of habit.

"You're very pretty."

"Thanks." I looked down at the floor. I hated that he used that word—"pretty." I knew I was pretty. He could have said I was painfully beautiful. He could have said I had a great nose. "Pretty" meant he wanted to have sex with me. That's all.

"Would you like to catch a basketball game sometime? Maybe this weekend?"

"No thanks," I said, like a robot.

I walked ahead to the classroom while he followed behind, clunking. I was so angry I could hardly breathe. I knew he was a pedophile, we all knew it. It wasn't like he was trying to hide it. I just didn't know when he was going to make his first move. I was always on guard, waiting for him to ask me if I needed a ride home. We all watched him carefully, wondering who he would hit on first, Gabe or me. I felt stupid for even putting myself in such a position. I thought pedophiles had more style. They were supposed to win you over with a great irresistible charm or something. They were supposed to turn you on to Mozart and classic literature. They were supposed to buy you things. I was so insulted.

don started off the class with a lecture on HIV and sexually transmitted diseases. It was fifth period and everyone was tired, the lunchtime marijuana had worn off. This was the class to chill in, write love letters, draw, stare at newly arrived body hair. It wasn't a smart group. Smart kids knew how to get out of Health by getting their parents to write a letter. Most kids took it because it was an easy A. Unlike the people in the nerdy Gifted-and-Talented courses I always had to take, these kids were attractive, unsubtle, and sexy. Lip liner and good haircuts, adolescent boys without bad skin. Kids who are fucking. They look better. My stomach started to gurgle; I shouldn't have had three cups of coffee. Don began setting up the charts and graphs. The students might as well have been watching TV, the way they stared at him blankly, too tired and bored to even get a good laugh out of it. Don introduced me.

"This is Skye, she's in our peer education program." His hand rested on my shoulder, bothering me more than it should have. "She's going to talk to you about birth control."

Suddenly the room became electric. People sat up in their seats. The guys especially were very interested in what I was up to. I stood with a ripe banana dangling from my left hand, for a moment unable to speak.

"Um, hi. People tell you you should wear a condom but they never say how to put one on. So that's what I'm going to do." I was thinking that if someone doesn't have the dexterity and intelligence to put a condom on correctly, what in the hell are they doing having sex?

"Make sure not to use condoms that have been lying around for a long time. Don't use a condom that's been in the sun." I opened the package and took out the rubber item. "Hold it in your hand like this and put it over the tip of the penis," I said, holding the plastic circle on the tip of the banana.

"Girls, you can do this for him, too," Don said, a little too gleefully.

"Pull down and make sure it rolls down evenly as far as it will go. And that's it." I held up the smothered banana for all to see.

A few guys were elbowing each other in the back of the room. At least they had come alive.

"Do you have a question back there?" Don asked. The guys shook their heads no and sobered up.

I showed them diaphragms and sponges. I demonstrated how to use spermicidal gel. For the sake of history, I showed them an evil IUD from the days of old. Everyone finally indulged in healthy laughter when I brought out a female condom and attempted to demonstrate its use in my hollow fist. The only one in the room with a straight face was Don, who looked at me with serious concern for the plight of women and their contraceptive devices. If teenagers don't use condoms because it's not cool, our little demonstration didn't help any.

"Any questions?"

"What are you going to do with the banana?"

"Eat it after class."

Two boys enjoyed a cheap snicker. I didn't really mind.

"What kind of contraceptive do you use?" a leering jock asked. It was a question intended to provoke a titillating answer. Don looked at me, practically drooling for my reply.

"Nothing," I said. Don's half-smile drooped. "I'm not heterosexual."

Two girls in the back busted up laughing and the others looked down at their tables nervously. I saw Don out of the corner of my eye. He was utterly confused, a deep line that I had never seen before formed between his eyebrows. I had tripped Don up and most of the guys in the room could sense this. They had a kind of respect for me.

"Don, don't you want to answer some questions about your personal life?" I said.

"I don't want to interrupt you," he replied, flustered.

"You go right ahead. Educate us."

He moved slightly and knocked down a graph of the healthy orgasm that was balanced precariously on the chalk tray. He set it back up then took his place in the center of the room.

"Any more questions?"

No one said anything. They slouched in their seats, chewing on pencil erasers, staring at their own shoes. I slipped out the door just as Don was attempting to make small talk with the students, something about rock concerts and large crowds, a summer he spent touring with the Eagles. He heard me go and turned to look at me with this hurt/angry look in his eyes. For a moment I was afraid of him, like he might hunt me down and catch me in a dark alley on my way to a movie.

two

mom. blond. thirty-nine. divorced. Depressed. Into
New Age and ceramics. Seeking God, preferably wealthy and not
into independent filmmaking.

The root of all evil lay in independent filmmaking. That was
where she met Dad, after all. Dad, the cause of all suffering, at
least until she found out about me.

In 1976, Steve Berringer pitched Anna Mayes his film idea
by the beer cooler at a beach party in Ventura. She thought it was
a brilliant idea and offered to raise the money for it. It was an op-
portunistic union. They had sex at the party that night in the
broom closet. I wonder why my parents tell me these things. They
got divorced after Dad's film, *Subjective View*, came out—an art film
about a businessman who lives a double life as a painter who is sexually obsessed with his models. I guess it was kind of autobio-
graphical. It was shown at an L.A. film festival and it drew a good
turnout. Someone who was running for governor came, as well as
a famous playwright visiting from New York. People hung around
for a long time drinking champagne until the place closed and the
party moved to El Nido.

They didn't have a sitter so I went along. My parents hardly ever had a sitter. They figured ten was old enough to be home alone or go along to a party. Sometimes Polly, a neighborhood girl who was bulimic, came over and took care of me, but Mom didn't like it that she always left the house in the spare car to go buy more ice cream.

I was drunk at El Nido from sips of other people's drinks. I remember Mom crying. I saw her through the window of my dad's car as we drove off, running along the rain-wet street screaming then breaking a heel. Mom says she never broke a heel and that it was a dry night with warm winds but I don't remember it that way. Dad took me to the house of a woman I'd never met before. I threw up in the bushes by the pool and slept on the couch. They divorced a month later.

mom lost it. She was a mess for months after the divorce. She was briefly institutionalized, no big deal, really. After that, she got her life together. She took up ceramics and got a job raising money for the L.A. Center for Contemporary Arts. Still, she would get so depressed she'd stay in bed for a week sometimes. She'd break her bowls and plates in fits of rage soon after she made them. I suggested she get into mosaic tilework, she could use all those pieces to do a backsplash or something. She didn't laugh. In fact, she lost her sense of humor almost the same time I hit puberty. Suddenly, in a period of only a few months, nothing was ever funny. For me, everything became ironic or sarcastic. For her, everything was traumatic or ecstatic.

She got on Prozac, which gave her some breathing space from her chronic depression. She found Matrix, an organization that put on personal-growth workshops dealing with LIFE PURPOSE. It changed her life. For almost a whole year, she took everything they offered and usually I had to come along. We did

Warrior I and II, Harmonics, Mastery I and II, Being Human, Actualization, Manifestation, and Humor. Two of the workshops were held in Jamaica, another in Pennsylvania. In Pennsylvania I got salmonella from a fast-food chicken restaurant and I had to go to the hospital for three days while Mom had an affair with Bruce, a man who said he was Mom's supervisor from another planet. He was a hulking guy who wore sandals because most shoes hurt him. He and my mom came into my hospital room every day with at least six others to chant and do energy work over my disease-infested body. They seemed evil. Bruce rested his thumbs at the top of my head and chanted to Archangel Michael while my mom and the rest of the people made toning sounds and flapped their arms around in a kind of music television interpretation of modern dance. Horrifying.

I calculated how much she spent on workshops and it comes out to somewhere around the sum of $100,000. Her dead parents had paintings. I guess she sold them.

Things got complicated when she embezzled money from the art center to pay for Harmonics II and got caught. The organization let her off easy. She just had to pay back the money and resign, but bad rumors spread around town and she needed to move out of L.A. if she wanted to have a social life. We moved to Santa Barbara because Matrix had its headquarters there. She couldn't stay sane without Matrix, she said. Santa Barbara was a more expensive place to live, so Mom had to move into a smaller house. The whole thing was a blow to her ego, though she blames her biggest descent into darkness on one particular phone call from my boyfriend Riley's mom.

riley and i met on my first day at my new school. I was standing in line to get some papers signed. Other students waited in chatty groups while I stood alone, feeling self-conscious. Riley came out of nowhere and introduced himself. Instant social life. He was gorgeous and philosophical. We liked the same music, wore the same clothes. People thought we were brother and sister. We were so perfect we made everyone sick.

My mom and Riley's mom, Heather, were never really friends. They were in the same aerobics class once. Heather didn't rat on me because she liked my mom all that much. She didn't. She did it because she had something against me. She used to tell my mom in aerobics class that she thought I was dyslexic or had some kind of learning disability because my attention span was short. She based this on the fact that I would fall asleep while watching TV at their house. She thought she was some kind of child expert because she had taught at Montessori schools all her life. Anyway, Riley told his mom about my bendable sexuality and the very next day she called my mom to vent her "concerns" for me.

I got home from school one windy day in the fall to find my mom sobbing on the bed.

"What's the matter?"

"Get out," she said with icy bitterness.

"What?"

"You freak. You liar. Get out of my house!" Spit flew from her mouth.

"What are you talking about?"

"Why do you lie to me? Heather called me today," Mom managed to say between heaving sobs. "She asked me out of the blue how I felt about you being . . . gay." She said the word *gay* as if it was some gastric outburst, then sobbed again.

"She doesn't know me."

"I'm the one who doesn't know you."

"You know me."

"No, I don't. I don't know you at all. You're a stranger." As if it was the most corny moment in the worst *After-School Special* she asked, "Are you a lesbian?"

"Maybe, yeah. Actually, I'm bisexual, I think. Whatever. What's the matter with you? It's no big deal."

Then I witnessed Mom just break into pieces. It was old pain. It had a smell. All the parts of her that were hidden, secretly anguished, and unfulfilled came bursting up to the surface like some monster pimple. Seeing Mom in such a state sent me into shock. I saw Mom at different ages, as a teenager, as a young adult, in her prime trying to be glamorous. All her pain was a black hole full of sludge and she was putting it all on me. I knew right then not to take it personally, she'd gone insane. I thought she would snap out of it eventually. But I was mistaken.

She came in and out of my room, yelling at me all through the night. She ripped pictures off my wall. She picked up my copy of *Vogue* 'zine and screamed, "What is this, your *Playboy*?"

Her image of me was so sordid. I tried to ignore her until it just became too much to take. About four in the morning, I calmly walked into the living room and in one swoop knocked a long row of stacked CDs off the shelf with my hand. The cases made quite a racket as they split apart and cracked. Mom's CD collection always pissed me off. She just bought whatever was shown on television.

"Why did you do that?"

"I don't know. You're making me crazy. You have to calm down. I can't stand this."

"*You* can't stand this! Do you know what you've done to me? Do you know?"

She got down on her knees and started picking up her CDs—half of which were lesbian contemporary-rock singers. What a hypocrite. I didn't say anything. I went back into my room. It just didn't make sense. Mom was countercultural. A vegetarian. I wouldn't have expected her to act like that in a million years.

The next morning she wouldn't talk to me. I sensed her venom before I even woke up and decided to pick up a muffin on the way to school instead of making a bagel in the kitchen. That became ritual. Mom's mood didn't change.

returning from my planned Parenthood fiasco, I hoped with all my heart that Mom wasn't going to be home. Unfortunately, her car was in the driveway and the front door was ajar. I didn't want to talk about anything. If she was sitting in the kitchen, she would definitely want to talk.

She looked up from her book when I walked in the door. She was highlighting certain passages with a neon-yellow pen, an act that gave her great satisfaction. For a moment she looked like a schoolgirl, then morphed into the thirty-something woman she was—with all her excessive pride in self-education. I put my backpack down on the floor and started heading toward my bedroom.

"You don't have to go straight to your room."

"I have homework."

"I'm not going to bite your head off."

"Are you sure?"

"You don't have to be curt with me. That's unnecessary."

It took every ounce of energy in my body to sit down at the kitchen table with her. I figured that sitting there for ten minutes would satisfy her need for bonding time. Maybe she wouldn't lecture me.

"So what did you do today?"

Needless to say, I didn't tell her that a pedophile had made a pass at me and I had come out to the sophomore Health class. She might have asked why I turned down a date with such a nice man just because he was middle-aged.

"So you're reading Deepak Choprah?" I said, thinking it was an innocuous topic.

"We're reading it in Group. The people in Group have helped me a lot."

"Really?"

"It's like I've found a long-lost family. It's really uncanny the way we all came together, like it was meant to be. They remind me all the time that I can't change you. That I have to give it up to a higher power."

"That sounds so Christian."

"I think Deepak is Hindu. Anyway, 'higher power' is really an AA term."

She started talking about chakras in a lecturing tone, never pausing long enough for me to comment. Her face became fierce as she talked about Polarity.

"The male body has a positive energy and the female body has a negative energy. The two come together and form a whole. It's a magnetic cosmic process, it's a celebration of universal life. People of the same sex have the same charge so there is no coming-together of two people creating a whole."

"People aren't refrigerator magnets."

"It's a subtle energy field. It can't be measured. Our times are very confusing. Men are still so unevolved and the pain of that has created confusion in your second chakra, the sense of identity is obscured . . ."

I didn't want to start a fight so I heard her out. I studied her face. Her eyes that were once full of soulful pain had become hard and distant with spiritual fervor. At one time she looked like a sailor's girlfriend, an only slightly washed-out blonde who wore her sex appeal on the surface along with her dubious sanity. Watching Mom talk in the kitchen that day, she looked like a stern and unbending principal who can't change the rules even if they don't make any sense. Getting herself together did not look good on her. Who had Mom become? I would have told her to go see a therapist but she was already seeing one, Dr. Walker, who she had a crush on. He was the one who started her on Prozac. She was less depressed, but her personality had become cold and industrious. She still wanted to change me. No longer displaying symptoms of mental illness, she behaved like a member of a cult.

"So what do you think? You know it's true, don't you? I mean we're created as male and female bodies for a reason."

"Maybe I'm a man in a woman's body."

"But you're so beautiful, you're so feminine if you'd get out of those jeans for one second. Tell me, honey, honestly. Did anyone abuse you? Did your father do anything to you? We did so many drugs back then. It's all a blur."

I just wanted to shut her up, put a towel down her throat, and tie her to the refrigerator. Why couldn't she just be a normal mom and tell me I was going to burn in hell? The tawdry sexual-abuse stuff made me feel dirty.

I told my mom I would give my chakras some serious thought, which gave me permission to go to my room. I had to pick a topic for my English term paper, most likely it was going to be something on Virginia Woolf. I'd been in English Lit for a whole year and Mr. Tenasky hadn't presented one female author. Virginia Woolf was a glaring omission and it gave me no choice. I looked through the books I checked out from the library. One was about Virginia Woolf's experience with incest and how it shaped her personality and her writing. One of the inside photos fascinated me. It was of Virginia and her uncle. She stood stiffly in a lace dress while he put his arm around her thin shoulders as if he owned her. He was so smug and casual.

I tried to focus on a term-paper topic but couldn't get Mom's voice out of my mind, her speech about a positive and negative soul. Male and female, plug and socket, night and day, good and bad, willie and beaver. How many people thought like this? No one is just one thing. No one is straight and no one is gay. Sexuality is supposed to be no big deal anymore.

i tried to take Mom's mental lapse lightly. There was nothing I could do about it. Sometimes when it got bad I'd cry and pound my head on the wall but that just made it worse; she'd accuse me of fragmenting and threaten to take me to her psychic healer. When I pretended her anger didn't bother me, she'd say I was in denial.

Ever since her breakdown I had walked around with a rock lodged in my heart. Things just didn't feel right, like I was at the wrong place at the wrong time, like I'd forgotten something. I was scattered and when I sat still for any length of time a sadness would come upon me so engulfing that I would start to panic. I felt like if I went under I would never come back up again, so I spent most of my time with Riley. We had a way of escaping from the world. It didn't take much—a good tape, a little TV, some sex, if you want to call it that. Instant comfort.

"if you could be with the perfect girl, what would she be like?" Riley asked me after eating his last quesadilla. He wiped the grease from his lips.

"It's hard to answer that question with you picking tortilla out of your teeth."

"Sorry," he snapped. I had hurt his feelings. I never knew when I was going to hit a raw nerve with Riley. He put up with so much.

"You shouldn't eat so much cheese," I said.

"Why are you so afraid of food?"

"Cheese clogs you."

"It does not. Have they proven that? I mean, have they really opened up a dead person and found clogging cheese?"

"I can feel it, like in my pores."

"Cheese isn't bad for you."

"Whatever."

We bickered while we washed the dishes. In all the time we were together, we never cooked anything but quesadillas. Well, maybe once. We had a dinner party and invited over some friends when his mom was away. We made salmon. It was the best dinner in my entire life. We drank white wine and lay on the floor listening to his mom's vinyl records. The people at the dinner were just some of Riley's friends from the football team and one girl who happened to come along, but it was sweet. We climbed up to the roof and looked at the stars and the football-player guys talked about dying and what they would do for love and how they would feel about having to kill someone.

We watched TV while standing in the doorway, knowing that if we sat down, couch-potato syndrome would set in. We wasted too many Saturdays like that. Feeling the threat, we went to his room. I watched him from the bed while he looked at himself in the mirror, flexing his muscles and pinching at the fat around his waist. His room smelled like something alive gone dead and rotten but it was a familiar smell nonetheless and I sank into it for the feeling of safety and comfort it gave. I let my eyes rest on the various posters of rock bands and his psychedelic drawings done in watercolor. Riley came over and lay down next to me. I adjusted myself so my head was resting in his armpit that smelled strong but pure. The room lacked anything that could be described as feminine. It made me a little lonely, so I began describing my fantasy girl to him as an invocation, a way to send a charge into the stagnant air.

"She's got long black curly hair, blue eyes. She likes sweaters. Her sweaters smell like her sweat, perfume, and the ocean. She's really feminine but she's got these intense hawk eyes, full lips. I don't know. I imagine her so clearly it's as though she's real but I can't really describe her."

"Try. Just make it up." Riley pulled my shirt up over my breasts, a gesture no more surprising than his flipping the quesadillas.

"I can't talk when you do that."

"Yes, you can. What do you want from her?" He sucked my right breast and kneaded the other with his hand. It was slightly annoying, though beneath my irritation was pleasure, pure and simple.

"I just want to meet her, I want to kiss her."

"Where would you meet her?" he said, my breast in his mouth muffling his speech.

"I don't know. She'd just be in my class. She'd ask to borrow my pencil or something. We'd get to be friends. We'd be in love but we wouldn't say anything till we'd find ourselves accidentally touching."

"Where?"

"Outside."

"Then what?"

"I'd hold her hand and bring her fingers to my mouth and kiss them, then I would feel embarrassed for a minute, thinking I'd ruined everything. That's when she would touch my cheek and turn my face to hers and we'd kiss."

Riley was already down between my legs licking me, my jeans at my ankles.

"What next?"

"I can't talk when you do that. Don't make me."

"I wish I could be in your mind right now."

I went deep inside myself to a place where I could be alone with my imaginary lover. She was overused and fading, an angel put together with pieces of my history, movies, books, the gestures of strangers. Each time I thought of her there was something new—the smoothness of her forehead, her eyebrows just a little overgrown. She might bite her nails, an otherwise perfect girl, but she feels too much so she bites them. I thought of those fingers, strong but bitten-down and that was what took me, what grabbed my heart and made her real for me. Falling into that, I let my breath and the movement of my hips take me along the familiar hills and valleys of a definite climax. I was getting good at that.

I came hard in Riley's mouth. My spirit orgasmed into oblivion in the house of some ghost. Split apart. A short moment of frustration melted into sadness. Then a friendly feeling came, gratitude for Riley in my life; then again, who couldn't appreciate a sex slave? Riley came back up and kissed me on the mouth.

"Do you like the way you taste?"

"Oh, shut up."

Riley situated himself against a pile of pillows. He licked his palm and I watched him jerk off. I liked that, being able to relax and watch, not having to do anything. He had a nice penis, just the right length—thick, with a nice knob, aesthetically pleasing. I was glad Riley stopped asking me if I wanted to fuck him, just to try it. I kept telling him I hadn't even been with a woman yet, being with him would seem like some kind of defeat. You don't have intercourse with someone for the first time as a booby prize. After many plot twists and subtle nuances approaching epic mall-movie grandeur, Riley came, taking note as usual of how far his sperm shot.

"That was far."

"Past your nipples."

"You're turning red."

"I got embarrassed for a second."

"You? Nothing embarrasses you," he said. "You're the least shy person on the planet."

He grabbed a sock, wiped himself with it, and dropped it onto the floor along with a few other sacrificial socks that lay stiff and victimized on the floor. I wondered how many women knew how men treated their socks, the sordid history behind the crusty ones poking out from under the bed.

three

gate english was an advanced course comprised of mostly
white jocks, hip geeks, and pampered rich girls set on a college ca-
reer. There was the occasional genius that came out of nowhere.
Sam was that, a funny skinny guy whose parents ran a deli. They
were obsessed with him becoming a lawyer. He had every nervous
habit you could imagine and some you couldn't. For instance, he
ate the wire used for sandwich-bag ties. We sat next to each other
and passed notes, bonding out of our unspoken outsider status.
Maybe it was the fact that we were simply middle class instead of
rich or maybe it was just our sick sense of humor that made us
friends. If you ask almost anyone, they'll tell you they are an outsider.

GATE stood for Gifted-and-Talented English. I don't know
who decided I was gifted and talented. The class was on my computer printout, so I took it. If you weren't in it, it meant you didn't
want to go to a good college. Parents took GATE very seriously.
If someone didn't get in the class based on skill, I am sure panicked
parents showed up on Mr. Tenasky's doorstep with checkbooks
and cherry pies. Sam and I decided that GATE really meant Good
Anglo Training Experience.

Mr. Tenasky did the job our parents wouldn't do. He made us terrified. He talked about the SATs constantly and invited reps from Harvard and Yale to come and talk to the class about their programs. College must have been the high point of his life because he got teary-eyed as he reminisced about rugby games, finals, and fraternities. I had a hunch he was painting a false picture. College had changed since his times. College today is just high school with beer.

"You're going to be writing a college-level term paper, not a report. You need to have a theme, an idea that you come up with yourself. Yes, children, you are actually going to have to have an idea. You're going to write introductions and conclusions. You're going to write outlines." He rolled up the sleeves of his striped shirt. We all felt our weekend plans dissolve into visions of crumpled-up paper and White-Out, library books spread out over the kitchen table. I felt sick. Brad, Justin, and Steve, the inseparable trio of smart jocks, were seriously taking notes. I'd never seen them without their smug and sarcastic expressions; this worried me. I was actually going to have to work.

"I asked you to come up with a possible topic. If you haven't gotten one by now, I'll suggest one and I'll tell you now it would be really fascinating to see a paper on *Beowulf* this year." The whole class groaned except Sam. Sam actually liked *Beowulf*.

"I'm doing something on Virginia Woolf," I said when it was my turn.

Mr. Tenasky scrunched up his forehead. " 'Something'?"

"Um, something about Virginia Woolf and madness."

"That is not an idea. You have to have an idea."

"An idea?"

He stared at me. I saw Sam out of the corner of my eyes, drawing a picture of crazy eyeballs.

"An idea," I repeated.

"Yes."

A bomb had already gone off in my brain, scattering my thoughts. I kept talking anyway. "Um, there are themes of madness in her different books. Um, she dealt with it with themes like androgyny in *Orlando,* the torture of childhood in some of the other books like *The Waves.* Um, memories kept coming back and she couldn't resolve everything. She drowned herself. There's all this water imagery in a lot of her books." I knew I wasn't coherent but I kept talking anyway.

Mr. Tenasky interrupted. "What books are you reading?"

"*Orlando, To the Lighthouse, The Waves,* and some biographies."

"Fine," he said with fatigue. "Stick to the texts, though, the fiction texts."

When the other students presented their topics, he drilled them endlessly on specifics. He talked to Sam about Chaucer for a whole fifteen minutes while Sam was drawing on his knee under the table. He let me off easy, probably because he didn't want me to embarrass myself any further. He wrote me off as being stupid. I just wasn't explaining it well under pressure. Virginia Woolf and madness. Why wasn't it an idea? Sure it's not a theory, but isn't madness an open-ended question to be explored more than resolved? She drowned herself in a lake, okay? There's reason to believe she left clues in her writing as to why, some kind of map to the source of her suffering. There. An idea.

having volleyball after gate English made my life an ego-crushing obstacle course. After Mr. Tenasky's class, we slouched away with an anxious feeling of impending doom, then I had to face Bob, who blew his whistle more than he spoke, and even though he didn't have the demeanor of a retired general like Mr. Tenasky, he was no less sadistic. In some sense he was even worse because he would make us run steps and watch us with such a casual laid-back attitude as our lungs busted and calves burned.

He was a Zen sadist. When I failed and had to stop and rest, instead of yelling for me to get going, he just looked down at his feet and said, "Skye, I'm really disappointed in you."

There were four of us who at different times wore the title of worst on the team. We'd always get to play at the start of the game, then get taken out early when we inevitably started losing points. I had joined the team kind of on a whim, because I was new at school and I wanted to make friends. I almost chose tennis, but I really wanted to do a team sport. I'll just say it, I joined because the volleyball girls are beautiful. They're nice, too, not snobby like the tennis players, more into just hanging out than the basketball girls, and softball just wasn't my thing at all. Nobody knew anyone on the softball team. They were thick-thighed emotional girls on the lower field, red-faced from alcohol and budding lesbian love. They got into fights. I was afraid of them. The volleyball girls were smart and levelheaded, this made being a bad player all the more miserable. I dreaded every point. Getting ready to serve, a team member would always be chanting, "Come on, you can do it!" Lorri was good at this. She looked at me with all the hope she could muster, "Come on, Skye, you got it!" Then I'd hit the ball into the net or something and I'd see a flame of irritation flicker in her eyes then disappear. She'd look at me with a cool politeness and say, "It's okay, Skye." She was so nice. Why did I have to suck?

Before the torment of volleyball class began, I hung out in the locker with Lorri, Tara, and Nina. They had been friends a long time, way before I joined the team. I'd gone to the movies with them once or twice. They were the closest thing I had to real friends aside from Riley.

"I want a horse," Lorri said.

"Why?" Nina asked.

"I've always wanted a horse."

"They are a lot of work."

"Everybody I know who has horses does crystal meth," Tara said.

"Everybody you know does crystal meth anyway."

"Have you ever done it?"

"No, but my brother does," Lorri said. "It's totally his scene, when he's home all he does is tweak and play Nintendo. I'm like, 'Jimmy I want to watch TV,' and he's like, 'If you don't leave I'm going to hit you, I swear I am.' He gets so violent when he's tweaking."

"Has he ever hit you?"

"Of course, but I'm worse. I like, hit him with a brick once, but that was when he was five."

"Shhh, it's Bob."

"Two minutes!" Bob yelled into the cavernous locker room, interrupting the story that was blowing up my illusion of Lorri as the princess of purity. Her wholesomeness seemed like it oozed out to the very corners of her family tree like she was a descendent of a clan of Jesuit dairy farmers from Wales. Luckily Bob didn't hear our conversation; we might have gotten another *Don't ruin your life with drugs, you can be anything you want to be if you just put your mind to it* speech. He seemed to think we were all perched on the edge of delinquency, which maybe we were, but we were still some of the cleanest kids in in the whole school.

I liked Lorri's style, the way she wore her T-shirt and shorts. Nina was always trying to look like a raver so she thought her clothes had to be huge. It just made her look dorky, she was so thin and white with such strange red hair. Tara didn't really care about her clothes. It seemed she wore whatever her mom bought her at the mall on some shopping spree where they drank frozen coffee and bought clothes for the whole semester just like in junior high. Lorri wore clothes like an adult, a real athlete, clean and airy. There was something about her body that was so . . . there. She was the only girl on the team with serious biceps and shoulder muscles that rippled, yet she wasn't huge or anything, just tall. She wore her long black hair tied back in a ponytail. She was unaware of her gorgeousness. No one ever thought of her as

31

"Lorri, the pretty girl" but her natural beauty made us all treat her with a certain carefulness and formality, like it wasn't beauty she possessed but just plain goodness that we didn't want to offend. Guys were put-off by her wholesomeness, girls wanted her friendship. There was something about her mouth, the way her upper lip curved up on one side like a sneer and stayed that way. It was unbelievably sexy. Guys are so stupid, their ideas of beauty so generic. If someone fell in love with Lorri that lip would drive them crazy, they'd have to cut an ear off for that lip. The bummer about Lorri was that she was unapproachable, she was into sports to the exclusion of anything else.

We practiced serves that day. I was relieved because I didn't have to face losing points for my team in another practice game.

"The fist, not the wrist!" Bob yelled. He came over to show me how to do it, holding my wrist and bending my palm up into the correct position. Being singled-out as the person in the whole class to receive his stern and nervous attention was humiliating but no one else seemed to care. He left me alone after that, ignoring me for the rest of the class, which was fine with me. Lorri, Nina, Tara, and I stood around till our turn to serve came up, chatting about things like shoes and Lorri's trip to Canada the summer before. We practiced outside on the basketball court instead of in the gym. There was a light breeze and the sprinklers were watering the football field nearby, making us damp with mist. The air smelled like mown grass and wet cement. I realized they might not mind me hanging around. Knowing that was enough to make my body feel strong and confident and for the first time in volleyball class I was actually coordinated and had a few good serves.

i was hoping lorri would give me a ride home but she didn't offer and I didn't ask. She went walking off with Nina. I heard them talking about the weekend they were going to spend together hiking in Red Rock and hanging out at Zuma's Electronic

Cafe. I could have asked to come along, I suppose, but if they had said no, that would have sucked. Making friends is such a formal thing. It would have been so convenient if we all drank. Puking is great bonding, holding your friend's head over the toilet seat is kind of an intimate act. Puking friends come and go, though, at least that was my experience in junior high.

I went to my locker by myself, still in volleyball clothes. I got my books and walked across the crowded campus lawn, through the parking lot full of people already starting to party near chosen cars. It wasn't right to be alone.

Full of habit and routine, I took the usual route even though I didn't want to go home. I didn't want to go anywhere except with Lorri to her car to go to wherever. I stopped and leaned against a tree, a private gesture of protest at my situation.

Across the street a girl was sitting at a bus stop alone. She had black hair pulled back in barrettes and a little ponytail on the top of her head. She wore an old black lace dress, too small, like a doll's, ripped in places. Necklaces weighed down with heavy pendants hung over her pale chest. One arm had bracelets up to her elbow. She looked like a sandbox doll abandoned by some immoral kid who cut her hair, fed her Lysol, and tossed her in the corner next to the Lego and Power Rangers. Like some *Twilight Zone* character. I imagined her eyes popping awake, haunted.

She leaned forward with her chin in her palm, very at ease with looking bored in an overenthusiastic crowd of kids walking home. She was beautiful, too, with dark eyebrows and deep-set eyes outlined in black. Her image was like sharp glass cutting into me, I rushed to the surface to meet her with an urgency bordering on hysteria. Someone get gauze and bandages. I'm falling out. She's some dream I had. She's got part of me I didn't know I needed.

I stared at her for the longest time, so much that I felt like a pervert freak. I'd seen cute girls who wore black before but she was different, more dangerous or something. I was sweating that peculiar rancid smell that comes from too much coffee, too much thinking. Introducing myself was not an option so I just pretended I was next to her across the street with my eyes and my imagination as if I had some invisible body I could just send off to do things my physical body could not. Just sitting there, she woke something up in me.

She stood and started to walk, rearranging the barrettes in her hair with one hand and holding her dress in the fist of the other. Unexpectedly, she turned and walked backwards for a moment as if to look back at a friend she'd said good-bye to. When she turned around to go forward again it was like I got caught by a fishhook, part of me got pulled forward with her and I began walking, following her down the street. Her 360, a little fairy trick, had cast a spell. After walking a few blocks I thought of turning back to avoid craziness but I didn't. She got to State Street and I still followed her, watching the back of her move through the after-school crowd. She held her left arm close to her body while her right arm swung about with her hand picking at everything from leaves, brittle branches, to her own ear. She walked past a cement wall and let her fingernails scratch against its surface, dislodging little particles. When she walked into Zuma's Electronic Cafe, I stopped and waited outside, all adrenaline and liquid fear.

I was possessed by one image. A girl in a too-small dress walking down the street, turning to walk backwards for a moment, then in two bouncy steps, back around again to continue traipsing. I fit everything I'd ever been into that gesture, all my desire, my sadness, my thoughts on God, into that one image, the most beautiful thing I'd ever seen. It could have been enough, right? It didn't have to break me open and leave me hungrier than I'd ever been. It could have been a little gift, just the right amount.

I was going to leave, I convinced myself of it, that I would just go home after that. But I didn't. My underarm sweat had saturated my shirt and the synthetic fabric was turning it into something posthuman. It was clear that I didn't have a socially acceptable expression on my face for a coffee shop—nervous and desperate, like a homeless person—but maybe no one would notice. I went inside anyway.

She was at a table with two other girls—one fat girl, the other frighteningly thin. All wearing black, they sat, one on each side of her like opposing alter egos, props for her enigmatic persona. I ordered coffee, got a weekly paper, and sat down at the one table where I could watch them without being seen.

In the span of one hour, I drank three cups of coffee. People were working on the computers that lined the walls of the cafe, clicking away in a frenzy of cold focus. A large monitor in the corner was displaying information from the Web, a snake was slowly devouring an egg on the screen.

Everyone at Zuma's Electronic Cafe seemed to know her, which disappointed me for some reason. They came up and gave her hugs. Sometimes she'd linger, still hanging on the shoulder of some boy or girl she seemed to know intimately. Being casual seemed the most strange and impossible thing. Her two friends had bad allergies or colds or something, they sneezed and snorted, their noses red. I couldn't hear their conversation, just the shrieks that punctuated the hushed mumbles.

"I don't think so!"

"Not ever!"

"He's a rapist!"

"She is so fake, I can't even handle her!"

Maybe I should have walked away. I was searching for some codes and signals but wasn't finding any. I walked close to their table to put my weekly in the stack with all the other old newspapers before leaving. She caught my eye.

"I saw you sitting at the bus stop," I said, suddenly becoming brave and stupid.

"Oh." She paused. "Yeah." She was distant and very blank,

her aura of hipness commanding silence as she practiced the sadistic law of cool.

I tried to manage a smile out of my stiff face, a little wave, then I walked out.

the coffee made me unwell, turned my blood to the lava that comes up in the throat during a liquid burp. I felt like I would never feel clean again. Walking down the sidewalk, I couldn't stop touching the oily film on my face. I'd scratch my skin and stuff would get under my nails. My thoughts turned metallic with obsessive repetition. Halfway home, I started to run fast, my backpack slamming into me with the rhythm of my feet landing on the sidewalk.

I walked in to find Mom sitting on the couch with a man I'd never seen before.

"You're later than usual."

"I went to the coffee shop."

"I want you to meet Paul. We've been waiting for you."

"I'm not psychic," I said.

Mom and Paul gave each other a knowing look.

"Paul's an astrologer friend. I gave him your chart. He has some insights I thought you might be interested in."

I could smell my own rancid body odor filling up the room from corner to corner.

"I need to take a shower. I have this paper I have to do for GATE English. It's impossible. I'm freaking out."

The man on the couch kept looking at me with a gentle smile. He wore aquamarine cotton pants and a pink golf shirt. His hair was white. He took deep, controlled breaths.

"It won't take but a minute," he said.

"I stink. I can't stand myself."

"Just sit with Paul for a while. It's not often we have guests.

He'll give you your reading and I'll give you privacy." Mom flashed me her Victim Face when Paul wasn't looking. This always churned my stomach. She wore her weakness on the surface so people would treat her with kid gloves. If that didn't work she would try rage or hysterics. I sat down on the couch, holding my arms close to my sides so my odor wouldn't waft. Mom disappeared into her room.

"Your mom is trying very hard, you know."

"Oh."

"You know that, don't you?"

"What?"

"That Anna loves you very much." He stared at me hard with his watery blue eyes. I wanted to look away but thought he might think I was being rude; after all, he was trying to channel cosmic love. I knew his type—a single guy too old to be a player with young women, turns to New Age tricks to get some power and control, to make them need him. I wanted to get it over with as soon as possible.

"You don't feel comfortable around me, do you?"

"I don't know you. I've never met you before."

"I'm just here to offer help. I have tools, that's all. I'm not trying to change you."

I sighed heavily. He was really pissing me off.

"I have your chart. You're an Aries. You're stubborn but also curious. You want to be the boss of the situation. There's a lot going on for you right now, there's a Neptune conjunction, a lot of changes, but the information is not going to help unless you want it."

"I'm just kind of distracted. I have homework. I wasn't expecting this."

"That's the Pisces moon. Your emotions are always pulling at you; you have a fear of going crazy but also a secret desire to go into those watery realms. You don't trust men, do you?" His focus was unflinching, I was caught in a high beam. Was this a yes-or-no question? I was confused.

"I don't know."

"Men frighten you, just a little. You feel like you have to be tough. Your Pisces moon needs protection, especially with the very masculine Sagittarius rising. It's very easy for you to be male. That's why you wear baggy jeans and shirts that don't show your breasts. You don't want to show your femaleness. It's not safe."

"This is how people dress. I don't know."

He smiled and chuckled to himself as though he held some secret about me. I hated him. He was so wrong about everything but I didn't have the vocabulary to argue my case. Girl walking backwards—is there anything in my chart about a girl, a crazy broken girl? I wanted to ask.

"Things are hard for you right now."

"It's just that we just moved here. It's taken a while to get used to things to meet people and stuff. What's my rising sign again?"

"Why are you looking down?"

"I don't know. I don't like being stared at." I looked up into his oily face, his eyes caught mine again.

"You're just lonely, aren't you?" he said, smiling knowingly.

I was hot at the core and kept sweating. His focus seared through my boundaries and it hurt. I started crying.

"I don't want to do this."

"It's okay, there's nothing to be ashamed about."

"I wasn't ready. I don't want to be crying."

"You're so open, that's a beautiful thing and very rare."

He was a stranger. He was all around me and inside me. I wanted to tell him to fuck off.

"Anna loves you so much," he said, and with those words my heart broke open. I tried not to breathe because I knew I would start sobbing in violent hiccups.

"You know if you don't breathe you will die. Breathe."

The sobs came anyway. Sucker. I was confused, not knowing what I was crying about. Mom came back in and knelt beside us. She met Paul's eyes in a love gaze. They both put their hands on my knee while I cried. I held my body in a tight fetal position trying to find privacy in some hidden secret place. Why had I let him do this to me? He had no right. Why couldn't I just shut myself down? Fuck.

"Tell her you love her," Paul said to my mom.

I wanted to leave but I knew the only way to get out of the nightmare situation was to play by the rules. I looked up at Mom, tears were dripping from her chin.

"I love you," Zombie Mom said, her lower lip trembling. I wanted to scream.

Instead, I said, "I love you, too, Mom."

Having to say those words chilled me on the inside but at least I stopped crying. I would be allowed to leave soon. The three of us sat holding hands. Make eye contact, take deep breaths, look loving. I was used to those situations. I just wasn't used to them being sprung on me. My head started to hurt and my own smell was stinging my nose. Didn't they mind? We stared at each other for what seemed like an eternity and I didn't even flinch, no heavy sighs, I don't even think I blinked. Paul gave my hand a little squeeze then let go.

"I really should shower."

"You do smell strong, you've let go of a lot of toxins. Remember how beautiful you are. Okay?"

"Okay."

Feeling like a rotting carcass, I walked into my room and flopped onto my bed. Girl walking backwards—had she been stolen from me by the New Age freak? What was left of me? Hand between my legs, I brought her memory back, touching my breasts, my lips. Conjuring. Ripped lace, hair pulled up, the sound of fingers scratching cement. Stinking and crying, I made myself come. Back to myself.

too tired to work on my paper, I nodded off to sleep. I woke up to find my room gray with twilight, a tinge of orange from the setting sun shone through the blue sea glass hanging from my window. There was a knock on my door.

"Yes?"

"Can I come in?" Mom asked.

"I guess."

"You guess? Can I or can I not come in?"

"Come in. Whatever."

"You got a letter from Reed."

I saw it in her hand, businesslike and cold. It was the spring of my senior year, colleges were responding to my carefully prepared applications. I had made a point of checking the mailbox every afternoon on my way back to school to avoid such letters getting in Mom's hands but I was too distracted on that day. Mom was still airy from our session in the living room.

"Thanks, Mom." I took the letter from her hand and inspected its return address printed in crisp letters.

"Aren't you going to open it?"

"Yeah." I began ripping the paper at the edge like I was watching someone else do it, like I wasn't there at all. I didn't want it to be that way. I took the paper out of the envelope.

"What does it say?"

"I got in."

"Oh my God. Oh my God," Mom gasped and put her face between her knees. Back up again, she held my face between her hands and kissed me on the cheek, staring hard into my eyes. She didn't say anything else and went back into her room. I read the letter over and over about twenty times trying to feel something till I finally mustered up some excitement. They think I'm smart. They must have liked my essay.

I thought I could hear Mom crying in the other room so I put on a loud punk tape to drown it out and read the first paragraph of *Orlando* by Virginia Woolf over and over, not able to take it in because I was so distracted. The main character was sword-jousting at the head of a Moorish Pagan, "the color of an old football," hanging from the ceiling. After reading it countless times, it suddenly struck me as the most horrifyingly racist thing I'd ever read. How could I do a paper on a woman who used phrases like the "barbarian field of Africa" without irony, just for atmosphere? Getting through the next paragraph, I realized that beloved Orlando wasn't slicing off the head of a Moorish Pagan for real, he was just imagining it. Maybe that was better.

There was a knock on the door again. Mom, obviously. She didn't ask to come in.

"Can you come to the kitchen for a minute, please?"

"Sure."

I followed her down the hall. Her body was stiff, too adult.

She sat down in the chair while I leaned against the counter. The setting sun was spilling into the kitchen from the west window, bathing Mom's ceramics and the aqua-and-yellow decor in an outrageous orange. We were on fire.

"Sit down."

I sat.

"I'm very concerned. You're very confused right now."

"I'm not confused."

"Let me finish. You don't know who you are, one day you're this, the next day you're that. You're in your room all the time. You're gay, you're not gay. You want to do English, you want to study architecture. This architecture thing, what's that? You're always in your room."

"I have homework."

"You're depressed."

"No, you are the one who's depressed, remember?"

"I saw you today in our session with Paul. I saw how hurt and confused you are."

"I was assaulted practically."

Mom tightened up, claiming her privilege of having the last word. "If you don't let me talk I'll just decide for you and college will be definitely out of the question."

"What?"

Mom went on to explain her position. She said I wasn't stable enough to go all the way to Portland to go to Reed. She said I would be influenced by so many things and, without a strong base—a support system, she called it—anything could happen.

I listened to her talk and I got the same feeling I had in the hospital bed in Pennsylvania. She was evil, she could ruin my life. She was in the process of it at that very moment. I didn't want to cry again but I did, I was just so beaten-down. She talked about a workshop she wanted me to go to and a hypnotist she wanted me to see. She told me I was repressing memories of abuse, possibly sexual molestation by some adult. She'd read books. She knew the signs. I was quiet and withdrawn and needed help. Being gay was part of my "acting out."

"And if I don't do these things I can't go to college?"

"Yes, I'm afraid so." She couldn't even look at me.

"Dad's paying for it. It's not like you can stop me."

"So you want to live with your dad? Go live with him, then."

The screaming-and-shouting match started right on cue with the mention of Dad. I got a few good lines in, most of them about how I just wouldn't go to college if I had to go see her healers. I'd move out. She always got the best of me in fights, though, by her sheer force of nature. She shrieked, she spit, she flailed her arms. Her hair seemed to tangle right before me. Her eyes seemed to cross. I guess it was kind of funny. It should have been funny but every word of it got in. Every word of it hurt: her claims that I was selfish and that I had no heart, I didn't believe it in my thoughts. But my body took her words in like I was being hit.

"So much for our cosmic living-room session."

"Oh, don't be snide with me. Why are you crying? You're not the one who's being hurt here," she said, before swallowing an aspirin with a gulp of Slim-Fast.

That fight ended at about two in the morning. All through the night she went in and out of my room with some last remark that was for her the pinnacle of realization, some epiphany full of spite and bitterness. The visits got more infrequent around midnight, then at two she put on her Balinesian music tape and after that she didn't come back in.

four

i walked to riley's house the next morning, like I always did when things got bad. He lived with his mother in a little casita by the ocean. It was a cheaply made stucco-and-drywall unit with a tar roof but it was cute like the beach houses in Baja, salt-infested and damp, but alive with the sea. The rent was unbelievably low for Montecito, the nicest area of town dotted with fat palm trees and white mansions. When Riley turned eighteen, his mother planned to move out and he was expected to take care of the $850 rent himself. Of course he could move out, too, but Riley wasn't good at taking the initiative in a time of change. He preferred to just let things happen. He would stay and work just to pay the rent even if he had to take on two or three jobs.

He was still sleeping when I arrived. He got mad when I woke him up.

"I just needed you to talk to me. I had a heinous night. Just talk. I'll listen. Say anything. Just words."

"Fine, I'm just not awake. You're too intense."

Riley held me, listened to me, yet there was something I wanted from him that he wasn't giving. It just seemed like we never really got beyond the first layer of who we were. When we were together, nothing transformed into something else. We were real, not magic.

"Leave or just ignore her," Riley said, Mr. Rational. "Go live with your dad.

"I can't just move to L.A. Plus, Dad's a freak. You know that."

"More than your mom?"

"I don't know. It's different, plus he's never offered his place. He's got the films and everything."

We kept talking. Riley touched himself under the covers. Our focus went from north to south as I did the same. Our conversation petered out organically while I started to make myself come. I had three orgasms before he came. He would always pause to watch me then resume. If I was a little mad at Riley I'd show off my multiple orgasms which usually elicited a speech from him about how women are so much more sexually advanced than men. This pleased me, especially if I was feeling insecure.

After he shot, he fell asleep and I lay in the bed staring at the delicate hairs on his arms, thinking that if I looked hard enough, something in him that was hibernating would stir and come alive. I was so bored.

Riley got out of bed way past noon. He walked naked around his room looking for a joint in the pockets of his pants strewn on the floor. He had a beautiful muscular body with a tan that always looked like he got it just the day before. He was a golden retriever in the form of a guy, loyal, loving, and beautiful. In a way, I was lucky to be with him.

"You're so slow, can't we go outside? It's a beautiful day. I've been here since ten."

"You can go out if you want. It's great you came by, but that doesn't mean I can't sleep in."

"But it's Saturday, you could at least get up and have coffee with me."

"Whatever."

I was getting claustrophobic in his room. Navy-blue plastic

blinds covered the window, dusty with the edges bent. Spiderwebs clung to the ceiling. My eyes had no place to rest in that room other than on his body. That was beautiful. I could watch that.

It was clear our relationship was getting too small for the both of us. A third party would have to be introduced and fast. Maybe we could share someone, though I knew I was too much of a romantic for that. I hadn't even told him about the girl walking backwards. Still, it would have been Riley's biggest pornographic fantasy come true. He always thought of himself as a male lesbian, wanting nothing more than to watch two women have sex.

I went into the living room and watched the nature channel—nontoxic TV. Riley came out later in wrinkled khaki pants and started making quesadillas in the kitchen. I had high hopes for that Saturday. I thought maybe we'd go surfing then go to Zuma's Electronic Cafe. Instead we watched TV till three, had more orgasms together till five, then had dinner, quesadillas again. I suggested that we walk down State Street, browse the stores, see if there was a crowd outside of Häagen-Dazs, maybe find out about a party. Riley suggested we rent a movie.

It was *Apollo 13*. We watched it on the carpet, devouring a large bag of potato chips. I was having some sort of existential-angst body-image attack while watching the movie. The chips were going to make me gain five pounds instantly if I didn't stop eating them. Heather got home in the middle of the movie and succeeded in making me feel totally unwelcome. She talked on the phone loudly while smoking a joint, ignoring me. Heather thought she was really deep, and didn't like small talk. One time she got furious with me for not recycling a soda can and I never really felt comfortable around her after that. My skin felt greasy and my blood was stagnating. I just kept quiet while watching the movie, planning to go on a juice fast the next day.

Somewhere, things were actually happening. The thought that I was left out was too much to bear. There were concerts and parties. There was sex and arrests. Social lives. Heather got off the

47

phone and passed Riley the joint. I got rip-shit stoned with them and forgot about all the potato chips I ate and how that room was just a pocket of nothing in the middle of a throbbing Saturday night.

my life wasn't going to move forward unless I stepped out. Riley called me up on Sunday morning, his voice filled with a vigor I hadn't heard in weeks, not since his big crush, Teresa, actually decided to speak to him. He had an urge to go surfing and asked me to come by. I said I'd already made plans.

I packed my backpack full of Virginia Woolf books and set up camp at Zuma's Electronic Cafe. Surrounded by hardbacks and spiral notebooks, I felt official, like I belonged. I leaned over the table and tried to work. I couldn't, of course, it's impossible to really work in coffee shops, but I made a valiant effort. *Valiant*—such a Virginia Woolf word along with *inscrutable* and *masthead*.

I picked up the weekly which I'd already read and looked at the parts I'd ignored, the letters to the editor, the garage-sale ads, a long article on the politics of the town water board. Hardly anyone was at Zuma's Electronic Cafe, it was Sunday morning, after all. I was an idiot. Everyone had hangovers and scandals but me. I was drinking coffee and trying to find the core of Virginia Woolf's madness lodged in the flowery language and aristocratic posturing of *Orlando*. I studied for about an hour, then started reading a 'zine called *Poof,* put out by a girl obsessed with Glenda the Good Witch. I was working on a crossword puzzle on *Wizard of Oz* trivia when she came in.

She was by herself. She walked up to the counter and started talking to the man making the cappuccinos.

"Where's Pooter?"

"Pooter's in San Diego."

"I have his Thumper shirt."

"He'll be back next week."

She wasn't wearing the lace dress. She had on some Victoria's Secret thing—a teddy. It was black lace and transparent enough to show her breasts. Over black tights she wore lightweight black bloomers that came in around the knees. Strands of her hair were bleached out and dyed blue. I couldn't help staring, her arms were so thin and white. She turned to go and saw me.

"Hey," she said.

"What's your name? I've been seeing you around a lot."

"Jessica."

"I'm Skye."

"That's a great name."

"It's a hippie name."

"What are you doing?"

"I was trying to get some work done but I can't. It's Sunday."

"I know what you mean. I'm so behind it's not funny anymore. I was going to look at these used shoes. I saw them yesterday. Go-go boots at the Salvation Army. You should come check them out."

"I will."

"I mean with me. You can come if you want."

"Oh. Great. I need a break anyway. Um, let me just put my books away. I guess I could leave them here."

"Whatever."

I couldn't believe my luck. She was out the door before I could get my books arranged in a neat pile on the table. By the time I caught up with her I was out of breath.

"You're in GATE English, aren't you?" she asked.

"Yes, how'd you know?"

"I just know things. I watch everything and everybody. That's what I do. I'm just a big eyeball. So you're smart."

"Not really. My mom got me in the class. She said something about my father being a graduate of Harvard, that he was saving up for my education or something."

"Your dad's rich?"

"Kind of. Not really. He works in Hollywood. He's a grip. He holds lights and stuff. He makes a lot of money, sort of."

She walked with a rhythm that made me feel instantly out of step. I watched her feet to get a sense of it. What if we ran out of things to say? I felt like a complete idiot in my jeans and T-shirt, like my mother dressed me.

"He didn't even go to Harvard. He went to UC Davis."

She ignored me and walked into a store that sold decorative items for the home like iron-and-glass candle holders, art posters, and gauzy bedroom curtains. I couldn't find her at first. Maybe she was getting a good laugh out of me chasing her around. After a frantic search, I found her by the candles.

"These are cool," she said, picking up one of the honeycomb candles and smelling it. On the top shelf was a collection of aromatherapy oils. She started unscrewing the caps and sniffing each one. "I like this one." She held it out for me to sniff. The skin on her forearm had red lines all in a row. Scars.

"You get scratched by a tiger?" I said, noticing the marks.

"What?"

"Your arm."

"Oh." She smiled and admired her arm for a moment, then suddenly became withdrawn. "Yeah, I guess so."

She disappeared to the poster section and I rushed to the counter to purchase the oil she had liked so much. Maybe I would give it to her if things didn't get too awkward. The cashier, an older woman wearing beige linen was very surprised that I actually bought something. Jessica was the kind of person that made cashiers nervous. I imagine they kept an eye on her.

I chased her through every thrift store and secondhand clothing outlet. I stood and waited outside while she got chocolate ice cream in Häagen-Dazs. I didn't want any because I felt fat from the potato chips I ate the night before. She stood eating it, contemplatively. After, she went into a record store and asked the guy at the counter about obscure punk bands and scoffed at him when he said he'd never heard of them. I thought maybe she was getting sick of me and wanted me to beat it. She ignored me, mostly. I considered leaving but every time I thought of telling her good-bye, she said something incredible.

"Culture is the only thing other than death that has the power to change you," she said, somehow escaping pretentiousness.

"But what about people? They can change you."

"They don't. Think about it. Like, let's say a teacher did something that changed you. She just gave you another way to think about the world. You can't separate that from culture, she just took you out of one box and put you in another box. No matter how huge a realization you may have, it doesn't mean anything if it's outside culture. A blue rhinoceros visits you, big deal. You have great sex, fine, but how are you going to use that? But if you get a visit from Elvis or write a brilliant song, there, that's something you can use. Angels only mean something because they're part of the rock concert called the Catholic Church. Without the Catholic Church, angels would just be these weird extras in an alternative-rock video, about as significant as a stoplight."

When she spoke like that her body became electric, like the light that fills a computer when you turn it on. She couldn't look at me. Knives danced around her. She was either a prophet or a lunatic, maybe both. A genius for sure, because when I understood her, I knew she was right.

"The imagination is geometric. It takes random occurrences and puts them into a kind of order so it looks like your life is predestined. It wants to protect you from the knowledge of death."

Maybe she read it all, got it from lyrics from a song. She was so good with words, it was more believable than all the New Age stuff my mom's friends talked about. I didn't like where it was going, though. To Nowhere. To Nothing Mattering at All.

"So you don't believe in magic?" I asked, trying to understand her depressing world view.

"Of course I do. I believe in The Force. *Star Wars*. My whole philosophy of life comes from *Star Wars*."

When she said something like that, it was accompanied by a nervous twitch, an adjusting of a barrette that deleted her seriousness and seemed to indicate she was just joking. At times she seemed irritated that I couldn't always keep up with her.

"You're like the desert, aren't you?" she said.

"Why?"

"You're airy and calm. Peaceful."

"What are you, then?"

"A tiger."

She looked right into my eyes. No one had gotten that close and so suddenly. The whole atmosphere was charged with her. She was like weather. As my thoughts plodded along the mundane and stupid, hers seemed to soar in some magical ether.

"I think that if you don't sleep, your dream life still has to express itself so it takes over your waking hours, making your actual life more like a dream. What's the longest time you've gone without sleep?"

"A night," I said, not even trying to act cool by that point.

"I've been awake for four nights."

"Just on your own?"

"Meth. It's wild. Really bad for you, though, that's why I'm so thin," she said with a hint of pride. So that's what my life was lacking. Drugs.

Gradually she lifted me out of myself and I soared with her talking and walking for a long time. We just wandered, passing some of my favorite houses. I took her five blocks out of our way to show her an austere mini-mansion that had a giant wooden statue of Saint Barbara in front of it and all these Christmas decorations that were still up. A life-size Santa-and-reindeer outfit was on the roof, lit up even in daylight, and weird plastic ducks and geese were perched everywhere. The work of some egomaniacal Republican, no doubt. We agreed it was truly sick and that the arrangement needed two inflatable fuck dolls at the entryway for a proper greeting.

Farther down the street there was an aquamarine stucco house with a Virgin Mary shrine nestled in the bushes near the driveway. We liked the people in that house and wanted them as adopted grandparents, concluding that the residents knew Virgin Mary shrines were tacky but they loved her so much they couldn't help it. Up Milpas Street, we passed the high school underneath the shelter of giant trees that grew on each side of the sidewalk. The leaves met and tangled together over the street.

"I've never met anyone like you," I said, after spending minutes mustering up the courage.

"Oh my God," she said, kneeling down by a tree. A dead bird lay in the fine sand. I saw it over her shoulder, peaceful, perfect, and very dead. It was a gray sparrow.

"Poor birdie, poor poor birdie." She cupped it in her hand and gently pet the feathers on the top of its little head. I was too moved by Jessica to feel much for the bird. I just wanted to touch her then, all dressed in black, her breasts showing through her opaque shirt. She was still the most innocent person, the most alive thing.

"We should bury it or something," I said.

Jessica started walking ahead without answering me.

"Its name is Heda," she said, looking back, no longer sad.

"Heda. Dead Heda."

"Heda's dead."

"Poor Heda."

We walked along discussing headstones and a proper burial for Heda. We came upon a convenience store and Jessica walked in, bird in hand. She got a Coke from the cooler and went to the candy aisle, stopping near the small selection of toys.

"I've got it!" she said.

She pulled something off the rack and as she came closer I could see that it was Barbie clothes, beach clothes, to be specific. She held the package between the fingers of the same hand that held the bird, absentmindedly, like the dead bird was some key-chain tchotchke. She put the package down on the counter along with her Coke. She had beautiful, strong square hands. I wanted to be the bird trapped inside.

We walked to a park just a few blocks away from downtown and sat next to the koi pond. I poked my finger in the murky water, thinking I was being brave. I thought the giant fish would bite me but they were wise and jaded and ignored me completely. She took the Barbie clothes out of the plastic wrapping and began to dress Heda. A little skirt around her waist, a pink brassiere over the bulging feathered breast, plastic sandals sticking over eensy talons. It amazed me how well the clothes fit. Jessica held Heda up for me to see in all her funeral finery. There was something so moving about the bird, something vulnerable and sad.

"Heda was a good bird. She liked the beach. She was loved by all her friends."

"She liked listening to the sound of people chatting in the park."

"She liked seeds."

"She was Buddhist."

"Really?"

"All animals are Buddhist."

We looked for a place to bury Heda but couldn't find a spot worthy of her magnificence. We concluded that she wasn't ready to be buried yet.

"But she'll start to smell," Jessica said.

"We can freeze her."

"I can't at my house. My mother's addicted to Tater Tots. She's in the freezer five times a day."

I insanely volunteered my refrigerator. What the hell. Mom

never used the freezer, only occasionally, for nonfat ice cream. I could hide Heda in the back.

"She can visit. When you come over you can bring her," Jessica said. "I gotta go." She hugged me good-bye and left. Just like that.

I stood alone, deciphering her hug, figuring out which part of her opened into what part of me, what was borrowed, given, even stolen, and what kind of future such a hug predicted.

walking home, i forgot that I left my stuff at Zuma's Electronic Cafe. I ran back and found it still on the table just as I had left it. I put the bird in the pocket of my backpack. It had the iron smell of warm blood. Lorri and Nina walked in and saw me and I was more embarrassed than I should have been, as if they could see I'd been up to something strange. They invited me to come sit with them. I did. Blushing.

I first started having a crush on Lorri in the fall, when she sat in front of me in history class, always wearing sleeveless shirts that revealed her strong arms. I stared at her constantly like a lech and was ashamed when my greasy stare once caused her to turn around during a test and ask if she could borrow my eraser. We became friends after that and my crush crept away with its tail between its legs, too afraid to risk actual rejection. "Come kayaking," Lorri demanded. For her, bossiness is a sign of real affection.

"I don't know how."

"It's easy, you have to come."

"I don't have a bathing suit."

"You can go in your jeans."

I couldn't turn down Lorri's command. If she told me to walk out in the middle of a freeway I would have gone, she had that kind of presence. I realized that although she was soft-spoken, there was something of a tyrant inside her. I liked it.

"And if I don't go?"

"You'll go. If you don't go we'll come in the middle of the night and kill your pets."

"I don't have pets."

"We'll poison the house plants."

"My mom would have an attack," I said. "She has them anyway but if the house plants died she'd probably take it personally. My mom thinks that everything on CNN is like a personal broadcast of the state of her own soul."

"My mom can't watch the news," Nina said. "She's too sensitive."

"We don't watch the news because my brother's taken over the TV," Lorri said. "He's got it hooked up to the computer. He's going to blow up something, I know it. He's like a terrorist."

"Right."

"No, I'm serious. The guy who he was putting on raves with was borrowing money from the Mexican mafia and he didn't make enough to pay him back. He's in hiding with some relative in Wisconsin and he communicates with my brother by computer."

"Scary."

"Totally. It's like he's in a gang."

They finished their coffee and we left to go kayaking. I couldn't remember a day so full of invitations. I fell from one event to the next as if I was being passed from one soft hand to another.

we stood waist-deep in the surf, trying to push the cumbersome boats over the waves so we could climb in. The kayaks toppled over even with the smallest amount of force and we trudged through the undertow to retrieve them. My jeans stuck to me and got warm from my body heat. I got over a wave that drenched me and climbed up into the kayak, grunting. I knew my wet T-shirt was turning into entertainment for the men on shore. Nina had an especially hard time. She let the whole beach know by screaming hysterically as the waves slammed the kayak back into her, knocking her over. She had to chase the boat back to shore countless times. I was relieved that I was better at kayaking than volleyball.

a blue, red, and yellow boat under a perfect sky, the islands in the distance. From our boats, the town was voluptuous with green hills cradling Spanish houses. The harbor was lazy with whites and blues, seagulls everywhere, a few pelicans. We lay back in the kayaks just watching everything until a seal poked its doggish head up near Lorri then disappeared. We started rowing, trying to find it again. Lorri, the jock, didn't stop and we got in quite a rhythm keeping up with her. My eyes followed the red Santa Rosa Ranch insignia on her wet shirt sticking to her back as she rowed. Her paddle touched the water at just the right angle, making a perfect sound. She took us under the pier, a murky maze of wooden beams covered with barnacles that we had to maneuver through, using our hands because the oars were too awkward. Our boats slammed into the living pillars. I grabbed hold of the sharp black shells and pushed off. Lorri and I got through quickly and waited in the sunlight while Nina was still stuck and screaming.

"Eeew! I touched a starfish! It was disgusting!"

"Cool."

"Don't row, just push!"

"I'm stuck!"

"Just go slow!"

"I just touched this squishy thing! Help!"

"No!"

"You suck!"

I looked at Lorri in her blue boat, her muscular body resting, her breasts busy being cold and awake under her wet shirt. The sunlight on the water was reflected back on her body in a quivering web of lines that made her squint. The beauty of it filled me from my toes to the top of my head. I had to close my eyes.

"When I get my horse, you should come ride. Do you ride?" she said.

"No, you'll have to show me."

"Nina's a mess. Look at her, she cracks me up."

"I'd like that a lot."

"What?"

"To come over and ride your horse."

"Oh. Yeah."

I could see thoughts come and go on Lorri's face. They didn't stay, they left her face uncluttered, the opposite of Jessica whose face was a collection of a zillion things she held on to. With the two of them in the world on a single day, everything was perfect.

such days stand apart from the rest, like the sky on the Fourth of July, a rare occasion of night swimming in a lighted pool, a day filled with light upon light. It's the Wheel of Fortune, a good day usually follows a horrible one. It goes the other way around, too, but why ruin a good day with thinking about how bad the next one is destined to be? All things good that we've ever done or thought are rewarded on the good days, as if the plants, the sidewalks, the sky, the strangers are all one thing saying thank-you to us.

five

i lay in bed with salt and sand in my hair, in my ears, never taking for granted the way the ocean lingers on the body. I counted in my head all the colleges by the Pacific. The colleges in northern California don't count, the ocean is too cold to swim in, and southern California colleges just aren't all that great. I would have to make a decision between my brain cells and the sea, my first great compromise.

The moments before sleeping have always been my favorite time. I go between worlds. I lay very still and feel the sensation in every part of my body, starting at my feet then going up to my head. My hands start to feel thick and parts of me open, beginning with a tickle or a little ache. My elbow, for instance, might spin into blue, then a memory of a dog I saw once. A left leg might become hopelessness, then melt into red dirt to become strong again.

That night I became a rushing stream and I had to breathe fast just to contain it. I knew how to let the world fill me up till I spilled out over the top. Usually I'd cry or make myself come, but that night there was just peace, finely cut and perfect as a diamond. I lay there in a white fire. Jessica was there as a red swirl going crazy. Lorri as the sun on the water above me.

Orlando was a man and then a woman, then a man again, through the ages, a soul never ending. This was the one part of the book I did understand. Being everything.

hardly awake, i stumbled into the kitchen the next morning to find Mom sobbing into her hands. Her hair was matted at the base of her skull. She wore an oversize T-shirt with paint splatters, and satin underwear. Her eyes were swollen. When she saw me, she motioned for me to come closer. When I got within reach, she pulled me to her and held me tight, her body convulsing into mine. The smell of her tears stirred my sleeping stomach and turned it to acid.

"Sit down," she said and she stared hard into my face at something that was making her eyes fill with deep despair.

"I got a call last night from Leslie. She was a friend of mine back when your father and I were together." She gathered herself and took a deep breath. "She said Robert was being arraigned for child molestation. Monster—that goddamn monster! I could tear his throat out with my bare hands! He's got a little boy and a little girl. Monster! Do you remember Robert, honey?" She spat out her words, possessed by a demon.

"Dad's friend?"

"Yes. You remember him. Tell me, do you remember anything, did he do anything to you?"

"No."

"We were so blind. Drunk and sick. Our babies just ran around those party houses naked."

An image flashed into my mind of me and a naked little boy, running through a house screaming and laughing, then ending up in the living room where the adults lay on pillows and rugs listening to *Abbey Road*, smoke hovering in the air. Someone told us to stop and stand still. I saw my father's eyes, so stoned that they were not his anymore, looking at me. People started to say stuff about how beautiful my body was, how me and the little boy were like the Garden of Eden or something. Mom looked proud of me and told me to turn around and show everybody what a cute butt I had. Then I was allowed to go.

It was an environment ripe for sordid interludes of all kinds. Anything could happen at one of those parties. Sex floated in the air heavy as smoke, but like all children, I instinctively avoided hot stove tops and vicious dogs in the same way I avoided adults exuding the sickly heat of sex.

"He did something to you, didn't he?"

"No. I didn't spend any time with Robert."

"You were drugged."

"Yeah, but I still remember stuff."

"Oh God, oh God. I'm so sorry. I've been blaming it on you all this time. I'm so sorry. Oh, God forgive me."

"It's okay, nothing happened. People don't turn queer from that kind of stuff anyway. It's a different issue."

"Don't say 'queer,' honey. That bastard! That monster! I'm going to tear his eyes out for what he did to my baby."

"He didn't do anything."

"Oh God. We were so blind."

"Mom. Nothing happened."

Mom wailed and heaved. I was numb again. She stole all the emotion from the room. I couldn't let her go on thinking that anything happened to me. It would give her permission to take control over my whole life. Robert. Tall. Wore plaid shirts. Jeans. I didn't like him.

i walked to the school with an uneasy feeling deep in my gut. My body felt like damp cardboard. I didn't want to identify the feeling as shame. I was ashamed to be ashamed.

Mr. Tenasky wanted our outlines which I didn't have. I didn't remember him asking us to do them. At lunch hour, I explained to Mrs. Stanley, the Special Ed teacher, that I was quitting my community service with Planned Parenthood and I wanted to do normal Study Hall like everybody else.

"It isn't going to be that easy," she said, making a strange sound with her tongue and teeth: I was going to have to get things signed. "Is anything going on at home?" she asked with creepy concern.

"Yes, we have cable now."

"i don't want any cheese," I said to Riley as I zoned in front of the TV.

"Are you on a diet or something? You don't need to lose weight."

"No. I'm just tired of routine. Our life together is becoming so habitual. After school we just sit around and space."

This pissed him off. He put the cheese and tortillas back in the refrigerator with exaggerated fury.

"What!" he snapped. "What do you want? Just tell me what you want and I'll do it."

"That's not it."

"No. Just tell me. Make something up." He was almost begging. Something inside him was deeply, devastatingly tired. I had an idea.

"Go in the bedroom."

Riley got instantly perky, visions of blowjobs dancing in his head. Wishful thinking. I followed him in.

"I want to show you this breathing thing I did once."

"A breathing thing?"

"It's something I did in a workshop. It's no big deal, it's just breathing."

I thought it would wake him up, make him more emotional.

I couldn't believe I was stooping so low as to use some New Age trick from Mastery II, but I wasn't good at blowjobs anyway, I only tried once and Riley lost his hard-on. I was glad he did because I really didn't want to do it. He lay down on the bed.

"Start breathing in and out with no separation from the in-breath and the out-breath, like you just ran up a hill."

"What is this about?"

"Just do it."

Riley obeyed me, his eyes resting on my cleavage. The breathing exercise often makes people slightly dizzy. Their arms and legs tingle and the hands can become temporarily paralyzed as they clench up into fists. After an extended amount of time, euphoria kicks in. It's glorified hyperventilation.

"Take off your shirt," he said.

"Keep breathing."

"This is making me horny."

I took off my shirt to appease him so he could focus. His breath turned into a lecherous pant. I lost him. So much for my plan. His brain faded into something reptilian, and mine was soon to follow.

"I want to watch you touch yourself, over there," he pointed to the wall covered with posters and his artwork. He was already starting to massage his dick. So much for my rebirth breathing plan for Riley's spiritual awakening. I did what he asked. I was happy to please him, there was so little I did for him sexually. I was merciless. I took off my jeans, sat against the wall and touched myself while Riley watched me from up in his bed. I never watched him from that angle before. His dick looked bigger. What a waste, I thought, and smiled. He'll find someone soon enough. We both will.

I considered the possible fantasies. Jessica was still too scared. Lorri was like my good friend so I couldn't think about her on the kayak in a wet T-shirt. The imaginary sweater girl would do but when I went inside my mind to think of her she was nowhere.

All I could think of was Mom talking about Robert. I thought about being nine years old, standing naked in a roomful of adults. The thought turned me on a little, all those eyes on me.

This was the fantasy I had: I am in a punk club that Riley and I went to once. It's dark, smoke-filled, and crowded. The music is loud. I wait for the bathroom and a tough Skinhead type pushes me against the wall.

"Touch yourself for me."

"No."

"Yes, you will."

"Not here, please don't make me."

"Come for me or I'll fuck you." He threatens to take out his dick.

I'm wearing a miniskirt and my underwear is crawling up my butt. There are people around already starting to watch. He probably has a gun or a knife or something. I do it. I touch myself in the hallway of the sticky, smoky punk club while he leers at me, his dick bulging in his black jeans.

Riley was grunting on the bed with his eyes closed. He opened them to watch me and I looked back at him but he was somewhere else, lost. We came at the same time without planning to. We lay there, silent and heavy, like sediment sinking to the bottom.

"What were you thinking?" he asked.

"Nothing."

"That's wild. I always have to think about something."

There are two kinds of fantasies, seedy fantasies and love fantasies. Sometimes seedy fantasies are hotter but after you come they leave you drained and feeling greasy.

"Can we order out for pizza or something?" I said, lying against the wall with my T-shirt on and pants off.

"Sure, you got money? I'm out."

"I don't really want to pay twenty bucks for pizza."

"Come here for a minute," Riley said. I got up and crawled

into his bed. "You're so beautiful. You're going to make a great lover to some woman someday. You're too sexy. I'll miss you."

"I'll miss you, too."

"No, you won't."

"Maybe not, huh."

I said a silent prayer that Riley would find all the love in the world. He would have denied it, but he had a sadness than ran deeper than any I'd ever seen. I always thought something horrible must have happened to him as a kid, there were giant chunks of him that seemed to be missing.

"You know when I was on acid and stuff?" I said. "As a kid?"

"Uh-huh."

"Maybe stuff happened that I can't remember."

"Like what?"

"Maybe someone did something. Like, sometimes I feel like maybe someone did something sexual. Like at a party."

Riley got tight all of a sudden. I felt the cogs in his brain move faster. "But you would remember. If something happened like that, you would know. It would make you feel weird."

"I do feel weird."

"I mean weirder than you already are, like gross-weird."

"Yeah. I'm not sure if I feel that. Maybe way deep down I might feel that but I feel a lot of other things, too."

"Like what?"

"Mostly just wanting things. Desire. That's mostly what I feel."

six

"ready? you psyched?" Lorri said in motion as she hurled her backpack into her locker. Swoop, slam, click. She was fresh. Like September. A new checkbook. Like starting over. *What's wrong with me?* I almost mouthed audibly, needing so much of her attention all at once, it hurt. Mom's moods were getting to me. Something in my body was working backwards, maybe my liver, putting poison in my system instead of taking it out. I just couldn't get clean. By the time I got to school for the volleyball game, I needed another shower.

"You okay?"

"I've had a hard few days. My mom's being strange."

"How?" she asked, as if the idea of a mother being neurotic was a completely baffling concept to her.

"I'll tell you later."

Lorri was in her getting-psyched-for-the-game mode, deep inside herself like a real athlete, someone who could pay attention to things. I left her alone and put my socks on over my still-wet feet. I forgot my uniform so I had to use an old one that was sitting at the bottom of my locker since who-knows-when. The fabric smelled like green apples, gasoline, and something alkaline like moldy wheat bread. Lorri took off her shirt and used deodorant on her armpits. She put on a clean T-shirt and rolled up her sleeves perfectly. Her socks were soft and fresh. In her presence I felt like a germ, like something growing in the grout between the tiles. Everything weighed.

The opposing team wore red. We wore blue-and-white. I tried to muster up hostility and disgust for the little quirks that made them different. The Other. This was going to help me focus. Santa Maria girls still wore scrunchies to hold their hair back. Old. They carried water bottles. How lame. They were all too blond; they must be Aryan fascists. Lorri walked to the sidelines and to my horror started talking to one of the girls like she was her friend or something. That shattered my whole approach.

My body felt weak. The more I thought of the game ahead, something hot and acidlike pulsed sharply in my veins. I couldn't think clearly. I thought an earthquake might be nice, or maybe an injury. I longed for an interruption, a small disaster, anything to delay and distract.

Up and down the bleachers, around the court, we ran until our lungs burned. *Bif bif* went everyone's practice serves. Mine went *thwick thwick*.

"The palm, Skye, the palm," Bob said. He stopped the exercise to show me again. At that point I weighed which would be the lesser humiliation, staying and causing them to lose the game or leaving and making a coward of myself. My inability to make a decision caused me to stay. It was Bob's fault; he shouldn't have let me on the team. I wasn't good enough.

I did the warm-up exercises feverishly, hoping it would all come back to me like it did only a few days before but something felt off. My shorts were too small and I was sure it was because I'd gotten fat. I couldn't help thinking that part of my butt was probably hanging out below the hem, vibrating like jello whenever I ran.

"Relax, girl," Nina said, sensing my tension.

The game began.

It started off well. I was pleased at my ability to make myself invisible on the court, dashing out of the way to let the better player get the ball. Dodge-ball was what it was called in grade school. I sucked at that, too.

"Skye, you get it!" Tara said to me, as a gentle lob approached the ground. No! Not me! I dove down to the ground elbow-first and popped it up into the net.

"Nice try," Lorri said. It looked cool. If all else fails, fall and grunt a lot.

I actually hit some shallow lobs back over the net, though usually right to the sweet spot of an especially mean-looking Santa Maria girl who slammed it back impossibly hard.

Santa Maria was winning. They were, after all, one of the better teams in the area. With their cocky attitude, they made winning seem ugly, making me take pride in the soulful state of being a loser. Lorri, Nina, Tara, and some of the other good players got focused and called each other's names out during plays. "Nina, slam it!" "Lorri, go!" "Dive for it!" And to me they'd yell, "I got it!" "Move it!" "Let it go!" Sometimes I heard them, sometimes not. I felt like a pedestrian who'd kind of wandered into the game. A photographer maybe. A drunk.

The game was almost over and it was my serve. The coach had Zen resignation all over his face, not a good sign.

"Just get it over," Lorri said.

I served. The ball eclipsed the sun as my fist came to meet it, hitting it with the sound of a flame flickering. Not a good sound. Still hoping, I watched its feeble arc until it hit the net. Point lost.

We were one point away from losing the whole game. Lorri whispered something under her breath and looked down at her sneakers.

At least the last point was an impressive rally that seemed to last forever with me dodging the ball every time it came near.

Lorri and Nina were majestic, moving as a unit, setting up the ball for each other to slam back with a grunt, sweat flying. Santa Maria won the game with a last slam that hit Nina in the leg. Nina and Lorri practically fell into each other's arms hugging, knowing they'd done their best. They walked off the court arm in arm to the water fountain without talking to me. Thank God.

I didn't stick around to hear the coach give his usual scolding-yet-philosophical speech. I went to the lockers by myself, got my backpack, and left without looking at myself in the giant mirrors that lined the cinder-block walls. Bob was going to be pissed off at me, but it didn't matter. I wasn't planning on coming back.

i looked for jessica, of course. She would fix everything. Whatever monsters dwelled under the surface of my skin, she would get along with them. She was creative and artistic. I didn't really know this, I just assumed it. She was probably a painter or a writer and if she wasn't, her life was art, she didn't need to prove it by actually doing it.

I was walking toward the lawn, composing my own definition of art, when I saw Jessica in a crowd. A raver girl who couldn't have been more than thirteen was sitting on the grass leaning against a tree. Jessica was lying with her head in the girl's lap. She was tying Jessica's hair into little braids. I didn't know what I felt, but it was loud. Screaming. If I was an animal, I would have run off but I was me so I walked forward, pretending to be normal.

People were standing around on the lawn wearing ripped overcoats, black lipstick and tall hair, vinyl sneakers and baggy jeans. They were a mishmash of goths, ravers, and punks who weren't cool enough to hang out with the elite of their given crowd so they were happy enough to lurk with each other peacefully. They were all stoned. I felt intimidated and superior both at once. They ignored me as I casually plodded toward Jessica.

"Hey," I said. Jessica screamed and got up and hugged me. No one seemed to notice. She pulled me down on the grass and without letting go of my hand she continued talking to the raver girl, some gossip about a particularly wild night. A band. Someone puking. Something about stolen nail polish and a girl who was mad. As I listened to the voices around me, it seemed like everyone else was having the same conversation. I zoned out and the words became atmosphere, entertaining and a little draining, like radio music. I wasn't used to it. I didn't know what to say back.

They were all waiting for information about a party. A band was playing and there was a rumor that everyone would go to The Barn after the gig. A blond girl in a low-cut black dress and boots told her friend how she would never do heroin, only coke, and she wasn't addicted, she didn't even like it that much, in fact she'd never bought it, it was always just given to her. I eavesdropped for a long time, hiding in my anonymity.

I stared at a boy who was wearing a tweed jacket and hat even though it was a hot day and felt Jessica's hand pulsing in mine. I tried to pretend it was nothing, that her hand there wasn't saving my whole life. The boy was skinny and his face was so long and white that it seemed his skin had no blood. Next to him was a girl in a long ivory dress. Equally as pale, her eyes were wide and empty. They looked as though they were from another time, a young version of the classic painting of the midwestern farmer and his wife. I couldn't stop staring at them. The boy caught my eye. It was strange because I didn't feel the usual jolt of energy I get when my eyes meet someone else's. It was a cold stare. He raised his arm up and made some sign with his fingers. His face opened up like a dry pod and let out something evil.

"Hoto," he said in some foreign, unrecognizable dialect. The words went right inside me, I was so open. He said it as a curse.

"Fuck off, you freak," Jessica said. She turned to me. "Satanists. Be careful. What did he say?"

"I don't know." Terror made me speechless. Minutes passed

and I just stared at the sky, bathed in the sound of talking voices and cars going by.

"Jessica?"

"Yes?"

"Can we go somewhere for a second?"

She said yes but I knew she didn't want to leave her friends. She followed me to the mural of Spanish settlers and the Chumash Indians on the library's west wall that was was strangely free of graffiti.

"I think that guy put a curse on me."

"Oh, stop it. They're just creeps. He was just trying to freak you out."

"No, really. I felt it go inside me. They did something. I can feel it."

"Think of white light, Jesus Christ. Whatever." Her lack of understanding was out of character and very disturbing.

"I need to do something to undo it. Think of something."

I was surprised at Jessica's suggestions, they were so storybook. Wear a cross. Eat some garlic. She was so imaginative with Heda, where were her brilliant ideas when I needed them most?

"Maybe Heda could help?" I suggested.

"Is she in your freezer?"

"Yeah."

"Maybe you could eat some dirt or something."

"That's it!"

"Dirt?"

"Grass, I think. Grass is innately good."

I picked a clump of grass with my fist from the center of the lawn, shoved it in my mouth, and started chewing. Jessica just stared like I was nuts. I felt the evil curse on my tongue and in my gut. The bittersweet taste of grass strangled it like an army of sacred Easter bunnies. It was the taste of my childhood. My self. The evil left.

"It's gone."

"How do you know?"

"I just know."

After the crowd dispersed, Jessica invited me to her house. I went with her on her usual route home, beneath the eucalyptus and oak trees, beneath the sun smiling. When she was walking her face was the most free of anger. She looked like a saint from a Renaissance painting, pale and lit from within. Few people are that white in California. The sun is so insistent, how she avoided it was beyond me. As we walked, she acted like a spoiled debutante in a gothic castle, then in the next moment she was a lewd Skinhead with a Cockney accent. I always thought it was best to just be myself, be authentic. Being with Jessica made me realize that being real was horribly unsophisticated. Subtle nuance took precedence over honest gestures and I never was quite sure if she liked me and yet something drew me to her, held me like a fist clenched around my spine. A glass of red wine held up to the light, that was the color of my feelings for her. Until then I had been aqua, light blue and green. She erased me.

Her nylons were ripped, showing her untanned leg. I liked how she was always coming loose, leaving pieces of herself everywhere like a thread, a barrette, a curse. We got on the bus and Jessica stared at the floor as we rode through town. I looked at strangers, took in everything—an old woman in a nice blue dress, a mother who was sitting next to her child, holding a Ninja Turtle toy from ten years ago. Used toys make me sad, they are always sticky, dirty, and filled with just one child's feeble love. Pathetic.

"You said the first day we hung out together that you watched everything, saw everything. Remember?"

"Yeah," Jessica replied.

"Do people ever make you sad?"

"All the time."

"What do you do? To stop it?"

"I don't. I drown. I'm always drowning." She said it like a

drunk girl at a party, with a smile and a swagger in her shoulders. She met my eyes in a challenge. I didn't know what it was. Something about the drowning.

her house was suburban ranch style, the kind you find outside of L.A.—drywall and factory cabinets, an arrangement of brown and white. I watch houses like I watch movies, looking for the story. Houses reveal everything. People aren't that complex really. When you meet someone, after saying a few words you know pretty much who they are. It's the same with houses. I could tell from Jessica's house that her parents put hard work before anything else. Her mother married her father as a second choice out of duty and necessity. They're slightly pathological, like most Americans, obsessed with appliances. They had maybe six thousand dollars of credit-card debt. Main psychological problem: sexual repression expressed through drywall, soiled lamp shades, and a lack of original art on the walls. Also, everything in their house was new, like old things would bring up a past that would be better off forgotten. Like some people read tarot, I read houses.

Jessica's house was huge, more expensive than my mom's for sure, but ugly. She had to get the key to the back door from inside the garage that smelled like basketballs and auto grease. Jessica was cursing and looking for the key under different empty coffee cans full of nails and other junk. Something about the garage told me that her mom and dad were still together, the garage being the domain of the married man who fixes things and leaves a small mess and collects sports equipment. I took a guess that her mom worked a home computer job while her dad was a salesman of some sort. Jessica found the key under a power drill. She seemed to be reading my thoughts.

"My dad's on a business trip."

"What does he do?"

74

"Sells hospital equipment."

"And your mom?"

"Herbalife."

I was close. Jessica let herself in, dropping her backpack on top of the washer. She went to the kitchen and drank juice from its cardboard container while I waited in the living room. I didn't put my backpack down. I needed permission or something. I guess I didn't really want to be there. I didn't want to think of Jessica having parents and a home. I wanted her to just be part of the world like people in the park, a mysterious stranger.

The whole house was filled with some suffocating invisible substance. I couldn't tell if it came from the old shag carpet, the TV, or the refrigerator. There was no air. I opened the sliding glass door that led out to the pool.

"Your house is so like, American. My relatives in Cincinnati have a house like this."

"Yeah. It's a house. Capital *H*."

"Your parents don't shop at Pottery Barn. How refreshing."

"They're from Kentucky. Dad likes history."

I noticed a bayonet above the faux-brick fireplace and a photo of a man in buckskin pants.

"Your dad?"

"Yeah. He's into Civil War reenactment."

"What's that?"

"A bunch of adults going camping without Velcro or vinyl. They make biscuits and play, like, mandolins and stuff. Drink cider."

"What's cider?"

"Mead, or something. A brackish blend."

A framed poster was the only other art in the room, an illustration of a large bass violin advertising the Vermont Jazz Festival. The kitchen, the couch, and even the plants seemed to be facing the entertainment center with a big-screen TV, hinting that television was the sole activity her family took part in together.

75

"Can I see your room?"

"Sure," she said with a look that I read as being flirtatious. She had that look often, a sharp immediacy, a warm come-hitherness. I didn't know if it had anything to do with me or if it was just a random flash of inspiration on her part. Her face became an elf's mask of mischief, like she was in on secrets.

jessica's room had different air, hotter and faster-moving. Wrinkled and torn movie posters from *Star Wars* and *The Empire Strikes Back* covered her walls. She had cheesy things lying around like a ceramic piggy bank and a doll on her table that looked like her grandmother brought it back from Holland or some other very white place. It was the room of someone two years younger than sixteen. At sixteen you're supposed to realize posters and parents' gifts aren't cool. You're supposed to evolve into a kind of minimalism, just pictures of friends, presents from friends, rocks picked up on hikes, a long piece of fabric decorating a bare wall. Maybe that was just me, though; even Riley had posters.

Jessica lay on her mattress. There were no chairs in her room. I didn't know what to do with my body. I wanted to lie next to her and be casual like all the straight girls seem to be able to do. They hug constantly, lie all over each other and kiss, and it doesn't mean anything. Instead, I sat at the foot of the mattress and leaned against the wall. We talked, sort of, but mostly I looked at her body, the tightness of it, the condensed electricity that buzzed under the surface of her anxious skin. Her black clothes made her instantly tragic and sexual. In comparison I was calm and closed. Whereas I had an inner world, a place to put things out of view, she seemed to wear her insides on the outside. Even her words seemed to slip out accidentally.

"Someday I'm going to go to Barcelona and like, paint. I

76

went there once in sixth grade. They have this church with Pepsi bottles in it, like mosaic tile everywhere and it goes on through all these passageways and the guy's been building it for five hundred years and I'm going to go there and work on it. My dad knows someone there. That's where I'm going when I graduate."

"I love mosaic tile. It's my favorite thing," I said.

"This church has blue glass and gargoyles and in some places it's cold, like a tomb. I was like, 'Get me out of here, I can see dead people.' My mom was there. She was like, 'Right, right Jessica, take your pill.' "

She talked without looking at me. Her tone of voice changed to something cold and urgent. Not her. It scared me.

"There's bats in here."

"Where?"

"In here, there's bats in here."

I didn't know how to play along with her game. I didn't get it. Her body folded up and she held herself, terrified, aware of a presence in the corner of her room. It wasn't like she was seeing bats for real, like a hallucination. She was imagining bats and she believed her imagination was real.

"I don't see the bats," I said, apologetically.

She was quiet for a while and in that space of silence my faith in her fell through. She might be crazy, downright nuts, and what kind of fool was I, then, thinking she was the new prophet of my world? Always the enigma, she lifted her head and said, clear-eyed, "There's bats in the church in Barcelona, too. I want to go there with you and we'll dance on pillars. We'll like, drink wine and emote."

"Okay."

She looked pained for a moment, then all of a sudden she was better. She showed me her collection of colored nail polish. She pulled my shoes and stinky socks off and began painting my toenails blue. We lay back and stared at the sprayed plaster ceiling. Her black silk shirt was hiked up above her waistline showing her bare skin and I saw the red tip of a scar. I couldn't take my eyes from it. It looked so unnatural.

"Ceilings are weird."

"Ceilings should show you something," I said. "They shouldn't be white. They should be like cathedrals with stories on them, you look up and you see angels and devils, you look up and you're afraid and you're in love. When you look up something should happen, not just nothing."

"You could draw on the ceiling if you want. Dust would fall in your face. Draw a birdie." Her hand rested on her scar absent-mindedly.

"What's that? Under your shirt."

She lifted her shirt up, faking confidence. She couldn't look at me. On her stomach was the word *IT* in pink scar tissue.

"Did you do that?"

"I did it with a razor. This girl Bella has it, too. She moved to Seattle, it was a going-away thing. She was the first girl I met who cut. She's cool."

I was baffled. I couldn't understand why anyone would want to do something like that to themselves. I was squeamish about it but tried not to let it show.

"This man wants me to model for his fashion shoot. I'm like, 'I'll do it on three conditions. That you don't alter my body in a way that I don't want it altered. Two, that you don't make images that are demeaning to women, and three, that I can make more money doing that than I can doing anything else.' "

"Are you going to do it?"

"He's going to call me back. I don't know. He's weird."

She was doing something strange with her eyes. They were speeding around the room, corner to corner, paranoid. For a moment I thought of asking her if she was on speed, then I thought it might be a mental thing and I didn't want to freak her out. She was so nervous. She was digging her thumbnail into her finger then biting it.

Showing me her scar was like telling me a secret. I was glad about it. She trusted me. Her secrets were like layers she stripped off each time I saw her. I assumed there was some core she wanted me to get to. Maybe she was seducing me, pulling me in with the story of her pain.

"Why do you do that?"

"Did I freak you out?"

"No, I just have never seen anything like—"

"I freaked you out."

"You didn't. I'm glad you showed me. I'm like honored or something."

We were quiet for a while. Both of us tense. It seemed like she was mad at me. I couldn't think of what to say to make it better. She felt like she shared too much too fast, I guess.

"Does it hurt when you do that?"

"Not really. It's a rush," she said, glad that I wanted to talk about it more.

"Oh."

"Actually, it does hurt but it feels good. Sometimes my thoughts get stuck thinking about something bad and the pain gets rid of it. The pain becomes this clear thing. It wipes everything else away."

"I don't like the sight of my own blood."

"The blood's the best part. I'll have a scab and I'll scratch it off at a party and bleed. It's so powerful. People freak out. It makes them like, deal, you know. They can't turn away from the sight of blood."

"But what about the pain?"

"The pain isn't that bad. It's like a hangnail. It's satisfying pain," she said, with an expert confidence in her voice. "Sometimes I can't stand to look at my own skin. I'll get out of the shower or something and see my leg and I'll want to dig into it with a pen. It's not depression or anything. It's a feeling of something coming that I can't keep away. Too much. A feeling of too much."

She was talking to the wall, like she'd said that speech a million times, it meant nothing to her. I wasn't sure if it was the truth. There was a deeper reason for her cutting but I didn't understand it and I don't know if she did, either. I didn't know if it meant she just hurt more than other people or if was it just something superficial, an indulgent ritual for a self-obsessed person.

"I wish I lived in a place where it rained more, where it was dark, and then I would sleep in the day and go out at night like in New York. There are people who don't even see daylight there. The less I see daylight the better I am. Sometimes I'll see a palm tree and I'll like, freak. Palm trees are obscene. My mom always wants to get me shoes. Does your mom want to buy you things like that? Shoes and stuff?"

She was almost incoherent, talking as if she was drunk. She picked a safety pin off the dresser and pushed the PLAY button on her tape machine. Punk music blasted. She held the pin firmly between two fingers and drew a line along the soft white part of her arm next to the rows of other scars in different stages of healing. Nothing. Then red. A Moses red sea spilling over. I wanted to kiss her. Instead, I just sat there and watched.

Blood. It brought a stillness into the room. Her body moved a little to the slam-dance beat, her mouth was in a half-smile. I wished I could make her feel that good. She handed me the pin.

"Do it."

"I don't want to."

"Not to yourself, to me."

"I can't."

I thought it was ironic that I was allowed to make her bleed but kissing her was somehow beyond the realms of etiquette. The long red line grew thick and broke off into tributaries that dripped down the side of her arm. Some drops fell on the carpet making a sound that made my mind stop thinking.

"Blood is beautiful. I like to see it. It's a friend. I'm like, 'Blood, where are you? I miss you.' "

She touched her forearm and got blood on her fingers. She played with the blood, feeling the texture, holding it up to the light. The color went from red to brown as it dried. She was a horror-movie image out of context on her flowered bedspread in front of the dirty white drywall. Out the window, I watched a branch quiver in the soft breeze but it made me totally sad so I just rested my eyes on her instead. There was something beautiful about her like that, with her insides coming out, the way intimate gestures like crying or waving good-bye are beautiful. I watched like I was looking at a painting. Her neck was bent forward, astonishingly white and vulnerable against her black shirt. Her eyes were fierce, her legs looked thin and abandoned. The light from the window kissed her left side as the shadows of the wind-bothered leaves danced on her body. She was beautiful and painful.

the sight of her blood did break the ice, I guess. She wiped herself off with a towel she kept hidden in a drawer along with a bottle of peppermint schnapps. The towel was already a brown color. It absorbed her blood and turned a deeper shade. I wanted to smell it. Mostly I wanted to cry. Of all the times I cried without wanting to, why couldn't I cry then? Something inside me was frozen, thick with bewilderment. We lay on the bed and drank while listening to her mix tape.

"Draw a picture of an angel on my ceiling."

"You're not supposed to like angels."

"Why not?"

"You're a vampire."

"I don't think angels are all that good. They just look good.

Angels are sex addicts, they're dangerous purveyors of lust. They have like, too much muscle tone, too much spirit, and not much brains."

Her left side touched my right side and it was warm. It was more than I expected.

"Tell me the story of your life," she said.

"I can't, that's huge. I have no story."

"Just try. Make it up."

The worst sin around Jessica was to be unspontaneous. I just started talking, saying bullshit. "I was born to two yuppie adults in the movie industry. By the time I was ten they were downwardly mobile and desperate."

"No, that's your parents' story, I want to hear your story."

"I was a smart kid who always had to take GATE English. . . ."

"Not what you did. Who you were. Who you are."

I was getting drunk. A fire started inside my tongue and spread to the surface of my skin. No one had ever asked me anything like that. I never knew I wanted anyone to ask me that until she did. I spoke slowly, choosing every word carefully.

"I was a child who listened to trees and felt the disappointments of the dead. I had friends but they weren't as real as those invisible things that inhabited secret places in my mind. I was as open as a flower and people saw that and always commented on it and they tried to take things from me. Then I found love and I realized how dangerous it was to wear love on the surface, so I kept it deep inside and learned to protect myself but then people couldn't see that I loved them and blah blah blah I don't know."

"No, that's great. You've been in love?"

"Maybe."

"With who?"

"A teacher."

"Scandal."

"I'm drunk. What about the story of your life?"

Jessica became instantly serious and withdrawn. She looked out the window. In the gray twilight, her expression was one of melodramatic suffering. I waited for her to answer.

"There was a girl who saw too many lies and then she died."

"Oh."

Then she laughed and I laughed with her. Very spontaneously. We threw a stuffed giraffe across the room and wished Heda was with us so she could tell us the story of her life flying across town, her days spent chirping. I schemed of how I could tell Jessica, sometime in the future but not then, that I loved her.

seven

the house was too quiet when I walked in the door.
Mom's car was in the driveway but she wasn't sitting in the kitchen
as usual. I went to my room and lay down on the bed, the smell
of Jessica's room still in my nose—magazines and peppermint
schnapps. I heard the sound of something crashing in the bathroom.

"Mom! Is that you?" I yelled from my room. "Mom?"

There was no answer. I heard the pounding of more objects
hitting the floor and another thud, soft and fleshy. It gave me the
shivers. I walked to the bathroom and stood outside the door.

"Mom, you in there? You okay?"

"Mmmmm-hnnn."

"Mom?"

"Mnn . . . fuck. Goddammit."

Thud! Bam! I heard the sound of the medicine cabinet slamming shut. I was worried so I opened the door. Mom was sitting
on the toilet in her yellow robe, her head leaning against the blue
wall. Her robe was open and I saw her small breasts and bones I
didn't know existed bulging from under the skin of her tight chest.

Her eyes opened, rolled back in her head, then attempted to focus.

"What did you take?" I demanded.

"Nothing. I got my prescription wrong. Had a glass of wine with my Prozac."

Her left hand kept flipping back and hitting the wall. I picked up the different prescription bottles strewn on the floor . . . codeine, Xanax, Valium, Prozac.

"You need to get in your bed."

"You're so pretty. My pree-ii girl." She reached out to me like an E.T. mother. *Phone boooome.* I laughed.

"Am I funny?" she said with a smile.

"Yeah, you're funny," I lied.

I didn't know if she was partying or dying, if she was suicidal or simply melodramatic. I went up to her and caught the scent of cheap body lotion and something chemical. I reached my arm around her body to help her up.

"Come, let me take you to your room."

"Yooor beu-ful. Beu-ful girl."

"Thanks, Mom."

I tried to lift her but she didn't help me any. She was heavy and slid across the toilet stool and fell onto the floor with a slow-motion flop, legs every which way. The robe was up past her butt, exposing her white underwear with little red flowers on it. Her butt hung past the panty line, dead flesh.

"Mom, you gotta help me. You're too heavy."

"I don' wan' go. Get out, you fuggin' bisshh."

"What did you take?"

"Bisshh."

I went to her room and looked through her address book. I got Dr. Walker's number just in case. Who knew what she had taken?

In the bathroom, she was lying on the floor just as I had left her, except she had passed out. I grabbed her wrists and swung her around on the black-and-white tiled floor. I pulled her a few feet toward the door. I stopped because I imagined what I must have looked like dragging my mom in her robe, her breasts jiggling and swaying. Whose movie was this? She had to get to her bed, so I pulled her all the way into her room, adjusting her robe so she wouldn't get rug-burn. I plopped her down just near her bed and thought of leaving her there. I went to the kitchen and got a root beer then came back in. I watched her for a while, her jaw open and relaxed, her beautiful blond hair. I wondered if Janis Joplin had looked like that when she was passed out. It all was a little less horrifying if I thought of Mom as a rock star. She had to get on her bed. If she woke up on the floor she would ask me what went on. If she was up on her bed she could pretend she had a little blackout. We could go on like nothing happened. I leaned over her body and tried to lift her like a baby, beneath the armpits, but she was too heavy. I laid her gently back down.

in the fantasy there's a knock on the door. I answer it and am greeted by a man in a brown suit.

"Are you Skye Berringer?"

"Yes."

"I have some bad news."

He looks sad. I know what he's going to say before he says it.

"Your mom's been in an accident. Her car went flying off a cliff and went crashing down in sparks till it blew up at the water's edge. Your mom is dead."

I break down in tears, fall on my knees, and he asks me if there's anyone to call. I shake my head no. Then I call a friend who comes over and comforts me, helps me gather my mom's things together.

The fantasy comes in the worst of times and I always feel bad after thinking it, like it's the closest to sin I've ever gotten. I'd be a different person if Mom was dead. I'd be full of guilt. Full of darkness, and free.

dishes clammered in the sink, like a bogus drum corps announcing Mom's awakeness. I sat up, forgetting my dreams. My first thoughts were that I was glad she wasn't dead. I just wished she could have stayed passed out for a few more days. I needed a break. The phone rang.

"Hello?" my mom said, her voice coherent but full of smoke. "Yes?"

It was for me. Probably Dad. I stumbled into the kitchen half-awake. Mom acted busy, going through the stack of bills on the table. She handed me the phone.

"Hello?"

"Hi, hon."

"Hey, Dad."

Mom's body stiffened. She tried to act uninterested.

"I'm on the set so I can't talk long, but I was in Brentwood this morning and I saw Harrison Ford in his pickup truck. So that's three down for me."

"That's not fair."

Dad and I had made a list of celebrities at a boring cocktail party. We started a bet. Whoever saw the most in a period of a year got taken out to Bacio for dinner. I was living in L.A. when we started the bet. Being in Santa Barbara was decreasing my odds at winning.

"It is fair. We changed the list. Steve Martin and Geena Davis live in Santa Barbara. I'm winning fair and square. Nya-nya," he said.

Mom let out a heavy sigh. The longer I stayed on the phone the more danger there was of Mom throwing a fit.

"So how are things?" he asked.

"Fine. I'm working on a paper."

"How's Mom?"

"Fine."

Dad didn't say anything else for a while and I heard background noise and chatter on the set.

"I gotta go, Hershey Bar. I had a second. I wanted to test my cellular phone batteries. And talk to you, of course. Love you."

"Love you, 'bye."

I hung up the phone.

"You get home okay? I think I was asleep," Mom said.

"You were."

mom felt guilty. I could feel it like underground seismic activity working its way to a massive catastrophe. All she had to do was apologize but instead she became manic. She filled her schedule up with endless coffee dates with people she hardly knew. Other people's dramas became her own. A woman named Alexis was losing her therapist's license because she'd asked her client to go on a wheat-grass diet and the client developed some horrible bowel syndrome that prevented her from finishing her Ph.D. thesis. Mom became Alexis's sole support system. They talked on the phone constantly. Mom even started a wheat-grass diet out of solidarity. There was nothing in the refrigerator anymore. I went to the market occasionally for things like eggs and milk. Mom looked at the food I brought in like it was contraband. I got lectured endlessly on the evils of dairy and cooked foods. It was a refreshing change from the usual lectures that were focused on more personal things.

I discovered that Mom hid Negra Modelo in the pantry and drank a six-pack every night while she thought I was sleeping. I am convinced her switching to beer was born out of a physical need for nutrition, vitamin B. She was getting thin and the bathroom floor was always covered with her brittle blond hairs. I pointed it out to her and she said it was part of the detoxification process. New and better hairs would grow back in.

"You need protein, Mom."

"Protein is a conspiracy of the meat industry."

"Protein is food."

"You can get everything you need from plants."

Somewhere in my memory I had an image of Mom sitting in a chair looking out a window while smoking a cigarette. Her skin was tan and her hair loosely pulled back with a peach scarf. I came in and asked for something. Her eyes lit up, she exhaled the smoke out of her nose, and as if she had to travel a long way back from where she was, she said, "What, honey?" She was a real person then. A time before the spinning started.

All week long she kept leaving pamphlets everywhere for me to find, stuff from Rolfers and massage therapists, to hypnotists and past-life-regression practitioners. Each was tagged with a little Post-it note with her comments. I threw them in the trash. The next day I came home from school to find the wrinkled, food-stained papers back on the kitchen table. Mom's note read:

> Why did you throw these away? Insurance will pay for this. Why not take advantage of it before you go to school? I've made an appointment for you to see Dr. Hayward and I signed us up for Cross the Line. Don't make any plans this weekend.

Cross the Line was brutal. It was one of those EST-meets-the-nineties experiences. All about confrontation. People come right up to you and tell you what a piece of shit you are. They break you down then leave you alone to pick up the pieces. Walking on hot coals was often part of the training, depending on whether Ben was in town from Hawaii or not. I don't walk on hot coals. Period.

Mom demanded I tell her yes or no. I consented to doing Cross the Line, minus the coals, but told her I wouldn't see Dr. Hayward, the hypnotist. The whole idea gave me the creeps. I pictured myself in a trance while Dr. Hayward said things like, "You find vaginas repulsive. The very thought of kissing a woman makes you want to vomit. Penises are kind and loving. . . ." Unfortunately, Mom wouldn't take no for an answer and she started making threats again. No Dr. Hayward, no college. It was a standoff.

A little war began. Mom followed a strict schedule of meditation, chanting, and preparation of food that involved such items as shiitake mushrooms and kelp. I played loud fast music and baked whole chickens in the oven until the house would fill up with that age-old smell of domesticity. Mom complained that she couldn't meditate to the "stench of death." I graduated to bacon but it was getting expensive spending my movie money on meat, plus it was just making Mom think that I was trying to psychically attack her, which I guess I was. It was so easy.

it was may and lust came on me like a habit, an addictive condition. In the afternoon it would get thicker, clouding my mind. When I tried to work on my Virginia Woolf paper after school, all my ideas just composted into erotic obsession. Dusty, linen-and-tea-saturated, I imagined Virginia Woolf as the kind of entity that would haunt the dorm rooms of students at ancient women's colleges, watching over timid freshmen girls as they tried to have sex under the covers, fumbling in their attempts at giving pleasure, yet still finding more grace than any boy.

Virginia Woolf heard voices. She liked water metaphors. She drowned herself in a lake in 1941. Constantly molested as a child by male relatives. I imagined her as a crazy animal girl, forced into a tight lace dress. I pictured her skin as dark, more Islamic than English. Even though she was articulate from a very early age, in my mind she was a preverbal wild child who ran off to the woods and chewed on berries whenever a relative came lurking around, horny and heavy breathing.

I lay in my bed, unable to study. I reached into my jeans and let my hand be there, holding on. I kissed my other arm, imagining lips. In the fantasy I am Virginia Woolf's next-door neighbor, another girl her age, just a little more free. I know that her hideous uncle is about to visit from some faraway place and I come over just in time to save her from the obligatory romp in the garden shed. In her bedroom with its odor of fresh soap, she holds on to my body and cries. I can feel her trembling beneath layers of white lace.

Strangely, she turns into Jessica then. From white lace to black lace, exposed arms and legs. I comfort Jessica as she cries. The romantic takes on a sexual edge and I'm really touching myself. Then there's Lorri, her arms, her clean physicality. Back to Jessica, her intoxicating darkness getting to me in a place that I wanted to call love. Returning then to Virginia Woolf and the threat of men and their penises in barns, toolsheds, and basements. Sleazy. A man is fucking me without my consent. I say no but he keeps going. Breaking in. Breaking me. The strange feeling of my own fantasy somehow crossing my own boundaries, raping me. I think for a moment, How can I imagine such a thing if it never happened? What if something did? If so, how would I be different? If such a rape existed in my past, it would give me permission to self-destruct, to be nothing but rage taking complete control. It could change my life. Such a memory could give me a power no one could touch.

I tried to think of Jessica before coming, my hand drenched in myself but I couldn't make her face into a picture, and surprisingly Lorri came back in my mind, sun on the water reflecting on her chest as I came, saved by her, everything in me coming out the top of my head like a fountain.

eight

my crush on jessica became sacred to me. I thought about
her constantly, stood up straight and took each step with care,
living for the moments I would see her even briefly, a hello and
a hug.

In Mr. Tenasky's class I fantasized about kissing Jessica in a
car, on a pier, on a sidewalk at night after walking to her house. All
day I was underwater. While Mr. Tenasky talked about playing
rugby at Yale, I got drowsy and my head slumped down onto the
desk. I could see my breath on the plastic surface, in and out, full
of sex. I napped. Sam drew a picture of me sleeping in a page of
his notebook. He gave it to me at the end of class. I especially
liked how how he showed the drool coming from the edge of my
mouth. Drawn in pen, the drool looked like blood, like I was a
vampire passed out from a good meal. Jessica would have ap-
proved.

riley was waiting for me after school in his favorite lime-
green bowling shirt. He waved. Even from across the lawn I could

tell he was in a manic mood. He would want Taco Bell. I caught up with him and he put his arm around me like a real boyfriend.

"Want to go to the kegger at Brian's house?" he said.

"I have plans to go to the rave. I'm sorry. I should have called you."

"With Lorri?"

"No, with Jessica," I said, realizing I'd never told him about her and that meant I had suddenly grown a private life apart from him. "You can meet up with us later at the rave if you want."

"I hate techno," he said, with all the spite he should have saved up for me and my flakiness. Sometimes it worried me how he never got angry at me when I blew him off. It was a character flaw, something that if unexpressed would turn him into the kind of person that would end up shooting off a machine gun in a crowded Denny's somewhere in Nevada.

"I'm starved. I'm going to get a Burrito Supreme and two tacos, and a whatever-they-call-it, those cheese things," he said, changing the subject.

"I'll see you tonight maybe."

"Yeah. Whatever."

"Don't get gas," I said.

"What do you care if I have gas?" he yelled over his shoulder.

I wondered if I did care. He was my best friend, but did I really care? Riley just accepted that I was self-obsessed. If he had any needs, he knew he would have to take care of them himself. I couldn't be counted on. I craved being with someone who would teach me how to give. Not giving is a state of psychic pain, and if he loved me he wouldn't let me stay there. It's the worst kind of abandonment, when someone lets you be an asshole.

i arrived at jessica's at nine o'clock, gift in tow—a plastic-goose lawn ornament I had stolen on my walk over from a particularly impoverished split-level house behind a Jiffy Lube. The sun had turned it yellow and it was covered in dirt. I set it down near the couch where she was watching TV.

"I got you a present. A goose."

"Thanks," she said. She didn't get up but kept watching, flipping the channels every few seconds with the remote control.

"I tripped on a rock getting it. I have grass stains all over my jeans because of you."

I realized how lame my comment was right off. For Jessica, blood mattered. Blood was the least anyone could do. I sat on the other end of the couch and stared at the hysterical television for a while till it made me dizzy.

Her mom was cleaning the kitchen like she was mad at it. Lots of banging and slamming. I made dumb comments about what was on TV and Jessica rolled her eyes and kept detonating these heavy indignant sighs. She was working herself up into a really nasty mood for no reason at all. I got up and went to the kitchen to say hello to her mom. It gave me an excuse to leave the couch of silence. Introducing myself was a good thing to do anyway, considering I was eating her potato chips and drinking her root beer. Her mom was very normal looking with brown hair, a puffy face, and quilted designs on her shirt.

"Hi. I'm Skye. Nice kitchen," I said, lying.

"Have I met you before?"

"No. I just met Jessica a few weeks ago."

"You want another root beer?"

"No thanks. What's your name?"

"My name? Mothers don't have names."

"Oh."

"I'm Martha." She put a container of food into the avocado green refrigerator.

"There's this stuff you can get to paint your refrigerator," I said. "It's spray-on. It looks like stone. It only takes about an hour and afterward the refrigerator looks like it's made out of granite. It's kind of cool. It would go with the countertops."

"Really? I've always hated that green color. It looks like baby poop. You want some frozen pizza? Tater Tots? They're good for snacks."

"No thanks," I said. She really wanted to feed me. Judging from Jessica's thinness, she'd denied her mother that last domestic pleasure. The idea of eating freezer-burned food was hardly appetizing or I would have accepted. Instead, I offered her my own brand of covert affection, interior-design advice. I told her that her cabinets were fine, but refinishing would make them nicer. I explained that underneath the brown carpet there might be beautiful hardwood floors. The little attention I was giving Martha was making her ecstatic. She was thinking how brilliant and polite I was, why couldn't all of Jessica's friends be like me? Jessica was probably seething on the couch, overhearing us.

I excused myself and went outside to the patio and stared at the pool, wondering if I had made a big mistake by coming. I wasn't even sure I liked her anymore, sometimes she showed a side of herself that was mean and just plain superficial. Maybe it was better to forget about her and keep the memory of the girl walking backwards, yet I knew it was too late for that. I wanted things. I was addicted to her. A deflated dragon floated on the black surface of the pool, an abandoned monster in the dark. I heard voices and the sound of the sliding glass door opening. Jessica came out with two others.

Jessica introduced me to Mol, a fat girl with a frizzy mane of black hair that she tied up at the top of her head like a palm tree. She wore thick eye makeup that made her look feline. Her face was beautiful, like something from a religious dream. She wore a big black cape. Around her waist was a belt that held a small knife in a sheath. The handle was made of intricately carved silver. Her presence inspired awe yet when she spoke, her voice was too young for her body. It had a forced raspiness like she was trying too hard to be tough.

Cathy, the other girl, was thin and distracted. Her black

hair was cut in an angular bob. Her nails were bitten down. I recognized Cathy and Mol from Zuma's, the first day I saw Jessica.

"I'm Skye," I said, introducing myself. They both kind of grunted. Mol was looking through her purse for cigarettes. She found them, pounded the pack on her palm about twelve times, pulled one out and lit it, an intimidating gesture. The fire at the tip of her Marlboro hypnotized me into submission. I was some kind of initiate. I kept quiet.

jessica, still distant even around her friends, got on her computer while Mol and Cathy looked through fashion magazines on her bed. I found myself staring at their arms, looking for scars. Mol had a triangle just above her wrist. I felt out-of-it and wished I could manufacture some instant dark side. I considered confessing to them that I'd been molested by a friend of the family. I could tell them the memory just came back to me, that it was really fucking with my head. I'd hold out my hand so they could see my fingers shaking. I could be the dangerous one.

The silence in the room was thick, reminding me of junior high when I partied hard. My friends never really became human until the first beer and in the early evening, we sat around catatonically, scheming how to get it. The computer keyboard clicked away as Jessica talked to people in the America OnLine chat rooms. Instant messages kept popping up on the computer screen, making their *bing bing* sound.

"Who are you talking to?" said Mol.

"OMO's on teen chat. He's my bud. I'm getting messages from these other assholes, too. They all want sex in private rooms. I mean, sometimes I wonder what these guys look like. Dan Rather or something. You know they're old. Teenage boys can't spell cunnilingus."

Bing. Bing. Bing. Welcome. Bing. She was typing fast, first with a light touch then with an angry pounding.

"I'm getting slammed. Suck my dick to you, too, fuckhead."

We couldn't resist getting up and staring at the computer over Jessica's shoulder.

A post flashed on the screen, it read: *Little princess. Let me show you my six inches in a private room.*

"Gross."

"Let me on."

"Wait."

"Beat it, Mol."

"Move over."

"No."

"Just let me say one thing."

Mol took over the keyboard and began typing.

I have a bloody pussy. Doesn't anyone out there like nice juicy steak?

We stared at Mol, her mythic face in the glow of the computer screen. We waited for a response. They came all at once.

I want to fuck your bloody hole, one said.

I like bloody cunt, said another, so creatively.

Mol responded, *No. I only want people who want to put their tongue in my big bloody vagina. I haven't taken a shower in days!*

Bing bing. The responses came flooding in.

I like brown blood in my teeth. Want to go into a private room? said someone by the name of WhamRod.

Mol tried to respond, typing fast, misspelling.

"Hey, Mol, you can stop now," Cathy said, grossed out.

"Wait a sec."

"No! Stop! That was OMO. You just told my good friend to swallow your thick red monthly placenta."

"Oh, sorry. I'll stop," Mol said, desisting.

Jessica took the keyboard. *Bing. Bing. Bing.* She repaired her rapport with OMO, stating she had a deranged psychopath in the room by the name of Mol and if there was a cut-up skinny guy in plastic pants who looked like the singer from Imperial Dada to send him her way, she would most definitely like to fuck him.

we got in mol's honda civic and smoked half a joint that was left in the ashtray. None of us liked pot but we had to have something. It was already midnight by the time we drove off. We lingered for a while in a pot stupor talking about daytime beauty versus nighttime beauty. They all decided that I had daytime beauty and Mol had nighttime beauty. Jessica had both. We weren't sure about Cathy. It depended on her makeup.

We decided to stop by a rumored house party before going to the rave. We could definitely get free beer and maybe score some Ecstasy or acid. That's what Mol was hoping. I was just happy to be in the backseat with Jessica. I didn't care what else happened.

We followed a curvy road lined with trees and expensive houses till we saw cars parked along the side. Walking up the driveway, we passed a brightly lit tennis court on our way to a huge white house with black-framed windows. Floodlights made it seem unreal, like a movie set. People spilled out the front door in small groups, tribes of boys in baseball hats, T-shirts, and shorts that went past their knees. The girls lurked just out of view in the shadows under the trees.

We walked through the crowd, following the noise. Mol, Cathy, and Jessica got a lot of attention, dressed in black like a coven of witches. Mol reached back and grabbed my hand. Everybody was drunk. Faces on fire, guys fell into us making the usual remarks like, "Get a tan," "Smile," and "Wrong address, the cemetery is up the road."

We tried to get in the room with the keg but it was too crowded so we went to the pool and sat down on the plethora of lawn furniture. Mol took some eyeliner out of her purse and told me to hold still as she applied it thick under my eyes. A peace offering. Her fingers smelled like perfume and cigarettes. "Look up and don't blink," she said. It was the first warm human gesture I'd felt all night. I decided to like Mol.

Something was bothering Jessica. She stood up and walked to a bush and yanked a few flowers and came back. She sat in the lawn chair all scrunched up, pulling the petals off one by one. Her silence got our attention. Cathy offered her a cigarette which she declined. There wasn't anything we could do. Mol asked her what was the matter and she said nothing.

We watched the boys throw each other in the water. Wet and bare-chested, they wrestled each other endlessly. The male bonding was reaching a level of hysteria.

All the girls hung off each other, forming little clumps of friends. That always bugged me. I don't know why. At the end of the night they would all break apart to go off with some guy, forgetting everything that came before.

We didn't have any gossip so our conversation deteriorated into drug stories. Cathy, who hardly ever spoke, shared how crystal meth helped her clean her room. "I can sweep, do my homework, and do step aerobics all in one afternoon and still go out all night. It helps you lose weight, too," Cathy said, like a ditz.

"Maybe I should try it," said Mol sarcastically.

I was going to say something about Mol looking great as she was, meaning fat, but I couldn't think of how to say it without sounding fake so I kept quiet. I thought Cathy was pretty stupid. I don't know why Jessica and Mol were friends with her, she just rolled her eyes all the time and acted mean and nasty like she was above everything. It might have been okay if she had some intelligence. She saw herself as being "put upon" by society and faked a kind of low-level depression.

We started sharing the inevitable "my worst trip" stories. Such storytelling has a certain competitive edge and I usually end up winning, since my acid stories happened when I was just a kid.

"My parents went to parties even on school nights," I said. "At this one party I drank something that was spiked and I was standing alone in someone's designer kitchen—"

"I know, I totally . . ." Mol tried to interrupt. No one listens to each other in "my worst trip" stories, they only remember their own stories and try to butt in all the time.

". . . I was trying to trip on the crystal hanging in the window. The kitchen was gigantic, all black-and-white Formica. The counter was covered with high-tech objects like a cappuccino machine, a breadmaker, and a juicer. It was totally clean. Like, scary."

"Cleanliness freaks me out when I'm tripping. Once I . . ."

"I started to freak out about plastic. Everything was made of it, the counters, the floors, the cabinet doors. It started to like quiver and turn into an oily sludge. Plastic was like, grease. Alien skin."

Cathy interrupted with an ever-tedious explanation of how her face turned liquid in the mirror when she was tripping. I think she was making it up. Talk of drugs wore us out till only real drugs could fill the void. Mol and Cathy wanted Ecstasy and told us to wait by the pool, they would find some and be right back. Did anyone have a twenty? Thank God Jessica did. I had one but I didn't want to spend it. I didn't trust Mol to not get ripped off. Plus, Ecstasy always makes me feel horrible the next day.

A loud punk band played in the house, from a room that was unknown. We heard them start songs, then stop after the first line, mumble something, then start again. Something slammed, then there was the sound of feedback that went on for a whole minute. More mumbling.

I looked at Jessica. She had a huge scowl on her face.

"I fucking hate these people," she spat. "Gang-rapist piss-heads. I fucking hate them." Her venom surprised me.

"I know. It's kind of stupid," I said.

I lay back in the poolside lounge chair and watched Jessica imploding with hatred by the second. She was still so beautiful in her black lace dress, the one she wore the first time I saw her. Her eyeliner was smudged like she'd been crying. I could have watched her sitting there all night, her chin in her hand, her face a mask of disgust.

"I'm so glad I met you. You're not like anyone else I know. You're real, you know what I mean?" Jessica said, not looking at me.

"I'm glad I met you, too." I knew it wasn't everything I wanted to say. I wanted to confess everything right then but held back.

"When I'm with you it's like we're possessed or something. Do you feel that?" she said.

"Yes."

"It's crazy."

"My life has changed so much since I met you," I said, beginning my confession. "I mean, I don't know who I was before. It's not this big thing or anything, I'm just . . . changed."

"You're strong," she said. "Not very many people are really strong, you know?"

"I'm not that strong." I wanted to explain how I wasn't strong at all, that if she didn't carry me in that moment I might break.

She stood up and reached out to me. "Come on, let's go somewhere."

I grabbed hold of her cool hand, our fingers entwined, and she led the way past the pool, through the keg room to the dining room where the band played.

They were set up in the corner. The drum set, amps, and punk guys wearing the usual outfits looked strange against the pink wallpaper beneath a white crystal chandelier. What parents let their kids have parties like that? A few junior-high boys were slam-dancing in the center; one had blood running from his nose. Another guy lay in the corner, passed out and twitching. The lead singer of the band had a stiff Mohawk, pierced nipples, and diagonal scars all over his stomach.

"He looks like he's on speed," I said, watching him bouncing around the stage.

"Why?"

"His face is twitching."

"I think I know a girl who had sex with him."

"Gross."

"What's the name of the band?"

"Global Anus."

No real punks were watching the band play, at least not the ones who hung out by the memorial statue downtown, collecting puppies and begging for money. It was the football jocks who stood and stared with dull expressions on their faces.

Jessica plopped herself down on a red velvet armchair and pulled me down on top of her. I arranged myself in her lap and suddenly I wished I was drunk. People stared at us.

"You want a threesome?" some guy said, leaning over, beer in hand.

"Fuck off," Jessica said.

Some of the clumps of girls took refuge in that room. There was a chaos of blonde in the corner. Serious breasts in tight tank-tops. Those girls scared me so I decided to hate them for a minute. Someone handed us a bottle of Jack Daniels right on time. I took about five swallows without breathing, gagged, and handed the bottle to Jessica. She did the same and handed the bottle back. She took my hand again and held on tight.

The whiskey hit my brain fast. I sank into her lap and listened to the band. The lead singer was screaming indecipherable lyrics into the mike. I was safe in the noise.

Jessica's legs against mine were making me crazy. I could feel her breathing and I paced my breath along with hers.

I saw Lorri through the crowd with Nina, looking lost but

happy. Lorri wasn't wearing her usual T-shirt. Instead, she had on a flowered sundress, like she was going to a Sunday brunch instead of a keg party. I thought it looked sweet. My reflex was to get up and say hi but Jessica's body held me back.

"People are staring at us," she said.

"I know."

"Lots of UFOs."

"Klingons."

"Look over there," I said, pointing to a flock of girls wearing the latest weeknight-sitcom haircuts. "Total Klingon rating."

"If I kissed you right now it would freak them out totally," Jessica said.

"It would. Totally."

Lorri moved through the crowd seeming lost, too innocent. She looked at me and I looked down, pretending not to see her. I immediately felt bad about it but when I looked up again she was gone. I could have at least waved. Team Blonde in the corner was passing around a Cuervo bottle and staring at us.

"I'm going to puke, Skye, these people make me sick, you have to kiss me or I'll puke."

I turned around. I was too high so I scootched down to be face-to-face. Her tongue was in my mouth before I had a chance to think. Her hand was holding on to my shirt. With a trick of the imagination I convinced myself we were the only ones in the room. I guided her tongue to slow down, to listen more closely. She was breathing fast. I was on the edge of something. I could have cried it felt so good.

It seemed like we made out forever yet it wasn't long enough. When we opened our eyes to take a look around there was not a woman to be found in the whole room. In fact, many of the guys had left, chasing after the pussy that fled. Some jock in the corner was staring at us, hiding his erection. The bass player gave us a little nod.

"Let's go somewhere, a room or something," I said.

"We should find Cathy and Mol. They're probably wondering where we are."

She got up and I followed her through the crowd, reaching forward to grab her hand.

mol got two ecstasy tablets and Jessica talked me into sharing one with her. Why not increase the bliss, right? We swallowed the halves with a beer on the way to the rave. I felt lucky but uneasy, like I just won money that could easily be stolen. I watched Jessica's every move for signs of affection. I thought a kiss was supposed to end all that. If you get a kiss it means they like you, right? I was more unsure than ever. Jessica was in the front seat and I had to get in the back with Cathy.

"This guy was there who I swear stole my VCR," Cathy said.

"How do you know?"

"We were going out for like a minute then things started disappearing from the house and then all of a sudden he was in jail. He has like a criminal record."

"Do you know Riley Ackerman?" I asked, wondering if they knew of my so-called boyfriend.

"No, why?"

"He knows everyone who's a criminal in high school."

"This guy's not in high school," she said with attitude. "He's like, thirty-five."

Cathy talked nonstop about the joker she used to date. She talked about the drugs he took, the music he listened to, the brand of shoes he wore. She thrived on the scumbag. The only time anyone got a glimpse of her personality was when she was complaining. She even exuded something bordering on sex appeal.

When we got to the rave, Jessica held Mol's hand on the way in. I ran to catch up with them and put my arm around Jessica's waist, leaving Cathy stranded. This made everyone awkward. Mol reached back for Cathy and we entered the club as some kind of teenage amoeba, hanging on each other and oozing down the hall. People had to step aside to let us pass. We were an enviable sight. I always felt insanely jealous when I saw girls hanging on each other like we were then. Girls like us looked happy. No one knew I was miserable. There's probably at least one miserable girl in any teenage amoeba. In fact, none of us were happy till the Ecstasy kicked in.

The rave was called Universe, held in a gymnasium at the community college. A machine filled the room with cherry-scented fog. Large sheets of paper hung over the walls, painted with neon spraypaint that glowed in the black light.

"Are we the only goths?" Cathy said.

"I'm not a goth, I'm a pagan," Mol replied. "The DJs tonight are supposed to be famous."

"Everyone looks twelve," Cathy whined.

"Everyone's so . . . happy," Jessica said with disgust. "I need more alcohol, the X is kicking in."

"It is not. You took it five minutes ago," said Mol.

"A contact high," I suggested.

"I have to pee."

I was waiting for Jessica to finish up in the bathroom when I got the first rush of Ecstasy. Disco lights made rods of green, blue, and yellow light in the fog and there I was, the loyal friend waiting outside the bathroom. I was patient and gallant. That was my role in the universe. I was innately good. Jessica, also innately good, came out of the bathroom with a flask of Smirnoff.

"You want some?"

"Of what?"

"This, dummy."

"I want you."

"Oh, stop it."

The sting of her words was felt as a faint tingle of unrest beneath the ice of Superman's crystal castle. The knowledge that I would do anything for Jessica took shape as a wave of love too much to bear. I could be happy being her dog or her household appliance.

I followed her onto the dance floor. It was full of people that were small and futuristic-looking. The music and lights seemed to emanate from a place beyond history. Everyone wore clothes that came from some TV show about space that maybe never existed. As I was dancing to the techno music I felt like I belonged to a tribe. We were encoded with a secret doctrine and we came together to celebrate the last days on Earth. The music made our bones pulse with the same rhythm and I knew that the dance floor was a vortex that the angels smiled upon. We were the chosen. I loved my tribe. I danced faster and harder to increase the love.

Mol came walking up to us with a huge smile on her face. Black hair, black coat, a friendly midnight coming to swallow me up. She put her arms around me and it was heaven in her vast chest, sweet as a child's dream. Blackness is friendly. We were peaking. Mol danced like a sixties rock-and-roller to the techno music, her arms flailing under her robe. Jessica and I couldn't stop staring at her and smiling till our faces hurt. She was the cutest thing, like a fat baby bat. Sometimes the ground seemed to turn into clouds and I had to focus on the music to keep from passing out from love.

"Jess, I need to pee," Mol said.

"We love you, Mol," I said.

"You do not."

"Yes, we do," Jessica said.

"I have to go to the bathroom."

"I was just in the bathroom. The line is forever. I'm so drunk, Mol, hold me up," Jessica said.

"Come on." Mol pulled Jessica away from me by her elbow. Our bathroom bonds were growing complicated. Jessica looked back at me with a forlorn expression as if to tell me I was her true bathroom companion. I telepathically told her I would die for her if she wanted me to. I was dancing for quite a while before I realized I was alone.

i glided through the crowd surveying my tribe and I was pleased. We were a worthy group for the end of the world except for a few white teenage boys who scowled in the corner, shirtless, wishing the DJ would play hip-hop. They had the emotional maturity of a fetus. Tortured by their own chemistry, they couldn't speak or smile, only lurk and smoke. The little child-boys on the dance floor, the ones who hadn't hit puberty yet, were like elf messengers. They danced so fast and sexlessly, like molecules.

I needed a task, so I began walking to the Smart Drink stand. For three dollars I could get an amino-acid concoction—not like I needed it, the Ecstasy was making me speed. Maybe a Brain Blast would take the edge off, make the trip more embodied, less cerebral.

Over by the table I saw Riley, though I wasn't sure it was him. The blond guy in the green bowling shirt and jeans waved at me. It was him. I ran over and threw my arms around his body, taking in his familiar smell.

"Hey, Skye."

"You. Look, it's you. You're here. You're a thing. This thing."

"I'm looking for Teresa. Have you seen her?"

"No."

Teresa was his big crush, a girl he'd grown up with who he always thought was out of his league. Her parents were Rainbow Gathering / Burning Man Festival people and I think he mistook her arrogant superiority for a fairylike sophistication. She wore her love beads like a supermodel, her long blond hair was always brushed smooth.

"I have to find Teresa."

"Just come outside for a second."

I pulled him through the crowd by his sweaty hand, my good horse, boy thing, my prize. When we got outside, the cool air caressed me and a eucalyptus smell wafted over from a small grove of trees.

"What," he said curtly.

His face was red and his eyes were swollen. His Technicolor personality, angry and surreal, led me to believe he might be in a blackout.

"I kissed Jessica."

"Really?"

"At the party."

"What party?"

"On Tunnel Road."

"I was there."

"You were?"

"Where were you?" he said accusingly.

"By the band, on a big chair and by the pool."

"You always do your own thing, don't you."

"You don't have to get sarcastic, I didn't know you were there."

"Teresa was there. She was crying and I asked her what was wrong and she wouldn't say anything and this asshole was with her. She said she was coming here so I came. I can't find her, though. I'm worried about her."

"Jessica's here."

"Whatever."

"What's with you?"

"Never mind."

"No, wait."

"You don't care."

"I do."

"No, you don't. You have your own thing and that's okay. You have enough to deal with."

Riley pulled away and began walking back to the rave. My Ecstasy force field wouldn't allow me to follow him. I watched him almost fall as he weaved his way through the crowd.

A film was being projected onto the side of the white cement-block building. It was an image of a microscopic cell. The white thing quivered, contracted, then broke off into two cells and they both oozed off in different directions.

I couldn't see Riley through the crowd anymore but I could feel him, as if he left pieces of himself with me. I walked to the grove of eucalyptus trees and bummed a cigarette off a kid wearing a metallic jogging outfit, my first whole cigarette ever. We talked about his dog, a Labrador mix who just got hit by a car and was at the vet getting his bones reset. He was so worried. I told him I had this psychic sense that his dog was okay. I could feel that his dog was thinking about him, loving him, thanking him for caring.

"You really feel that?"

"I do."

"Cool. I feel that, too. I feel like Bogart's right here."

"Does he have a white spot on his forehead?"

"He does. How did you know?"

"I just know."

"That's amazing. I'm gonna go home. I can't be out with Bogart hurting."

"He'll be okay."

"Thanks. Thanks a lot," he said, adjusting his baseball cap and walking off.

The cells on the outside wall were splitting off into fours and eights, filling the screen with little white circles. I went back inside. The building was humid from other people's sweat. I meandered through the fog, searching for Jessica on the dance floor and in the crowd. Underwater and weightless, my skin stretched tight over my bright happy body. I never smiled at so many people in my life. Time warped as I watched someone getting a tattoo of a bug on their stomach at a table lit by a single halogen lamp. Three minutes felt like an hour. I remembered my bathroom pact with Jessica. I would be there for her. Loyalty was everything. I continued my search for her, with a focus that took on epic meaning.

I waited in the long line to the women's room. The bathrooms had become coed; guys stood peeing with the stall doors open. The nerve.

"You can go next," a girl said.

"I don't have to go."

I leaned down and looked for Jessica's shoes under the stalls. I saw them, along with a pair of sneakers. I didn't think. I walked over and pushed the stall door open. What I saw made the room turn bright like a flash photo. Too much blood to the brain. My ears rang. Some asshole was down on his knees, his face between her legs. Her skirt was up and her underwear was down. Their bodies were a pornographic blur, the Playboy Channel caught accidentally at three A.M. in a bad motel.

"Riley!" I gasped, recognizing him in a double take, though it was Jessica's face that hit me like a fist. It was stark white without any defining expression. She saw me and kicked him away.

"What the . . ." Riley said. He looked at me and winced. "Skye?"

"Great," I said. "Fabulous."

"Fuck . . . Skye . . . get out of here," Jessica slurred.

I shouldn't have watched her pull up her underwear or exchange words with Riley before he left but I did. Riley tripped past me, looking at the ground and holding on to the walls for support. I couldn't move. Jessica's jaw was slack as she came out of the stall, paused for a moment, looked at me then turned back around to go back in.

"Oh shit," she said.

She had to push a girl aside to get back in the stall where she immediately fell to her knees and threw up with the stall door ajar, visible to onlookers. She wretched violently, her deposit hitting the toilet water and splashing up into her hair as if a brick had been dropped into the basin. I shut the door and waited outside for her to finish. Loyal. Riley came back in. Girls yelled at him for cutting in line.

"Skye," he said. I turned to him. His body was wide open and listless.

"Why don't you just go."

"You know her?"

The pain of it all surged up into my heart and down into my arms. I pushed him and he stumbled back into the mirror. Everyone in line got perky, waiting for a scene.

"Don't you fucking push me!" he said, regaining his balance and coming at me. I stared into his drunk eyes and kicked him hard in the shin.

"Goddammit!" He reached down to touch his leg, hopping on the other. "I didn't know who she was."

"So what happened to Teresa?"

"What do you care? You cunt, you kicked me."

I grabbed him by the shirt collar when two twelve-year-olds came up to me, both with the same haircut and light blue pants.

"Chill," one said.

"You just need some air," said the other.

I let go. Jessica came out of the stall, the girls held me back as she stumbled drunkenly past me and Riley without looking at us.

"Fuck you," I said, the words coming out full of sickness. I could have hit her.

"This is dank. I'm gone," Riley said, taking the opportunity to leave.

"Don't do this," Jessica pleaded, turning around and looking into my eyes. "You don't know." Her words mysteriously disarmed me. She walked into the lights and the fog and I followed. She was a zombie, totally lost.

everyone was still smiling. What was wrong with them? I sat in a metal fold-out chair and tried to figure out what to do next. Visuals faded and the room became a minimalist *thwomp*ing bass line getting into my bones, rearranging DNA. With my forehead in my hand, I tried to cry a little to clear my head but the drugs wouldn't let me.

"You want to dance?" a boy said. He was cute in his little red outfit, very gay.

"No thanks."

"Are you okay?"

"No."

His angular Latin face, too sensitive for Earth, twitched. He looked at me like a rabbit then sat down cross-legged beside me on the floor.

"Will you let me hold your hand?"

"What?"

"Let me hold your hand."

I let my right hand drop from my lap and he took hold of it. His hand was small and clammy but comforting in a weird way. We sat like that for a while. I scanned the crowd looking for Mol and Cathy then saw Jessica sitting against the wall, no more than a few yards away from me. Her body was curled up with her knees to her chest. She kept shaking her head back and forth like she was trying to get something out. No one saw her, she was pretty much in the dark. Her body was still, then all of a sudden it thrashed around. Some kids walked by, pointed at her and laughed. That was too much.

"Where are you going?" the boy said when I let go of his hand.

"I have to take care of a friend."

"Thank you for being one of the lovers," he said with complete seriousness.

"Thank you for holding my hand." I nodded and got up to go to Jessica. I sat next to her, reluctantly. She was so out of it.

"Bag. My bag. Where's my bag?"

"You don't have a bag," I said.

"Is that you?"

"Yes."

"Leave me. Just go."

"Are you okay?"

"Get out of here." She pulled at her black hair. Her face was streaked with tears.

"What was that about in there?"

"Somebody kill me. Bad girl . . . didn't feed the cat . . ." She let out a demon laugh. Something was really wrong with her.

"Are you okay?"

"I hate you," Jessica said.

"Great. That's helpful," I said.

I sat there in a rage while she mumbled nonsense to herself. It occurred to me she might have some serious mental illness but it didn't make things any easier.

"Jesus, Skye, what's wrong with her?" Mol said, coming out of nowhere like some winged thing.

"She's fucked-up. She needs to get home. Get Cathy."

"She went with this guy to get a beer."

"We have to take her home. Now."

Mol kneeled down and touched Jessica's cheeks. Her gesture was more maternal than anything I could have mustered up. I had a pang of jealousy. Mol looked at me. "What happened?"

"She drank too much. I found her in the bathroom with . . ."

"Are you okay?" she said, noticing my sorry state.

I lost it then. I wanted Mol to touch me like she was touching Jessica, a mother's touch, but I couldn't ask so all I could do was let down the floodgates.

"Baby, what happened to you?" Her round face, brown eyes, black kinky hair, beamed in my direction and I leaned into her sweaty large body, held on tight and sobbed.

"What is this, some personal-growth workshop?" Jessica said. "You ate too much lettuce. You got candida."

"Shut up, Jessica," Mol said. "Get yourself together. I'm taking you home."

"I don't wanna go home."

"You don't have a choice. Pull your dress down, your skinny little white thighs are showing."

i waited in mol's car while she tried to coax Jessica into the backseat. It was quite a project. Jessica was psycho, yelling things at Mol then breaking down and crying. I tried to get myself together before Mol got in but when I wiped my eyes clean, more tears would come.

"No, you don't mean that," I heard Mol say.

"I do too want to die," Jessica slurred.

"No, you don't."

"You don't know. I'm going to kill myself."

"No, you're not."

"I'm gonna die now, okay?" Jessica was sobbing by then. It was hard not to feel sorry for her.

We drove to Jessica's house and parked far enough away so the sound of the car wouldn't wake her mom up. Mol got out and opened the back door for Jessica.

"Oh shit."

"What."

"Her arms. Shit. Oh fuck. Fuck."

"What."

"This is my mom's car. She's going to kill me."

I looked back at Jessica. She held a pen in her fist. She had used it to ravage her forearm, ripping away scars that were almost healed. I don't know how we could have spaced it out. Blood was smudged all over her dress and her face. She reached up to touch her hair and blood dripped from her elbow. She seemed unable to speak. Her eyes were open and haunted.

"Her mom can't see this. I'm going to see if the pool door is open."

Mol left and I got in the backseat and sat next to Jessica. I ran my hand along her blood-wet arm, checking to make sure the wounds were only superficial. When I touched her hand, her fingers curled around and she held tight.

"Why do you do this?"

"I'm sorry." She forced the words out as if they came on her last breath. "I just wanna go. I just wanna leave this place. Let me die. Kill me."

I kissed her sticky face as if that alone could make her want to live. I ripped pages from a math textbook laying on the floor and put them on her cuts. The paper turned red and soggy. I buried my face in her hair. It was as strong-smelling and as oily as my father's scalp. I used to smell his combs as a child, amazed that something coming from a human could smell so strong, almost rancid. The odor of her hair mixed with the undefinable smell of her blood. I felt like I was inside her, closer than any person should be allowed to go. I was a thread away from screaming my head off when Mol came back.

"Let's get her inside."

"Mol."

"What. Are you going to throw up?"

"Mol."

"What?"

"Just wait."

jessica hung off our shoulders as we guided her quietly through the glass door to her room. We bathed her naked body with warm washcloths, ringing out the orange blood into the sink. The wounds weren't as bad as they looked. Jessica cried quietly the whole time, lost in her own impenetrable world. How could anybody be so miserable on Ecstasy? Even after all that had happened, I was possessed with an unwanted, almost demonic glee.

"I'll stay with her," Mol said. "You can go home if you want."

"I can't go home."

"I know what you mean." Mol tucked Jessica into her bed and climbed in beside her.

"You can sleep up here with us."

"I'm okay down here," I said, lying on the carpet.

"You need a blanket, though."

"No, I don't. I'm okay."

"Good night, Skye. Thanks."

"Good night. Thanks to you, too."

The light went off and I stared at a patch of gray on the wall from the light coming through the single window, too speedy to sleep.

nine

i wonder if it's possible to ever really know a person. I think we decide who a person is in the first few seconds of seeing them. It's a pure moment of recognition, almost animal-like. Over time things get piled on that image, the stuff of personality, psychology, and then I think that maybe I never knew them at all. A maze begins, a process of getting to know them and you have to really love a person to walk it. Like Mom—I don't even know what her favorite food is or where she goes when she wants to be alone. And Jessica. I thought I knew her because I could feel her inside me like some magical force but if someone came along and asked me if she was a good person or a bad person I wouldn't know what to say to them. I mean, those are important things to know about a person—whether they're evil or not.

I left Jessica's house at sunrise without saying good-bye. On the way home I stopped at the haunted house, a three-story on the corner of Mission and San Mateo. It became clear to me that if Jessica was a house she would be that one. It's an old house with white paint that has chipped and turned gray. Stained white curtains cover the cracked windows. Despite the fact that it's run-down, the house exudes romance. It's exciting to think that if someone just took a paintbrush to the building, it could be a house of dreams, a house that would change the person living inside it, making them somehow more magical and timeless. The house begs for someone to love it and remodel it but whenever someone comes along they get pushed away by the hassles that arise from deeper inspection—a leaky roof, structural damage, bad copper pipes. Even the most inspired decorators give up. They love the house, but not enough.

I walked the three more blocks to my house and stood behind the jacaranda tree to see if Mom was home before I went farther. I always had to stop and think if there was anything I was lying about that week just in case she started asking me questions. Luckily she was gone.

When Mom wasn't around, I loved coming home. Some part of me quieted down when I got the key from under the pot, opened the door, and smelled the kitchen. I love that house. I think I loved it more than Mom ever did. The exterior walls are made of thick white stucco with handmade tiles of Mediterranean color and design inlaid near the windows. The floors are smooth planks of blond wood. The kitchen floor is done in saltillo tile.

The living room catches the southern light. What I liked best about my room was the thick wood trim around the single window above my bed. It was sturdy and old-looking, chipped, revealing coats of purple, green, and pink. In the center of the window I hung a piece of blue sea glass, the neck of an old bottle, worn smooth by salt water and motion.

Our kitchen had the trashiest cabinets but I loved them. They were yanked out of a house that was torn down in the early sixties. They were white and made out of a soft curvy metal. Our cabinets looked like a 1956 Buick complete with chrome trim.

Mom complained about the kitchen the most. The whole house bothered her, really. It was too small. When it came to

Mom's social scene, the house might as well have had a neon sign out front—Downwardly-Mobile Cafe—we make our cappuccinos and sushi at home now.

My contribution to the house was a 1960s fold-out breakfast table. It was aquamarine with little black specks. I tried to talk Mom into buying it at a garage sale but she was too stingy so I sprung the forty dollars and bought it myself. It was the soul of the kitchen.

I was hungry and went to the refrigerator to eat some peanut butter from a jar when I noticed that Mom had left a page torn out of the local newspaper for me. The headline read, HYPNOTHERAPY HELPS RITUAL ABUSE SURVIVORS.

Mom had circled the name of the hypnotherapist—Dr. Hayward. I had seen his name before on the numerous pamphlets Mom gave me. I was scheduled to have a session with him in a week. The newspaper was called *California Light—Your Resource for the New Thought Network*. A photograph on the front page showed Dr. Hayward in a white lab coat. He had a gray beard that grew way past his chin. A quote in bold letters by the photograph read, "Of course your family will deny it, what do they have to gain from admitting they allowed a child to be tortured in their own house?"

A woman named Sue (a fictitious name) had discovered through hypnosis that her parents were part of a satanic cult. They injected her with drugs and drove her to a field where hundreds of other Satan worshipers stood in a circle wearing black robes. She was laid on a cold slab of granite and raped and sodomized by the Warlock at knifepoint. She then was forced to sodomize a male infant with a black candlestick. Her parents made her watch as the Warlock sliced the infant's chest open with a dull knife then took out its still-beating heart. "I don't know if I ate it. Oh God. Oh God. I don't know. I can't remember if I ate it or not. They gave me so many drugs."

Sue was part of a support group full of other ritual-abuse

survivors under the facilitation of Dr. Hayward. I pictured Sue after a difficult session with Dr. Hayward, going to the supermarket, to the gas station, to the post office, thinking about the baby's heart. Was it the size of a walnut? A kiwifruit?

I'm sure Satanists exist. In a world where Hitler can exist, Satanists exist, and I'm sure a few do their share of baby-eating, but I just couldn't believe Sue's story. How could someone repress something like that? Most people who have had horrible things happen to them can't get the memory *out* of their minds.

"Stories of ritual abuse are common, about half of my clients have experienced some form of ritual abuse. It's extremely disturbing," Hayward was quoted as saying. *Disturbing!* How can this man sleep at night?

It was hard to grasp the thought of these people's parents donning black robes at midnight and getting into the Volvo to drive north of Santa Barbara to some empty field. I mean, you can't even get away with growing pot plants in this county, let alone eat babies and rape prepubescent girls on granite slabs. How are people investigating these accusations? "Excuse me, sir, when's the last time you sold a granite slab to someone? Tell me, sir, did they look vaguely satanic?"

It was just recently that I had been cursed by satanic teenagers. Evil, yes. Baby-eaters, no.

I napped on the couch, swallowed by one of the worst hangovers a person could ever have, an Ecstasy hangover. I scolded myself for doing it at all.

"What is the story of your life?" Jessica had asked. I imagined her, a ghost in front of me, sunken eyes and still-bleeding scars like the resurrected Christ in a dress.

I tried to answer. "It's full of dreams. Nothing ever happens in my life. But the dreams are real. They can be as real as anything. Right?"

The Jessica Christ shook her head. "Wrong. What is the story of your life?"

"You kissed me, then I found you in the bathroom getting eaten out by my boyfriend."

"No, that's me. What about you?"

"I lost my faith then. Not like my faith was any big thing. It was as weak as a small tree planted in drought season. I didn't expect anything. I probably deserved it."

ten

i made a pact with myself to not call Riley or Jessica. The decision came with all the puritanical fervor of a "Lose twenty pounds *fast*" diet. I was going to get myself together, not like I had any idea what I was going to do with myself once I got there. My inspiration was born out of the classic California mantra: "If all else fails, self-improve." I always believed that aloneness was basically good so I set up my room like a sanctuary and prepared to burrow for as long as it took to feel in control of my life again. I lit candles, cleaned up all the scattered papers. I cut some photographs out of fashion magazines and stuck them on the wall. I noticed that I was drawn to Italian-looking women in sultry power suits which I analyzed as my own desire to feel like I was at the wheel of my own life again.

With the house all to myself, eight o'clock was pretty quiet and lonely. Even though I didn't want to talk to Riley, I was still furious that he didn't call to at least ask how I was doing. Maybe I'd kicked him harder than I thought.

Jessica called at nine.

"Skye, I'm sorry. I owe my life to you." Her voice sounded drugged.

"I don't know if I want to talk to you right now. I have some thinking to do."

"I understand," she said.

Then we were quiet. I heard her sniffle on the other end of the phone and assumed she was crying. This got me crying, too. We stayed on the phone like that for a long time, saying absolutely nothing. Things were communicated, though, in the silence. I don't know if that was the healthiest way to deal with it but we already knew the words that were scripted for us to say, so why say them? We were both sorry. The love could be felt. I wasn't finished with her yet.

"So do you want to come over?" I said.

"Sure. I've got magazines we can look through. There's this new trend in fashion photography where they make the models look like demon children. They have painted-on freckles and they hold little stuffed animals. It's so cool. I want to make a collage."

"When can you come over?"

"In an hour."

"Okay."

" 'Bye."

"Wear your coat. It's cold tonight."

"Yeah. Thanks. I'll bring my 1980s French Avant-Garde Film Coat."

Three hours passed. She finally arrived at midnight, without the French coat and without the magazines. We watched TV and ate what we could find in the refrigerator and the cabinets—Slim-Fast, baked tortilla chips, a Romaine-lettuce salad, and some non-fat Cool Whip that was in the freezer.

"We should have ordered out for pizza, this is disgusting," I said.

"I like it. Fake food is a conspiracy. It's encoded with information on little microchips. You eat it and information is released into your brain that says, 'Go to the mall,' 'You're ugly,' 'Get a nose job.' "

"And you like that?"

"It doesn't affect me because I'm an anarchist."

"How's your cuts?"

"Fine."

That was as personal as we got. I had a million questions but my throat felt plugged. She built a wall by making stupid comments about what was on TV. She had something to say about every outfit, every hairdo. She set the tone. Code language only.

"Did you ever have to get stitches?" I asked, one of those infantile nonthreatening questions.

"Yeah, once. My brother hit me with a board that had a nail in it."

"I didn't know you had a brother."

"He's in jail."

"For what?"

"Assault. Like, sexual assault. He's an asshole, you know what I mean? I don't really want to talk about it."

I knew right then that her brother fucked her. Or something. Something had happened to her. I was afraid to ask. Talking about things like that can make people crazy, right? You're supposed to save it for the therapist just in case a memory comes back and takes you over. You need someone professional to handle it.

"He used to make me give him head."

There. She offered. Just another fact, but she didn't want to talk about it anymore.

she fell asleep on the couch. Blank. I watched her until I got annoyed and then woke her.

"What?" she said, as if she didn't know where she was.

"You should get in the bed."

"Why?"

"You just should."

We walked down the hallway to my room.

"I'm so out-of-it," she said.

"No kidding."

"I'm on this medication, it makes me space out."

"What medication?"

"I don't know. It's good. It gives me space to think."

She climbed under the covers, still in her clothes, and lay staring up at the ceiling while I changed into underwear and a T-shirt. I turned on the tape player and climbed under the cool sheets, making sure I didn't get too close.

"Did you ever get stitches?" she said.

"Once. Potty-training. Weird."

"What happened?"

"I fell off the toilet and hit my head on the toilet-paper-roll thing and I sliced myself open. Blood everywhere."

"You poor thing."

"I know. It was horrible. I wouldn't go near the toilet for a long time after that."

Jessica's laugh was easy and deep, it surprised me and made me feel close to her for the first time all night. I could tell, though, by the way she lay packed like a fish in her own space that I wasn't going to be her lover that night.

"So how come you never told me about Riley?"

"Don't even go there."

"Whatever. Sorry. I didn't know it was him. I hardly remember what happened. Mol told me about it."

There she was, Ms. Direct when she wanted to be, always the boss of the conversation.

"So Riley's your boyfriend. He's cute. From what I remember."

"I'm sure you don't remember much. You were out-of-it."

"I was gone."

"You know everything about my life, don't you?"

"I know you want a girl."

My face flushed with blood. Was that an invitation? What could I tell from her chest rising and falling and her small hairs catching the light?

"I guess I do."

"That's cool."

I was afraid to even move. In my peripheral vision, the skin on her arms looked so white next to her scars. I almost wished she'd cut herself then, because it was such an intimate thing for her. Blood would get on everything, though, the sheets, the floor, and I couldn't think of a way to explain the mess to my mom.

Jessica said she missed her blood when she didn't see it. I was starting to miss it, too, just that part of her that was real, laid bare.

The red gashes on her arm were a third party in the room I didn't want to send away. She had asked me to cut her that day in her room and I had said no. Lying in my own bed with her, I could have done it then. But really, I just wanted to kiss her, that's all. There was the civilized smell of her shampoo and the muskiness of her black dress, so many layers to get under. She was always the one with secrets. It gave her the power.

"Riley and I masturbate together, basically," I said, trying to share something that was a risk.

"Oh."

"Does that freak you out? Me saying that?"

"Oh, come on, look who you're talking to."

"You slut," I said playfully.

"Bitch."

"Cunt."

The soft places where she used to hurt me were getting tough. I was learning how to not feel everything.

"When I was a kid," I said, "I got left in basements at parties. I was drunk. On acid. I think something happened to me down there. Someone did something sexually to me," I whispered, hoping my manufactured secret would have the mysterious power to open her heart up to me. She just used it as an excuse to talk more about herself.

"That stuff happened to me all the time," she said flippantly. "My brother's friends would come over. Get me shitfaced and stuff. Someone started a game. Fifty bucks to the guy who could get me to give him a blowjob, but then they realized they couldn't prove it because the guy could be lying so I had to do it with everybody standing around watching. But then nobody would win so they thought it was only fair that I got the fifty bucks anyway."

It fast became obvious that I couldn't compete with her stories. I didn't even know how to listen very well. I felt like a talk-show host trying to appear sensitive while interviewing the latest victim of tragedy. It was so hard to feel without at least touching her. I put my hand on her wrist and she look down at it, distracted, like a bug landed on her.

She told me some stories I didn't really want to hear about: sex with guys after parties. Too many guys.

"Did you ever have sex when you were sober?" I asked. She paused for a moment.

"Yeah, once."

I began to doubt if she'd ever really had good sex. She talked about it like it was some sort of calamity to be dealt with and laughed about the next day, like puking from too much alcohol. *Oops, I just puked. Oops, I just got fucked.* I wanted her to shut up, her words were pushing me away again just when I thought I had an in.

"This one guy came over to my house and brought two flasks of tequila," she said. "I couldn't tell him to leave. He seemed like a nice guy. I guess he could have been a rapist, I just met him in the mall the day before. He was in a band. Anyway, he passes out in my room and as he's lying there I see this condom that fell out of his jacket. I was like, 'You are so totally gross. I'm telling Mom.' "

"Did you?"

"Of course not."

"I don't tell my mom about anything having to do with sex. She doesn't even date. Since she's started therapy and Matrix, she lives this pretend life, like she only talks to people to work some inner thing out. She goes out dancing and it's like a test. She doesn't have sex because she's trying to avoid sex-addict behavior, but every now and then she'll be in her room with the door closed and I'll hear this . . . *bzzzzz*. The vibrator."

"Your mom has a vibrator, cool. I can't imagine my mom ever having an orgasm."

"Don't try. Really, you could damage yourself."

"I mean, I can't imagine myself coming, either, so . . ."

"Really?"

"Yeah."

I mentioned that my mom rejected her first vibrator for a more advanced Japanese model and the original was under my bed. Jessica wanted to see it. I leaned over and pulled it up by the frayed electrical cord.

"This is it?"

"It's the kind you buy in the store for your shoulders."

"Yeah, right." She turned it on, fascinated. It struck me that she was considering using it. I panicked. Did she think it was some way for us to have sex? I mean, we didn't kiss or anything but it's hard to tell what's sex for some people and what's not sex sometimes. Was I supposed to do something? She turned on the vibrator and pressed it to her nose. She sneezed. She touched it to her ears, her scalp, her shoulders. Maybe if I was holding the vibrator I could call it sex, but I was already so terrified I couldn't feel, so then it wouldn't be sex, for me at least. Rule number one, you have to feel something for it to be sex. I just wanted to kiss her, that's all.

She actually did it. She brought it under the covers and presumably put it between her legs. I wasn't under there to verify. I never noticed how insanely loud it was before, like a lawn mower.

It was definitely there between her legs. Her eyes fluttered, her face tensed. She was gone. Totally.

Why did my life have to be so pathetic? I was in bed with the girl I wanted the most and I couldn't even kiss her. I couldn't even get off on her masturbating with a vibrator. It didn't look like she came. She handed it to me. It was warm.

"Smell it."

"Fuck you."

"Don't you want to use it?"

"I have enough orgasms."

"Now you're making me feel like a freak."

"I'm the freak."

"You okay?"

"Yeah."

"You sure?"

"Yeah."

"I'm sleepy. I'm kind of out-of-it," she said.

It definitely wasn't sex. She turned off the light and I had at least enough guts to put my arm over her and spoon her as she slept. I must have been awake for another hour replaying our kiss in my mind over and over. I thought that if sexual abuse made Jessica the way she was, that was really fucked up. Even though I was in love with her, I had the clarity to see that she was a jerk. If sexual abuse made people jerks then I was glad nothing happened to me. If something did, then I was lucky to forget. Being a jerk sucks.

eleven

mom got home from her workshop at noon. She walked through the door radiant, on an emotional high from Mastery II and insisted on making breakfast for us. She gave us both hugs, told us we were beautiful children of the universe. She had bags under her eyes and looked exhausted yet still wired-up like a grateful survivor of a natural disaster. She wanted to make us fat-free pancakes with honey but we were out of the mix so miraculously she settled upon eggs and toast. We held our breath when she opened the freezer to get a block of butter. Luckily she didn't notice Heda behind the frozen tempeh burgers.

Contrary to what I expected, Mom was really nice to Jessica. Jessica was polite enough. I was glad she wore a long-sleeve shirt to cover up her scars. I was surprised at Jessica's ability to act normal. She asked Mom to pass the salt. She participated in the conversation about Mom's ceramics and even added that out of all the bowls on display in the kitchen, she liked the purple one with the yellow cat the best. We all got a private satisfaction from our noontime breakfast. We were perfectly civilized. I almost broke the spell when I told Mom the eggs were "smashing" in an English accent. A look of hurt flashed in her eyes and I regretted the sarcasm. I wanted her to have the normal breakfast. That, I could give her. When Mom raised the coffee cup to her lips, her hand was shaking. At the same time, Jessica and I looked down at the table wondering if we would make it through the normal breakfast, so many things were pressing in on us. A dead bird, hidden scars, a coffee cup perched between thumb and finger, and just two eggs, sourdough toast, and butter to ward off all the craziness in the world.

jessica took the bus home. After sending her off I started walking down the street with nothing but a five-dollar bill in my pocket. It was my intention to walk all day long, to hopefully walk Jessica out of my system for good. I didn't want to need her anymore. It hurt too much. I missed Lorri, felt bad for blowing her off at the party.

I walked downtown past all the shops, sometimes stopping inside to look at things but mostly I just kept walking, looking at the faces. I looked at everyone. It was like I was looking for a specific person, though I didn't know who that could be. Most everyone met my eyes. Housewives, children, businessmen, and young shoppers smiled back or looked away. Each of them held something inside. A little bit of it leaked out when they looked at me and I kept it. I was heavy with their secrets when I turned to go down a residential street.

There were some houses I especially loved and I built a walking tour around visiting them. It was a game I played by myself from the age of ten when my mom first let me take walks alone. I imagined that visiting the houses made them happy. There was the old Victorian with stained-glass windows on Garden Street, the Spanish hacienda on Milpas with the fish tank in the window, the gingerbread bed-and-breakfast with lace curtains, and the dark wood-and-glass monstrosity on Tunnel Road that was built in the seventies. My houses had nothing in common with each other. It took all day to visit them. I never took a short cut. It was important to walk down the same sidewalk every time as if I was tracing some mystical constellation with my walking feet. I went past the house I called Betty for no reason, the hippie house with the hammocks and the hanging dragons, and down to the beach houses perched upon barnacle-covered stilts. I stopped along my walk to eat sourgrass, oranges, and a red berry that tasted like an apple. I took that walk with all the obsessiveness I could muster, memorizing details, calculating the square footage of each house, making up stories about the people inside. I forgot about my life for a while.

There was something different about the houses that day. They made me sad. I hated that I couldn't go inside them. I couldn't see the floors, the walls, the doorways, and the way the light spilled in. Each house had a world inside, a Hong Kong behind doors, a festival in secret, and I was too much left on the outside. I considered knocking on a few doors to ask if I could take a look around. I'm not the suspicious-looking type but decided against it, figuring I couldn't handle the rejection if they said no. Instead, I ran up to each house, touched the wall, and ran back to the sidewalk, tagging each house in this way, like an autistic person's ritual.

I got home at sunset. Exhausted, I lay down on the couch in our small, rarely used living room. My body sank into the cushions, the Ecstasy sludge still not cleansed from my system. A state of relaxation came, as satisfying as a hot bath. I could feel my pulse in my hands and feet. When I closed my eyes, I saw houses and people's faces. They were inside of me, so many of them. I had to make myself bigger just to hold them all.

Mom came into the living room, frantically rubbing moisturizer all over her face.

"We have to go in an hour. Are you clean?"

I had completely forgotten about the Sunday-night Cross the Line training. "I don't smell, if that's what you mean."

"Brush your teeth."

"Okay."

I got up and went to the bathroom. Looking in the mirror, I saw a few zits so I started popping the good ones, moving on to the blackheads. After I was done I looked like I had some horrible heat rash. I washed my face with really hot water but it only made things worse.

"What did you do!" Mom said when I came back out.

"I'm just breaking out a little bit. It's no big deal."

"Stress."

"Yeah, stress."

we had a tense drive to St. Cecilia Elementary School. She kept asking questions about Jessica, like did she have a boyfriend? She asked me if she was anemic because she looked so pale. I didn't want to talk about her at all and my avoidance made Mom suspicious.

"Is she . . . that way?" Mom said.

"What . . . 'way'?"

"You know what I mean. Is she gay?"

"It's none of your business."

"It is my business. I wouldn't let you spend the night with Riley and you always understood that. If you and that girl are sleeping together I don't want it to be in my house. That's my right." She gripped the steering wheel till her knuckles turned white, her lips pursed.

"She's not gay."

"There's something strange about her."

"She's not strange, Mom."

"I don't know if you're telling the truth most of the time. Go ahead, bring your lovers over to my house, have sex with them in your bed, I don't care."

I wondered what medication was making Mom so crass. I couldn't believe the things that came out of her mouth sometimes.

"Can we not talk about this now?"

"Are you fucking her?"

"No! God! Stop, okay? I agreed to come to this thing, so can you please not freak out? I don't want to walk in there with tears running down my face."

She pulled into the lot with a screech and parked the car. Cross the Line was being held in the carpeted lecture hall adjacent to the library. The smell of Frito's permeated the whole building. Children's drawings of endangered species lined the long hallway.

A fold-out table was set up at the entrance. Mom paid the hundred dollar fee and we were given nametags. I recognized some of the faces from other workshops, women and men in their thirties, smiling more fiercely than the drugged-out kids at the rave. Everyone had a new look. They were all striving to be very up-and-coming. Gone were the African mud-cloth vests and Guatemalan sack dresses; they all had discovered the glamour of mall-wear. Synthetic polyester shirts in the latest colors were worn with last year's silk skirt. The men proudly sported long-sleeve turtlenecks and sideburns. It was the "I've already made it to the top and can afford to dress down" look except no one had made it. They were going on the Course in Miracles' "Pretend you already have it and it will appear amazingly out of nowhere" look.

I gave Mindy a hug. A long time ago we had bonded in Warrior II during the Emotional Roller Coaster Game. In a fit of rage, I got nauseous and started throwing up. She retrieved a bucket from the utility room a little too late. She calmed me down by holding me till I started crying softly. I always liked her but she was starting to get really fanatical about the workshops and she pulled this superiority thing on me all the time.

"Are you okay?" she said, deeply concerned. Her question

was intended to make me feel like shit. Feeling like shit was the preferred emotion at Cross the Line, signifying you were out of the denial phase. You were only allowed to be happy near the end of the training and when you had signed up for one of the advanced workshops.

Despite my attempts to play it cool, I was actually very afraid. I hadn't been to a workshop in a while and I was out of practice at keeping people at a safe distance. Matrix people had a way of getting under your skin when you least expected it. To avoid having to make polite conversation, I sat in a row of empty fold-out chairs. A giant chart was displayed in front of the room. It looked like the same chart Planned Parenthood used to provide a visual image of the human orgasm except that this one was called "The Astarus Continuum." On the low end of the graph in red was Antagonism, Anger, and Overt Resentment. I guess that meant me. Yellow and orange were Covert Resentment, Boredom, Somatising, and Fantasy moving into the yellow-and-green of Curiosity, Pleasure, and Excitement. The graph ended in a splash of purple and the words JOY, UNIVERSAL LOVE, and POWER in capital letters. Unlike the graph of the human orgasm, this one didn't have a lull after the climax. There was no POST-JOY. I guess if you got a bad vibe you got demoted back to the red, orange, and yellow zones and you just had to work your way back up again.

I sat there staring blankly ahead of me, taking note of how fluorescent light makes everything look flat, like a show on public television. The tape on the stereo played Whitney Houston's "The Greatest Love of All" and a women's choir singing "Om Nama Shivaya" and a Native American chant. People sat down exactly at seven and the lights were dimmed.

Marilyn, the head trainer, started off the evening with a story about her first hang-gliding experience. Ben, her cofacilitator and sometime lover, shared some insights he got from the Harmonics workshop held on the island of Kawaii. He was wearing white cotton slacks and a flowered shirt. His tanned face was open and expressive, like a very unassuming elf. He told his story like a pro. Apparently the sun and sand along with intensive muscle-testing therapy uncovered memories of abandonment he experienced in the early stages of life.

"It was a miracle. My trauma was healed immediately," he said, tears streaming down his face. "I danced under the most beautiful waterfall with other beings who had also realized their belovedness in the eyes of God. We sang, danced, and made sounds that were at once both animal and celestial."

Apparently at the moment his damage was healed, the planet underwent a sort of chiropractic adjustment as a result of their revelry that was unprecedented since the Rainbow Workshop when the Samurai Game caused a peace treaty to be signed in Bosnia. He channeled information for a whole other seminar, Harmonics II, that was to explore sound and its relationship to the Inner Avatar and the Celestial Spheres. Pamphlets were already made and could be found on the table by the hallway. The seminar was scheduled to be held in Jamaica for $6,000, airfare and accommodations not included.

The soundtrack to *Rocky* came on the stereo and Marilyn appeared on the platform wearing a boxing outfit. She bounced around taking shots at an invisible opponent. Marilyn was over fifty; her bright red lipstick leaked along the wrinkled crevices of her mouth. She was once a soap opera actress who did walk-on parts. Mom liked to call her "a very sassy lady."

I didn't trust Marilyn because she touched my crotch once during a rebirthing process when my body went into paralysis from not getting enough oxygen. My arms, face, and chest began to tingle and go numb. I couldn't move and my face was frozen in a painful extraterrestrial expression. She put her palm between my legs, "to ground me," she said. It kind of worked, that's the embarrassing part.

In her little performance she gave us the metaphor of being

a fighter in training. You can never rest. You must push on and be stronger . . . faster.

"No fancy processes. No therapy. Just confrontation. Just cross the line. Fucking cross the line!!!" she said, a madwoman in spandex.

I looked at Mom. Her face was beaming. She was inspired by this woman.

I knew the routine. A person volunteers to go up on the platform and everyone confronts them, meaning they tell them what a piece of shit they are. The facilitator wanders around mediating everything.

My strategy was to be invisible. To create any conflict with Matrix people was an invitation to catastrophe. I kept telling myself I'd do it for Mom. I'd sit there and be a good girl.

A thin man wearing athletic pants and a T-shirt got up on the platform first. I didn't recognize him. He was probably a recent Matrix graduate, so full of energy and enthusiasm he made us all look sick. An older man stood up and took the first shot.

"Oh please. You're a space cadet. You're just a little boy. What do you do for a living, massage therapy?" Everyone laughed.

"What's the judgment?" Ben said.

The older man took a deep breath. "You're a flake. You don't mean anything you say. You're a fly-by-night."

"Thank you." Ben, the facilitator, nodded and looked to the ground.

The man on the platform stopped smiling. He shook his hands out and cracked his neck.

"Good, let that in," Ben said. "Next?"

A short woman in her twenties with blond hair and a sunburned face stood up and faced him.

"You just seem . . ."

"No no no, remember your language," Ben said. "No *justs, buts, like, seems,* none of that."

"You're castrated. You're a boy that's never going to become a man."

The blond woman broke down into tears as did the man on the platform. He stood with his hands at his sides, just sobbing, a real pro at the confrontation process.

"We have to move fast. This is just a touch-up. Thank you, Jerry," Ben said.

Jerry walked back down to his seat where he was comforted by two others.

An overweight woman in a white jumpsuit with southwestern fringe took the stage. She was already crying, full of an ancient self-hatred. The participants raised their hands.

"Why don't you just stop hating yourself, it's so boring."

"Your fat isn't going to keep you from getting fucked. Look at you, there's a sexy woman in there."

"Stop being a victim."

"You just never go the distance. You're lazy."

"You're afraid to be powerful."

I saw each statement sink into her thick skin. She'd been around the Matrix scene for years and she always had the same look on her face, like she was lost somewhere looking for her mommy. She returned to her seat unchanged.

Then Marilyn looked at me. "Skye, how about you?

I considered declining the invitation but I knew it would provoke something even worse. I could fake it. I would prove my ability to feel nothing. My mom put her arm around my shoulder. I recoiled. I walked up and stood on the platform, a blond sixteen-year-old girl with her hands in her baggy jeans.

"You're beautiful but you wear these ugly clothes, what are you—"

"What's the judgment?" Ben said.

"You're hiding your femininity."

Marilyn nodded in agreement and gave me a look that bor-

141

dered on lascivious. "Why is that, Skye?" she said. I didn't expect to have to speak.

"Um. I don't have time to shop for clothes. I'm too busy writing my term paper. Um, it's comfortable."

"You know you're beautiful, don't you?"

"Yes."

She snickered. "No, you don't."

"You're not a dyke," said a man in the back row. "You're just afraid of men."

"Take a deep breath, Skye."

I took one. I thought of Jessica, her mouth open with the vibrator between her legs. The memory had become more erotic than the actual event.

My mother stood up. She couldn't speak at first. Marilyn let her take a pause to pull herself together. "It's okay, Anna, tell Skye."

"I don't even know you anymore. You're just a stranger to me," Mom said.

"Take it in, Skye."

I saw Mom crying. Everyone looked at her with this feigned love, then turned to me to respond.

"Take it in."

"No." I said it under my breath so no one could hear. No. Never. Never again and for the first time no one could hurt me. I had found a place to hide. Deep breaths, deep breaths. Don't let them see the lie behind your eyes. A fake tear would have helped. Whatever. I was allowed to step down and return to my seat after giving Mom a long hug. Someday, I thought, I would be old enough to leave this all behind me. I would be old enough to say *Fuck off* to anyone. And I wouldn't have to pretend anymore.

when the training was over, Mom took forever giving everyone hugs and good-bye love stares. My impatience mounted. I could hardly take it. Just when Mom finally got her coat and we were about to leave, a woman broke down into hysterics. Everyone gathered around her in a circle. I saw a tear-stained face frantically rocking back and forth in the center.

"Get out! Get out of my body!" the voice screamed. She gagged a little then I heard her sing a child's song.

" 'Puff the magic dragon lived by the sea' . . . *sob sob.*"

People began *omm*ing a long monotonous tone that went on forever, drowning out her singing and crying. A man held the woman as she rocked, lost in a trauma. I stood by the door and watched as some of the assistants picked up the plastic cups and threw away the crumbs from the store-bought chocolate chip cookies. They cleaned out the coffee machines, pausing in their task to acknowledge the spontaneous healing by holding their palms out to the circle to give energy. They'd glance over at me as if looking for approval. When no one was looking, I went outside and got in the car and waited.

I looked out the car window at the playground and tried to remember fourth grade. There was lunch hour, Fruit Rolls, sticker trading, and a girl named Chelsea who was my best friend. Where'd she go? Maybe I could find her in the Los Angeles phone book. I hate the way people fall away. When memories start to dissolve and you don't know what's real and what was a photograph or some story someone told you, people are the only thing left to prove the past ever happened. Sometimes the past is the only thing that brings you back to yourself when you're lost. Chelsea and I stopped being friends because of some stupid thing like the French Club. People should never stop talking unless something really horrible happens. You don't even need to like the person, just don't lose them.

mom came out an hour later and we drove home in silence. I thought I was going to be able to go to my room in peace when she said she had a present for me. She went into her bedroom and brought out a medium-sized box wrapped in last year's Christmas paper. She placed it on the kitchen table. An opened business letter rested on top of it. I picked it up. It was from Mills College.

"How long have you had this?" I asked.

"You got in."

I read the acceptance letter. It was typed on thick linen paper. *Mills College* was printed in raised type at the top of the page.

"But you don't want to go to an all-women's college, do you?"

"I just want to go to the college that's best. They have a good architecture program there."

"I thought you were studying English."

"I changed my mind."

"Figures," she said bitterly. "Well, at least it's in California. Open the present."

I took the paper off, revealing a Nordstrom box. I opened it to find a neatly folded white lace dress. It smelled like an old house.

"It was my mother's. I thought since you're growing up . . . I mean I could wait for you to get married but . . ."

I took it out of the box. It was thick and heavy, almost damp.

"Thanks, it's beautiful." I kissed Mom on the cheek.

"Your appointment with Dr. Hayward is on Wednesday. You might have to miss volleyball."

"I can't miss volleyball. We have a game," I lied, hoping Mom didn't already suspect that I quit volleyball.

"You can miss it once."

"No, I can't."

"The appointment can't be changed. You'll just have to deal with it."

"I'm not going to see Dr. Hayward. I don't want to be hypnotized."

"That's what I thought. At least you admit it. Are you afraid of losing control?"

"I think Dr. Hayward is a quack. I'm hypnotized enough already. If anything, I need to come out of a trance rather than go into one. I'm not going."

"Then you're not going to Mills."

"Fine, I'm not going to Mills. There's a nice community college in Fresno. I'll work at the Wal-Mart and take night classes. I'll sell HerbalLife on the side."

"Don't be snide."

"I'm not."

"Why are you afraid of men? Does penetration frighten you?"

It was the way she said the word—*penetration*—that made it seem like something that came and got you . . . a pterodactyl casting its shadow then picking you up with its talons. Penetration—pterodactyl—genital—coital. Mythical—mutant—macabre. It's just a dick, what's the big deal? Mom viewed every act of the body as a ritual, some ancient rite of passage. When I got my period she had a potluck with beets and tomato soup. She invited the Matrix people. I had to participate in a ceremony that included a string made of hemp, a drum, and a bowl of water. Maybe I didn't want to fuck Riley because I had an irrational fear of my mother showing up in the doorway at the moment of orgasm with a smudge stick and a drum.

"I'm not afraid of men or penetration." I didn't tell her about the victimized vegetables, flashlights, and acrylic-paint tubes that upon close examination could be evidence on my behalf. "I'm not going to see Dr. Hayward. I hardly ever refuse to do anything and you know that. You can do what you want."

She picked up the letter from Mills, crumpled it up in her hand, and stomped off to her room with a loaded silence. I was expected to follow, throw some sort of tantrum, but I'd learned how to shut off my feelings. I knew when it wasn't worth it.

twelve

being that it was nearing the end of the school year, the campus felt trampled—every teenager's hormonal plot seeming to cause the molecules in the taken-for-granted halls and lawns to be drunk, creating a contagious dopiness and laziness that made everyone either horny or depressed. I seemed to have a mixture of both. The fact that I was graduating didn't really affect me. I wasn't planning on going to the prom. Even when Riley and I were a "couple," we talked of making opium tea out of poppies and dancing in the floodlights at the Old Mission on prom night anyway. Mostly, I feared the long summer days ahead, alone with Mom. I didn't have any sentimental attachment to high school, but at least it provided a safe place, a *before*—a *before* that would soon be over.

Spending my lunch hour alone, I walked around campus noticing the plants, trees, and all kinds of greenery. On my way to class, I ran into Lorri on the path near the tennis courts. It wasn't her usual route. She must have gone out of her way, because I never saw her after fifth period. I expected her to just wave and walk by but she stopped. I was self-conscious, wondering if I looked okay. It's not like she looked great. Her face was a little broken-out and she looked tired. She wasn't perfect for a change and therefore she was more approachable, more human.

"Hey," I said.

"How are you doing?"

"I saw you at that big party last week."

"Yeah, I saw you, too," she said.

"You did?"

"You seemed to be having a good time."

"Yeah. It was a bad night, actually."

"Yeah? Me too. I got in a car wreck."

"Really?"

"Just a little one. But it was Dad's Lexus so it kind of sucked."

The second bell rang. We were supposed to be inside.

"Hey, don't disappear on me," she said. "Give me a call."

"You can call me, too, you know," I said, a little defensively.

"I will."

She walked on and I stayed behind, wanting to follow but too afraid. She said she'd call and that was good, the event of the day that would carry me through. It was conspicuous how much it mattered. The hot sun was making the grass wilt, forcing it to give up its moisture into the air, onto my skin, smelling like green.

i sat down at my desk in GATE English class, glad to have Sam sitting next to me to take my mind off my own life. In the beginning of the semester, he made my skin crawl because he wore expensive designer dress-shirts and had a Swiss watch which he fiddled with constantly. It took a while for me to realize he was a tormented genius. His parents had succeeded in pressuring him into going to Harvard Law School, yet it was obvious that Sam's true calling lay elsewhere, in monkey-training or dressmaking— who knew what eccentric vocation boiled under his skin making him chew pencils and tap on the desk till Mr. Tenasky made him stop.

Sam leaned over and whispered in my ear, smelling like expensive cologne.

"We're in for one of Mr. Tenasky's inspired classes."

"Is he going to tell us about his freshman hazing? Underwear stories?"

"I think it's about this flyer."

I noticed the green flyer that was lying facedown on everyone's desk including mine. I turned it over and read, "This man is a rapist." There was a picture of a guy with a buzz-cut playing guitar in a band. "His name is Billy Haddock and he rapes girls. His band is called FRED. Do not go and see FRED. They are into raping girls." The flyer was put together amateurishly. It was hard to make out Billy's features.

Mr. Tenasky entered the classroom wearing a seersucker blazer and a sarcastic smirk on his face.

"He's on a mission." Sam handed me a flask he took out from his backpack. When Mr. Tenasky wasn't looking I took a swig. It was Bailey's Irish Cream.

"Thanks."

"I bet Mr. Tenasky's favorite movie is *Dead Poets' Society*," Sam said.

"No, I don't think he's the Walt Whitman type."

"The Dead Something Society."

"The Dead Skin Society."

"The Limp Dick Society."

"Men's Hair Club."

Mr. Tenasky was writing furiously on the chalkboard which gave Sam and me an opportunity to have more Bailey's. When he finished he stood back revealing the word PROPAGANDA, written in bold letters on the board. He drew our attention to the flyer on our desks with a sneer on his face that made him look on the edge of nausea.

149

"Who made this flyer?" he said. "Is their agenda clear? It's simple. It works on an emotional level. It's hard not to just think, 'Oh, Billy here, he's a rapist, let's go lynch him.' "

He went on to talk about the use of propaganda throughout history, citing the Nazis, the Pro-Life Movement, and the Feminists. He claimed political correctness had taken over every educational institution, killing it like a fungus from within. He fought against it daily with an almost maniacal fervor. Most students didn't know what he was talking about. I raised my hand to comment.

"Yes, Skye?"

"I think it's incorrect to call this flyer propaganda. Propaganda is information put out by a group with a political agenda. It's meant to sway you into thinking something. This thing seems to be made by a bunch of girls and maybe some guys, too, who are trying to let people know this guy Billy's an asshole. There's no political agenda. It's like a sign that says, 'Don't drink the water, it's contaminated.' That's not propaganda."

Mr. Tenasky scrunched up his face strangely, as if my comment was a multivitamin going down his throat sideways.

Sam raised his hand to speak. Mr. Tenasky nodded at him, hoping to hear a voice of reason.

"It seems like this flyer bothers you in some way and you want to convince us that it's propaganda. I mean, I really doubt these girls are trying to frame an innocent guy. It's just incorrect to call it propaganda. The admissions pamphlet from Princeton is propaganda. This isn't."

Mr. Tenasky's face got red. He went off on Sam in a language that was supposed to be intellectually intimidating but upon closer listening simply didn't make any sense. He used words like *infrastructure, methodology,* and *amalgamate.* The jock guys were trying to calm him down by saying he shouldn't make such a big deal about a stupid flyer but that didn't help. His heated lecture segued into a speech on the faults of multiculturalism and the fall of the university system. He was fascinating to watch, especially since I was drunk on Bailey's. Sam drew his rendering of the Limp Dick Society in his notebook and I developed a theory on the benefits of alcoholism, something about it being a painkiller, a buffer against annoying people. Beneath the fuzz, however, was the kind of anger that gathers inside you like a very organized flock of birds, each an idea, the beginning of a political consciousness.

mini-theories and revolutions faded when class ended and all I could think of was that maybe Lorri would cross my path on the way out, just one small good thing to take the angst away from the fact that it was time to face Riley, to break up with him once and for all. She wasn't around, though. No golden advantage for me, no imagined ally. I walked down the railroad tracks past Hammond's Meadow to get to Riley's house. Surfers walked that path, boys in wet suits carrying boards twice their size. I could have slugged their carefree oversexed faces, I was so full of bile toward boys and the privileged access to pussy that's awarded to them by nature. They don't even know what they're doing. Pretty boys. Easy pussy everywhere.

I wasn't sure if I was supposed to apologize to Riley or curse him. I knocked on his door before making up my mind.

He answered wearing a pair of red boxer shorts. That settled it. I was going to kill him.

"So. Nice outfit. What have you been doing? Lying around wanking over what happened on Saturday night?"

"Fuck you," he said, and closed the door in my face.

He might as well have hit me. My pain came flooding to the surface in one giant wave. I walked a few yards away to a big rock, sat on it, and cried. A woman came out of the house next door, walking her three terriers down the path. I tried to hide my face from her.

After I pulled myself together I knocked on Riley's door

again. He opened it, this time wearing a T-shirt from a reggae concert.

"I don't need your judgment today."

"I'm sorry. Can I come in?"

"Yeah."

His mom must have been out of town on a crafts fair because the house was a mess. Pizza boxes, clothes, and cans littered the floor. The air was so moldy it made me cough. He sat on one end of the couch and I sat on the other. For a moment we watched the television with the volume turned down, catching a fleeting moment of peace.

"Before you say anything, I just want you to hear me out," Riley said. "I didn't know you knew that girl, let alone that you had a crush on her. Teresa totally blew me off. I saw her right after I talked to you and she told me to stop fucking stalking her, can you believe that? So I was just trying to get my mind off things, I guess. I was really drunk. I mean, if I walked into a stall and you were doing that to Jessica I'd be happy for you."

"Yeah, but . . ."

"No, hear me out. You hit me. In public. No one does that to me."

All my rage went out of me at that moment, leaving nothing but the most shitty feeling I've ever felt in my entire life. I was moldy cottage cheese. A car seat covered with melted videotapes. I had no recollection of any particle of goodness in me. My badness seemed to reach back past the day I was born, finding its origin in some rancid soup that was my soul. The badness erased any ability in me to imagine a future. I was experiencing pure, one-hundred-proof guilt.

"I'm sorry."

"I don't know. It would be different if you didn't hit me. You didn't even call me the next day."

"You don't know what it's like." The tears were coming again. Riley stiffened, not wanting my emotionalism to sway his attempt at self-protection. "I really loved her. I don't know if it was real love, it probably wasn't, but I built up this huge world around her, and when . . ." I couldn't talk anymore I was crying so hard.

"You let your emotions run your life. You shouldn't give in to them so much."

"I just got so mad. I'm sorry."

Riley was quiet for a long time. When he finally spoke, he seemed to choose his words with great care. "I suppose I can't hold it against you. In a way it's like a crime of passion. I see how you couldn't help yourself. But there's a way that you're careless about our friendship. It's like your last priority, like flossing. It's not right. I forgive you for what happened but this changes things. It will never be the same with us now."

I couldn't believe what was happening. He was breaking up with me. From the beginning it was always clear that I was the boss of the relationship. I called the shots and there he was, leaving me. I was the one who was supposed to leave him. That's why I went over to his house. To break up. The fact that it was me who was being left, in the midst of a giant crisis of guilt and grief, turned me into the worst cliché of a sniveling, begging, abandoned female. I choked on my tears and begged him to forgive me, to not leave me, to give our relationship another chance. The more intense I got, the more emotionally distant he became until it became apparent to us both that we were acting out some ancient boy-girl drama that was completely irrelevant to who we actually were. I calmed down and actually managed to laugh.

"I wanted her. I really did."

He held me as I tried to cry a little bit more but couldn't. He talked about Teresa, the same story of unrequited love I'd heard countless times before. It took every ounce of energy I had to follow. I counseled him as best I could, then we drifted off to sleep. I woke up to the sensation of his hand wandering under my shirt and massaging my nipples. I didn't want his hand there. My original intention of breaking up with him came back to me.

"Stop," I said.

"Why?"

"My skin, everything is still so sad."

"You want to stop this?"

I knew he meant everything. Us.

"I don't know." I wanted to tell him I did. I did want to stop seeing him for good.

"If you ever need me, I'm here, you know that?"

"Yeah."

I felt it happen. He let me go right that second, without any fuss, like a boat untied from the dock floating away in the middle of the night with no one to witness it.

What was between us wasn't about company or conversation. It was about our bodies making a safe place for us to be ourselves. We had no friendship beyond sex and we both knew it.

"You know, sometimes I think we keep each other from the world," he said.

"We have to not see each other for a while."

"I know."

Even as I lay there memorizing his smell, his every muscle curve and hair, I was anxious to be free.

"I want to show you something," Riley said, getting up and walking to his closet. He opened the sliding door and reached for a stack of magazines on the top shelf. Mixed in with the *Rolling Stone* and car magazines were copies of *Hustler* and *Penthouse*.

"I don't want to freak you out. It's weird that I never mentioned them. I like to look at porn when I jerk off alone."

I looked at the two-foot-high stack. He knew I wouldn't touch it so he picked up a *Hustler* and started leafing through it, showing me stuff.

"You've taught me so much about women, what they want and everything. Like the football guys at school, the way they treat women like they're not even people. They just make me sick. I don't think this stuff is bad, though. Does this turn you on?"

154

He showed me a centerfold of a blond woman sitting against a barn, moving her fringe shorts aside with her fingers to expose her pink cunt.

"No. It's too slick. I've never really related to porn."

"What about this?" He showed me a picture of a brunette in a cowboy hat standing naked beside a black stallion. "They have lesbian stuff, too. Here."

Two women doused in baby oil faced the camera, their only point of contact, their two snakelike tongues.

"Gross. They're so fake."

"Does it freak you out that I have these magazines?"

He had made a confession and I was supposed to forgive him. I could tell he felt bad about it. I scared him with my lectures on how to treat women right. He worked hard to be a good guy.

"No, it doesn't freak me out."

What did freak me out was the finality of our conversation, like we were trying to say everything as if it was the last time we would ever see each other.

"It just feels sad. The magazines and stuff, the way you save them and everything. It's sad."

"It just turns me on, that's all," he shrugged, a little irritated.

He was so intelligent, not with brains so much—intelligent like an old grizzly bear. He felt things and he knew how to react. He knew who was friend or foe. He knew how to be kind. I worried about him. Something about him was already falling down a long tunnel, away from the world.

"Do you know that you're sad?"

"Sad?"

"I don't mean sad as in pathetic or anything. Just sadness."

"I'm not sad."

"You're such a Gemini."

"I don't believe in that stuff. You don't think I'm sick or anything, do you? 'Cause it's really a normal thing for a guy to be into. It doesn't mean they don't respect women."

"No, but there must be some better magazines, I mean those outfits are so Minnesota."

"I'm not looking at the clothes."

"Right."

"hi, this is jessica's friend skye," I said, hating myself for being so weak, for giving in to calling her at the first pang of loneliness.

"Yes?" her mother replied, her voice shaky and wan.

"Is she there?"

"No." She sounded fearful. It was contagious.

"Um. Where can I reach her?"

There was a long pause on the other end of the line.

"Jessica's had some trouble."

"Is she okay?"

"Yes, but she had to go to the hospital."

I'd never experienced a real emergency before. Adrenaline shot through my veins and I wanted to climb through the telephone wire and get the whole story out of Martha, even if I had to shake it out of her.

"Did she try to kill herself?"

"We don't know. She cut herself up pretty badly."

"Can I go see her?"

"No. She needs her family right now."

"I'm her best friend."

"I know. I'm sure she would appreciate your concern, she just can't have visitors."

"But if she saw me, she would get better."

"That's questionable," she said, her tone suddenly changing.

"Excuse me?"

"I'm sorry, Skye. This has been hard for all of us. I can't help you."

She hung up. Bitch. Didn't she know our talk in the kitchen

meant we were bonded? I called back but she let the phone machine get it. I listened to the insipid recording—*blah blah blah, leave a message and we'll call you back* . . .

"This is Skye. Actually this is a voice. A voice on tape. But in reality this voice is attached to a person who is attached to your daughter being okay. If you could please call me back and let me know when's the best time I can come and see her that would be great. Sorry to bother you in this difficult time. 'Bye."

I hung up the receiver. I hated her mom then. She probably knew everything that was going on the whole time her child was forced into giving blowjobs in the basement. Was she screening her calls then? And where was Jessica's father, that invisible force of financial confidence and bad taste in interior design?

by the time i got to the hospital, I was hot and sticky with sweat, and my fantasies of helping Jessica escape had taken on ridiculous dimensions. One fantasy included tying sheets together à la Rapunzel so she could climb out the window to freedom. I would seduce the guard while Jessica escaped just at the moment of an imminent blowjob. When I got to the fourth floor my heroism dissolved when I saw her father sitting at a desk going through papers. I recognized him from photographs in their house. He was thin and pale, wearing a hillbilly shirt with pens in the breast pocket. He looked like a little boy with a saggy baggy face. His short gray hair was greased back. He wore tan shoes with his pale blue pants, like some kind of antique dad you'd find sitting at a Denny's in Idaho. That out-of-place-, out-of-time—ness I always took as a sign of perversity. I decided it would be best if Jessica's dad never knew I existed, not wanting to become another character in that crooked little head of his. I read *Newsweek* for a whole hour in the waiting room before he got up and left.

I approached the nurses' station, prepared to be curt and demanding. The woman behind the desk said that Jessica was in, but she wasn't allowed to see anyone.

"When are visiting hours?"

"It won't be for a few days. Her doctor doesn't want her to see friends right now. I'm sorry."

She was so nice I couldn't get mad at her. She looked me in the eye as if to personally apologize that she couldn't help me. Despite her white polyester outfit, she was hip, with a lavender scarf tied around her neck and reddish black hair pulled back in fashionable braids.

"Who are you?" she said. Her voice was a little croaky, like a party girl.

"You can't tell anyone that I came by, like her parents."

"I'm not a nurse, I'm just the secretary. I don't have to say anything."

"How is Jessica doing?"

"She's doing good. Usually patients don't have visitors except for family for a while. She's having counseling sessions with her parents every day."

"Gross."

She smiled. "They do come out of that room looking pretty haggard. After therapy, her mom's hair is like, out to here." She gestured with her hands to indicate Martha's frenzied Anglo-fro. "Jessica's not being all that cooperative. . . ."

"That's not surprising."

"Dr. Bromberg doesn't think it's a bad sign, though. It's better than being depressed. He always comes out of her room with a big smile on his face. Apparently she's doing well enough to cuss him out on a regular basis. So you're her best friend?"

"I guess. My name is Skye."

"I'm Joanna," she said with familiarity, making everybody else in the room seem unreal, like extras.

"Can I give her a note?"

"You could, but I can't guarantee it won't just get thrown

away." She rolled her eyes and bit the end of her pen, making a clicking sound as if to tell me the fourth floor was a fascist regime but she was on my side. I asked for paper and she gave me a three-by-five card.

Jessica, Heda and I miss you. Love, Skye.

I handed the note to Joanna. It was pathetically short and meaningless, but I didn't know how I felt about Jessica then, so why attempt poetry? Still, I wanted her to know I was thinking of her.

"Please, it's important."

"I can't promise it will get to her. Sometimes they don't let them read anything."

"How lame."

"Isn't it? I'll try to get it to her."

"Thanks."

"You take care, all right?" she said, with a warmth that stayed with me all the way down the elevator and onto the street.

I was so lit up with Joanna's kindness that my only thought of Jessica was a sick and selfish one. When she cut herself . . . was she thinking about me?

thirteen

"you don't have to come back if you don't want to,"
Mom said stiffly. She was at her worst because it was time for my
monthly visit with Dad. She sat rigidly perched on a chair in the
kitchen, strangely composed. She was wearing a flowered dress
and sandals. Her hair was in a braid.

"What?"

"Why don't you stay with your father? He's so much more
hip than I am. You can all have a giant orgy with some Heidi
Fleiss people."

"Can we just skip this?"

"Get in the car," she said.

She was well put-together despite the fact that she had been
throwing up all night. I had heard her flushing the toilet constantly until the water kept running with a gurgling hiss, keeping
me up. I got my backpack full of a weekend's worth of stuff and sat
in the hot passenger seat. Mom got in and slammed the door shut
with unnecessary passion.

"What are you mad at?"

"I'm mad that you're throwing your life away. You need help,
Skye. You're not gay. You're just doing this to hurt me. You think

you're going off to college when you treat me this way? I don't think so."

"College is more than a year away. God. How am I treating you?"

"I am a person," she said. "All I want is to be treated like a human being."

"You're my mother. You're supposed to take care of me, not the other way around."

"How dare you. You have never taken care of me. Never. You don't even know how to take care of anybody. You think you have these . . . friends. . . . They don't care about you."

Everything she was saying to me was something I could have said back to her at one point or another. Her talk confused me and filled me with guilt.

"We used to be friends," she said. "Remember?"

"Whatever."

She pulled into the parking lot of the bus station, turned off the car and stared straight ahead. I couldn't move. I waited for the grand finale attack. Instead of becoming more angry, Mom softened.

"I need to take care of myself," she said. "I'm floundering in my life the way I worry about you. It's draining all my energy. I was going to wait to tell you when you got back but I think you might as well know now. It came to me in a meditation. I tried to avoid it but now I know it's what I have to do. I've decided to become a trainer."

"Oh God."

She couldn't have said anything more horrible. The Matrix trainer course was a yearlong series. It was the highest you could go in the organization. She would have to lead countless workshops and be enthusiastic to the point of fanaticism and, like Marilyn, she would have to do performance art. She would be virtually worshiped by a throng of idiots. Plus, the whole thing costs thirty thousand dollars.

162

"How are you going to pay for it?"

"Are you worried I'll spend your precious college tuition?"

"No, I just thought we didn't have money. The kitchen table's covered with bills."

"What, are you spying on me now? It's not about the money."

"No, I—"

"I put the house on the market. People are coming over today to look at it."

There. She said it, a seemingly benign sentence full of words, yet to me it was a sacred confession in code. She was evil. There was no turning back. My body was electric with anger as I got out of the car.

"So? You're going to just say nothing?" Mom said.

"No, why bother? You have no soul. There's nothing I can do about that, can I?"

my life would never be the same. With that comment, I thought I cut the cord that tied me to my mother. It was a very melodramatic bus ride to L.A.—a Walkman and earphones would have been helpful to give my rite of passage its necessary soundtrack.

A production assistant named Brad picked me up at the bus station because Dad was busy on the set. He talked fast about parties he was going to that weekend and asked me if I'd like to come. I explained I didn't have access to a car. He said he'd give me a call but by the time I got out of the car I knew he'd blow me off. I didn't give him any signs that he'd get anywhere with me. Production assistants move fast and don't like to waste time. I found the key under a rock near the doorway and let myself in.

Dad lived in a concrete building in the Hollywood Hills nestled into the side of a sandy cliff where oak trees seemed to grow sideways out of the dry dirt. It was a fire hazard and hardly earthquake-safe, not to mention it was ugly. The concrete driveway was so gigantic it looked like a utility tramway in the back lot of Universal Studios. At least I had my own room. Over the years I had decorated it with Indian tapestries, beads, and garden statues of birds and Buddhas. Dad's friends took an interest in my shrine and brought me all kinds of things from movie sets. Above my bed was a headboard originally made for a music video. A giant Bacchus face was carved into the center, surrounded by vines and grapes. Above it, I hung red velvet curtains decorated with Christmas lights.

My room was the main attraction at parties. The rest of the apartment looked like a college dorm, all drywall and sliding glass doors. It was littered with lighting equipment. Cords were strewn everywhere ready to trip you at night. Gaffer's tape was stuck to any exposed surface, the wall, the refrigerator, the bathroom mirror. A movie poster for the film *Killing Zoe* hung over the fireplace. Dad always said that if you weren't working in Hollywood, make it look like you're working. "People who vacation are written off—like that!" he snapped.

Dad arrived later that evening. I heard the garage door open and the sound of voices. He carried in a case of Red Dog beer, followed by a bunch of his friends from the set of *Casualties*, an independent film on relationships in the 1990s.

"Hershey Bar!"

Dad had called me that ever since I was eight, it had something to do with a line in a Laurie Anderson song. He put down the case of beer and hugged me. I was really not in the mood for a party. I had to work on my paper.

"This is Skye, my daughter," he announced to his entourage. Everyone looked up from their immediately opened beers to give me a little wave. They were all in their twenties, three women and one man, sporty college kids doing an in-the-field internship. As usual, he had the role of God among them in his black jeans, black T-shirt, and Doc Martens. His black hair had streaks of gray making him look sophisticated like a New York fashion designer. He always said the key to staying young was to hang around with young people. They were getting younger and younger.

We all sat in front of the TV to watch the outtakes. Smoke filled the air. Everyone got blitzed, me included.

"So, Skye, tell us about your life," Dad said.

"I've started doing crack. I give blowjobs for some extra cash."

Everybody chuckled. Having a clever daughter was extra points for Dad. I've played that game since I was very young. Not like there wasn't anything in it for me. For one, I got to drink beer.

One of the girls handed me a Red Dog. Dad flashed me a peace sign, meaning two was my limit. We watched the video and everybody made in-jokes that I couldn't understand. Dad started to get his loud football laugh which I always hated.

"Look at him looking at his shoes!" Dad screamed.

"What's wrong with his shoes?"

"Leana drooled!"

"She did not."

"Yes, she did. I swear she drooled. She opened her mouth and she drooled. You don't believe me."

"Shut up. Shut up," a girl names Christie yelled, cracking up until she had tears in her eyes.

"Then we yell, 'Shoot!' and Jim like, looks at his shoe. He's not horrified or anything, he's just like—'Leana's spit is on my shoe. She drooled. Can someone get it off my shoe?'"

The occasion of hysterical laughter inspired the rolling of a joint. It came around to me and I passed it on to Christie who winked, took a long hit, and held it in her lungs. Dad smoked in the same way, choking on his words as he exhaled. I don't see what the big deal is, why all the drama. Just inhale and exhale the smoke. God.

Cliff stood up and pulled down his nylon shorts that had ridden up into his crotch and, regrettably, joined me on the couch. He started in with questions.

"So what are you studying?"

"English, but I want to study architecture."

"What are you reading?"

"Virginia Woolf."

"I saw the movie *Orlando* on video. It's probably not as good as the book. The book's probably better, right?"

"Actually, no."

He then ran out of words and started staring at my breasts, not like there was anything to see. My T-shirt was huge. Dad was too busy entertaining the girls with a story about losing an actress at an airport who'd just gotten in from Germany to notice that Cliff had become a pervert and was boring me to death.

"What do you like about Virginia Woolf?"

"Her nose. Stop asking questions. Make a speech or something."

"What do you want to know about me?"

"Why do you wear nylon shorts?" I asked.

"I don't know. They're comfortable."

He took a vial of white powder out of his shorts pocket, pulled the cap off and poured the contents on the flat ridge of his hand near his thumb. I didn't think anything of it. It all seemed part of the plot.

"Jesus!" Dad thundered. He stood up and in two giant steps, he was in Cliff's face, slapping the powder from his hand and lifting him up by his Nike T-shirt.

"It was for me! I wasn't going to give her anything!"

Dad pulled him out into the garage and started cussing him out. He was saying things like, "That's my daughter. Are you a fucking idiot?" *My daughter* this, *my daughter* that. I was a little princess. I couldn't help but have a half-smile on my face which seemed to give the girls permission to start laughing even though we could hear Cliff in tears, pleading for his job back. It was pathetic. He didn't have the sense to know if he just calmed down and kissed ass, it would all blow over. Dad took pride in his tantrums and liked to stay in practice. He never let it rip with me, though, not once.

"So my dad still knows how to throw a fit."

"Absolutely," Amanda said, "but he never does it without a reason. That's why he's so good on the film set. I mean, can you believe Cliff did that? That was so out-of-line."

"No pun intended?"

"Your dad doesn't do coke. Cliff knows that. None of us do coke and I'm sure you don't do coke," Rachel said, looking at me.

"Only on special occasions," I joked.

"Coke's lame. Don't ever do coke or heroin," Rachel said.

"Don't lecture her," Christie scolded.

"Sorry."

"Your dad is the greatest."

"He is. He's amazing."

"Thanks," I said, not knowing how to respond to such a comment. "I should go to bed. I'm kind of tired."

"No," Rachel said drunkenly, holding my hand. "We need you."

"Beer always makes me sleepy."

"We'll tuck you in," said Christie, as if it was the evening's most brilliant idea.

I trudged upstairs and the drunk girls followed me like distracted geese. When I opened the door to my room, the smell of sandalwood incense poured out. They stood at the threshold, amazed at the other world that lay within.

"It's a shrine."

"What a cool room."

"You are so amazing," Amanda said, picking up a statue of

the Virgin of Guadalupe on my nightstand. The three of them snooped around while I changed into a fresh T-shirt and underwear and got under the covers.

"This is the Voyager deck," Christie said, picking up cards on one of my altars.

"What's that?" Rachel replied.

"A tarot. It's totally like the best tarot."

The three of them plopped down at the foot of my futon. I felt their weight making the blankets heavy near my feet. They laid the cards out. They each picked a card and I told them what it meant. Christie was overtaxed creatively and if she didn't slow down she might have some kind of accident. Amanda was in the sex-goddess phase of life which she said was totally appropriate because she just met this great guy. Rachel's card said that she might meet someone who would lie to her. I didn't want to pick a card for myself, so I picked one for Jessica and got the Two of Crystals—Equanimity. How vague.

"Who's Jessica?" Rachel said.

"This girl. My friend. She just went into a mental hospital."

"What for?"

"She cuts herself, like with pins and razors and stuff."

"Gross."

"Why would she want to do that?"

"I don't know."

Amanda and Christie saw that I was upset about it and they felt bad for me. As my thoughts began to drift they pulled the sheets up just under my chin, tucking me in. I felt about three years old.

"She's so amazing."

"I wish I was that together when I was her age."

"Let's sing her a lullaby."

"I don't know any."

"What about 'Puff the Magic Dragon'?"

"No, not that one," I said, opening my eyes.

"I thought you were asleep."

"Just don't sing that one, okay?"

They made an attempt at singing a song by the Beatles but quickly realized that they didn't know the words. In the candlelight they were quite beautiful, like celestial sisters or Charlie's Angels, three different personalities and hairdos forming some mythical whole.

"What about 'O Holy Night'?" Christie asked.

"Man, Christie, you are so drunk."

"You say something better."

"What about a Disney song?" Amanda suggested.

"No!" the rest of us chanted in unison.

" 'O Holy Night' is my favorite Christmas song," Christie chimed. "I didn't even get to sing it this year because I was volunteering for the soup kitchen."

Rachel began in an off-key voice. " *'O Holy night, the stars are brightly shining. It is the night of our dear savior's birth.'* " She brushed her long brown hair out of her face. "Help me here."

They all joined in. " *'A thrill of hope a weary word rejoices, for yonder breaks a new and glorious morn . . .'* "

"This is my favorite part," Rachel said, right when Dad opened the door and came in, Cliff following close behind.

" *'Faaaaaalllll on your knees and heaaaar the angels' voices.'* " Dad and Cliff kneeled at the foot of my futon and held hands with the girls.

" *'O niiight deviiiine O O niiight when Christ was born Ooo niiight deviiiiiine O night O niiiiight deeee-viiiine.'* "

I opened my eyes just halfway to see everybody looking at me like I was their little baby. They continued singing as sleep took me into a place where they became a dream.

occasionally waking, I was aware of a few things. Dad kissed Amanda at the foot of my futon then went downstairs with her. Cliff fell asleep on my floor. Rachel and Christie climbed under my covers, one girl on my left and one on my right. Christie put her arm around my ribs and cuddled up close. Rachel was facing me and even though her breath smelled like Red Dog, it didn't prevent me from edging up so the warmth of it was on my cheek. Beneath the smell of beer was an animal aroma, hormonal and sweet. She was wearing a tight black sports bra and her breasts touched me slightly. I let my arm fall around her waist and fell asleep in a screaming tornado of lust. Scandal in Dad's house had its benefits. I couldn't complain.

billie holiday played on the stereo as I trodded down the stairs in the morning to find Dad in his robe, humming and stirring eggs over the stove. He was in an annoyingly cheery mood—sex with Amanda must have been successful. If so, I sure hope he would keep that information to himself and not tell me like he often did when he was proud of himself and there was no one else around to brag to.

"Is anyone around?" I asked. Rachel and Christie weren't in my bed when I woke up. The house was lonely without them. I thought maybe they might have left their phone number for me or something.

"They all went to the set. Amanda stayed downstairs with me last night and got up and showered at the crack of dawn," he said, trying to repress a gloat.

"Which crack was that, Dad?"

"How you doing, Hershey Bar? Hungover?" he said, ignoring my sick joke.

"No."

"Good girl. Sorry about that."

"It's okay."

Breakfast consisted of eggs and toast which I ate on the

living-room floor because the dining table was covered with light-ing fixtures and tangled wires. From my vantage point, I noticed a photo album on the floor, used to prop up an anemic potted plant. When I finished my eggs, I retrieved it and opened it up on the carpet. They were mostly party photos. There weren't the usual mundane holiday pictures you see in the photo albums of most families. The pictures were of red-eyed adults, holding cock-tails, a hand or a leg in a blur. I wondered if Dad even knew half the people. The pictures of me were all out of focus. There was one of me with a cowboy hat holding a water pistol with no shirt on, looking mean, another of me dancing at a reception in a blue dress.

"So Robert's in trouble," I yelled from the living room.

"Robert who?" Dad said, sitting at the kitchen table reading the *L.A. Weekly.*

"Your friend from the eighties."

"Oh, him. Yeah. He's in deep shit."

"What was he like?"

"Robert?"

"Yeah."

"He was one of those guys who was in your life and you thought he was your friend but when time went by and shit hit the fan, he was always one of those peripheral kinds of people. You know what I mean? What do you want to know about him?"

"Mom thinks that since he molested his kids, he might have done something to me."

"That's nonsense," Dad said. He stood up and poured him-self more orange juice. "Do you remember anything?"

"Not really."

"Well, there you go." Dad came over to me and handed me a glass of juice, end of dialogue on that subject. "If you need any-thing, I'm here."

"Yeah."

"You know what I mean?"

"What."

"Your mother."

"Yeah."

"I know how she can be."

"Whatever. Yeah."

What was he offering, his fatherly help? The usual lip service, more likely. Once, when Mom had a particularly traumatizing breakdown, I ran away to his place and he left me alone in the apartment with money to order out for pizza while he took a two-day trip to Ensenada with a girlfriend.

In the photo album I found a picture of Robert. He was standing in a group with all my dad's friends, posing like they were still in college. He didn't look like Chester the Molester. He just looked drunk. His kids, one boy and one girl, were my age but I never hung out with them. They never wanted to play the games I liked, so I stayed away and when we were at Robert's house I played in the garden by myself. I avoided their bedroom that was filled with too many dolls and smelled like cabbage.

Seeing Robert's picture didn't stir anything inside me. No repressed memories came flooding up to the surface to wreak havoc on my psyche. I looked at more pictures of myself—holding puppies, drawing with pastels, skiing in a white down outfit so huge that I looked like a swollen larva. In one of the pictures I was definitely on acid, maybe mushrooms. I was ten and I stood by the pool, naked with a serious expression, looking into the water as if I'd dropped something.

dad left at noon. I had the rest of the day to get some work done on my Virginia Woolf paper but I couldn't manage anything but lying in bed and looking at the tapestry patterns on the walls. Maybe I shouldn't have come, I thought. Jessica's sick. Mom's not well. A really bad kind of self-hate was waiting to pounce on me if I didn't at least move, do something.

I took a walk a few blocks to the south near the smaller Spanish haciendas and Hollywood ranch houses. In my dad's neighborhood, all the houses look like the places coke dealers live in on cop shows from the seventies. Ugly. The neighborhood to the south was nicer. Unlike many areas in L.A., old ladies watered flowers outside in their garden and people walked their dogs.

Turning a corner, I came upon a house I hadn't noticed before. It was a small boxy house, very Moroccan with carved plaster trim in the shape of swirls and sickles. The phallic-shaped entryway was trimmed with lush vines of jasmine. The plaster was a bright salmon color. Where the flat roof met the sky, a thin line of blue tiles sparkled in the sun. Gorgeous. I'd never seen anything like it. All the houses I'd ever seen prepared me for that one. It was me, my secret self.

I couldn't help noticing that a side window was open by a large pepper tree. My usual thoughts about sneaking in turned quickly from fantasy to pure desire. I wanted in. Bad. No car was in the driveway. I sat on the curb and the insanity increased. I could go in and out. Just like that. Take a quick look around and no one would know. I didn't look like a thief. If I was caught I'd claim ignorance. Wrong address, sorry.

I had to do it. I couldn't just think about it. Imagination wasn't enough. It had to be done in one smooth, confident swoop.

I crossed the street and walked right up to the side of the house. I rested my hands on the sill for a moment, then I just went. Pushing up, I swung one leg over and did a little roll. The cotton curtains brushed against my body like a cool hand. I was there, standing on the floor.

I was in what could have been called a master bedroom though it wasn't an ordinary one. The walls were yellow and the floor consisted of large wooden planks painted a glossy blue. The focal point of the room was a bed covered in a ripped antique quilt. Dirty and half-dismembered stuffed animals infested half the bed and were scattered atop the dresser and chairs in the room. Two men, arm in arm, smiled out from a photo on the wall. One had white hair, the other red. They were shirtless, sporting vivid psychedelic tattoos. They must have been the residents of the house, a couple. Above the childlike bed was an array of rubber straps hanging from a sturdy hook in the ceiling. There was no one around as far as I could tell. Adrenaline pushed me farther into the hall, painted a sickly lavender, and into the living room where I was startled by a mannequin covered from head to toe in the small mirrors used for disco balls where I saw myself, the criminal, as hundreds of small dots reflected back at me. The barely furnished room had about six child's tricycles in the corner and more dolls—sad and dirty apparitions. A windowless wall made a home for a giant painting made of thick black wax poured over a canvas of various colors. A line drawing was crudely cut into the wax of two large people embracing, a giant penis and giant vagina fucking as if a child had drawn it. Sun up in the sky. A single flower springing from the ground. Sick.

The place was so bizarre that I forgot for a moment I was trespassing. A recessed window made a home for a collection of bottles, Mexican orange and lime soda that caught the light like neon, and old Pepsi bottles that looked like they had washed up from the sea. I couldn't help it. I took one of the Pepsi bottles that glowed opalescent in the light. Maybe it wouldn't be missed. It was a souvenir. A gift for Jessica.

Secretly I wanted the people who lived there to come home and find me, thinking they might even find my presence endearing. Maybe they'd ask me to stay for dinner, a meal of macaroni and cheese perhaps. Being in their house felt intimate. Their absence created a vacuum, making me want to know them even more. They had something I wanted. I stood for a few more seconds, pretending I belonged there, before leaving the same way I came in.

tick tick. I lay on the couch and didn't get up. Los Angeles is not a place to be inactive. The lethargic in L.A. are punished with bad vibes wherever they go. After a self-punishing marathon of chip-eating and TV-watching, I decided to go home early. I called my dad on his cell phone, expecting him to be irritated at my change of plans but he just told me to make sure to lock the back door and call when I got in. Maybe I was imagining it, but I thought I detected a note of relief in his voice.

The bus dropped me off in Santa Barbara and I lugged my bag of books and clothes all the way to the hospital, not wanting to go home just yet. Jessica's gift was in my backpack, my apology. I needed to see her really bad, to touch her hand while she lay in her bed or sat up in a chair. Everyone in my life was scattering to far corners. I thought her eyes on me would be like getting my picture taken for good luck, something I could refer to when I was lost and didn't know where I was. I could be the same for her. The thing that keeps her here.

Joanna recognized me immediately. She waved from the nurses' station and motioned for me to come over. Her hair was done up in a series of chunky braids that poked out from all sides of her head. The other nurses were really conservative in comparison. I wondered what they thought of her, if they ever gave her a hard time.

"Why don't you put that bag down, it looks heavy."

"It is." I glanced down the hallway at the doors that were open. Televisions were on and the nurses walked up and down the hall pushing trays covered with drugs.

"Jessica's been transferred," Joanna said with a look of concern.

"Where?" I sank into failure that was waiting for me as punctually as a probation officer. I should have never gone to L.A.

"I don't know. Let me see if it's in the book. What's her last name?"

For a moment I thought I might not know her last name, but then it came.

"Jessica Gilbert."

She looked through her papers. "It could only be one of two places. Here it is. She's been sent to Rio Rancho. It's a long-term facility."

"Where's that?"

"It's in San Diego. It's a nice place."

She seemed familiar with Rio Rancho. Maybe every depressed teenager was sent there to recover.

"Do you have an address?"

She nodded and wrote it down on a notepad. The fluorescent light sucked something out of me as I waited. I felt invisible. For the first time since meeting Jessica, I had no plan of action, no scheme. Without that we were nothing.

"Here. Don't mail any sharp objects or anything. What do you have in that bag? It's stuffed."

"Books and clothes, something for Jessica."

"She got your note."

"Really? What did she say?"

"She's kind of heavy about things right now. I think it meant a lot to her. She wasn't into talking to me, though."

I stood there, unable to bring myself to leave. Joanna offered me some fruit which I accepted, eating her apple as if it was an extension of her niceness. We talked for a while between her various tasks until I thought maybe I was bugging her and left. There is the instinct to go home after the end of a day's events. It rose up in me, animal-like, then fizzled out in a burst of conflicting information. What was home anyway? Did I even have one?

fourteen

i felt like i'd abandoned jessica in the worst way. Before I left, I could have at least held vigil outside in the waiting room if they weren't going to let me in to see her. Someone would have let me in eventually. Guilt just increased my unrealistic reverence for her.

When I got home I saw that Mom's favorite duffel bag was gone, meaning it was likely that she was at a training and wouldn't come home till the end of the weekend. She thought I was still in L.A., anyway. I had a chunk of time where no one knew where I was, that gave me a certain sense of freedom.

Lying down on my bed, I thought of the smell of Jessica's scalp and the way her lower back was wet with sweat the night of the party when she kissed me. I remember putting my hand there, not expecting her skin to be cold and drenched. Those two memories, the smell of her hair and the feel of her sweat, became larger than they needed to be. They made her too real in my mind.

I went to Zuma's Electronic Cafe to be with the ghost of her. I sat down at a small table with a cappuccino, a weekly, and my spiral-bound notebook.

After reading for a while, distracted by an inner white noise, Mol came in and ordered a bear-claw with authority, wearing a velvet jacket and silk pants. The night of the party she was Jessica's friend. That day I needed her desperately to be mine. That's why it meant so much when she turned and waved, picked up her plate and joined me at my table like it was the only possible thing she could have done.

"What's going on?" Mol said, casually holding her plate.

"Nothing. So Jessica went away to some place called Rio Rancho. What is that? Is it girls' camp? Betty Ford for teens? What is it?"

"I don't know, her mom wouldn't talk to me," Mol said.

"She wouldn't talk to me, either. It's weird. One minute we're together, the next she's in the hospital."

"Are you okay?" Mol asked.

"I don't know. Things happened so fast."

Mol was a good listener. Better than me. She left her bear-claw untouched and didn't look around the room to see who was coming in. She pulled the truth out of me.

"I have to just say that I had a big crush on her," I said. "Maybe I was in love with her, whatever, I don't know. She kissed me that night, a real kiss, you know?"

"That's just Jessica."

"What do you mean?"

"She's out there. She does that to everybody, makes you think you're the one she can't live without. She did the same thing to me. I'm not trying to say she's not cool, she just has some problems. She has to bring everyone into her own world, you know?"

Of course it hurt to hear Mol say that. I tried to edit it out of my mind. She didn't know everything—the miracles that existed in a kiss, for instance. There are things that can't be explained.

"I love her."

"I know you do," Mol said, "I just don't know if she knows what love is."

"How long have you known her?"

"Just a year. I don't even know her that well. You sure you're okay?" Mol said, taking hold of my hand. Her long black finger-nails looked strange against my white skin. Her deep brown eyes held me safe. There was something about Mol that I could trust, that I could fall into.

"I think I'm okay. Do you think her freaking out had anything to do with us? Me liking her and everything?"

"She never mentioned it."

She was silent for a long time then she looked at me with these mad-scientist eyes, like she had a master plan.

"Jessica's on an online mailing list. She was always telling me about it. It's for this band called Thumper. Jessica posted on it every day. It's like a support group. It's intense. All these girls talk about being raped and being on Prozac and stuff."

"You're on the list?"

"I just read it once. Everyone was trying to talk this thirteen-year-old-girl out of doing heroin with her boyfriend. Sometimes I wonder if people are telling the truth; I mean, you could make up anything if you wanted to."

"How can we get it? I know it's like snooping but it's so strange how Jessica just disappeared. If there's anything we can find out it would be great."

"Just go online. A girl named Sheila runs it. I have her e-mail address."

We went up to the counter and bought time on the computer. I didn't know how to work it so I just let Mol do everything. She clicked around on the thing forever while I drank a double cappuccino and read a whole article on deforestation in the weekly newspaper before she found anything.

"Skye, I got Sheila. She's online. How far back do you want to go?"

"Two weeks, I guess."

"Do you want to read it online or do you want to print it out?"

"You mean put it on paper?"

"Yeah."

"Paper's good. Will it cost a lot?"

"Not too much."

Mol downloaded sixty pages before she was finished. I couldn't wait to go somewhere alone to read everything, but Mol was in manic mode and wouldn't stop talking about computers, goth clubs, and all the drugs she'd taken in her life. She drank cup after cup of coffee. I was distracted but pretended to listen, not wanting to be rude.

"I can't read this here," I said when Mol handed me the downloads. "I have to be alone. Maybe we can meet up later."

"Go and leave me, then. After all I've done for you."

"I'm sorry, I didn't . . ."

"I'm kidding, stupid. Go read the damage."

Mol asked me to come to a party with her later, adding that I could stay at her house for the night. I accepted. We agreed to meet back at Zuma's at nine o'clock.

obscure references to star wars and a hatred of football jocks made it easy to figure out that Jessica's screen name was Jester. At the public library, I read slowly by the window that had a view of the courthouse lawn. There was so much to read, most of it was guitar tabs and tour dates for Thumper. It seemed like a waste of time, then I found what I was looking for. I guess.

```
To Elsie . . . I cut myself too. Sometimes I
do words, sometimes just do long lines. When
I was fourteen I tried to kill myself with
```

Valium and Tylenol. My brother found me
passed out in my own throw up. It's good I
took the Tylenol b/c that's what made me
throw up and probably it saved my life. I
went to the hospital and they pumped my stomach . . . not something I recommend to anyone. Suicide sucks, people have the right to
take their own lives but they don't think
about how it will affect other people. I
didn't. It's not cool or romantic. It's a cry
for help but then sometimes it's too late.
It's just tragedy and death.

—Jester

Wake up wet in the big blue sun, you got
everything, some got none.

—Thumper

Jester,
    My thirteen-year-old brother tried to
kill himself last night with pills I don't
know what they were. He's in the hospital
tonight. We went and saw him but he wouldn't
talk to us. If you say something he just
nods like he hears you but he won't talk
back. My older brother (16) and I have always
thought he was gay. All he does is listen to
The Cure and the Pumpkins and Thumper and I
feel bad because I gave him all those records
for Christmas. we knew he wasn't okay and I
feel guilty for encouraging him to stay in
his room and listen to the music. Our parents
are totally homophobic and if they found out
they would kick him out of the house or
worse. So needless to say I didn't tell
everyone I was pregnant at the hospital.

love,
clambake

I'm a bitch . . . but you don't know me
. . . you don't know me . . . so you can't
call me . . . a bitch

—Thumper

Clambake,

Your brother needs to get out of the
house and fast. I don't know why people still
have such a problem with people being gay. It
made me cry when I read your post. When I
first came to this school I thought I'd made
some cool friends then they started bugging
me about the clothes I wear, ripped up
dresses, Thumper T-shirts. They were into
flirting with jocks. I trusted this one girl
and showed her my journal. She took it and
xeroxed this part about how I gave my
boyfriend head in eighth grade, and posted it
in the bathroom, gave it to people and stuff.
I'd walk into a room and even the friends I
thought liked me still would be talking about
me, they'd laugh and keep whispering. They
made a whole life out of hating me. I was
practically being stalked. But that's life
in cinderblock hell. I have different
friends now. One is a gay girl. She is cool.
It must freak them out that she's my friend.
They drove by the other day and yelled
"Dykes" at us. I liked that I could piss
them off like that. Also, did you know that
bloodletting is a sacred ritual in some cul-
tures, a kind of initiation thing. We are
tribal people even though we drink Diet Coke
and buy videos at Blockbuster. I haven't forgotten and I grieve for it with my blood.

—Jester

```
Sometimes you have to take the wrong road
sometimes you have to feel nothing at all
sometimes  you  have  to  turn  away  for  no
reason
that you can explain at all
```
                                            —Thumper


```
Hey grrrl,
     Jester, are you bisexual? I picture you
with short blond hair and Doc Martens.
```
                                            —Gigi
```
P.S.   BILLYHADDOCKRAPESGIRlSHEISINTHEBAND-
FREDDONTGOSEEHISBANDBILLHADDOCKRAPESGIRLS
```

```
Gigi,
     No, I'm not bisexual. I'm definitely
straight, though this seems to be an unfor-
tunate fact for my best friend who would love
to get me in bed. Ha;). I guess you could say
I'm mildly bi-curious. Guys with nail polish
rule. And about blond hair and DM's. I have
black hair and I wear old witch boots from
thrift stores.
```
                                            —Jester


```
even though I was dead . . .
I wanted you to touch me
```
                                            —Thumper

I had to put the page down then. Everything was in writing.
There wasn't much else I needed to know. I was just her gay friend,
her new cool life. It's strange how you can feel so passionately
close to someone and they can feel nothing at all. Her last post
was a long one. I almost didn't read it, afraid I might find some
other harsh insult.

Today was the most horrible day ever. My brother called and my parents were out. He's an ass-fucking rapist who always calls and asks for money it makes Mom freak out and Dad has to go work in the garage for five days and not talk to anybody so I told him to never call the house again or I would go to the jail and kill him or have someone do it and he got freaked out and started making threats so I threw the phone and broke it . . . my parents didn't get home and I went to my room and nothing was happening so I carved the word bitch into my leg and fuck me into the other leg and I felt better. I lit a cigarette and I was looking at it and I thought hey here's another way so I burned the top of my hands but instead of making things better it's making things worse because I'm remembering everything that happened and that's not very good so I came online . . . ta da here I am . . . I need a drink . . . I wish my friend was here . . . I want to tell her I'm sorry . . . I'm so horrible I make everyone leave because they always say I am cold and remote then once they get to know me they can't handle who I am I tell them about my brother and they think I'm lying because I'm not all emotional and freaked out about it all the time . . . and after I tell them I get needy I need more than any person should need anything I'm like a black hole that sucks everything up there are so many things that can cut and burn I think I need them now. . . . There's this knife a really nice one.

jester rhymes with molest her . . . and fester . . . oh fuck . . . fuck me . . . sorry to ramble. . . . bye mol read the downloads in the bathtub while I waited in the living room with her mother, Amelia. Mol had the coolest mom, a therapist with a Southern accent and a round and open face, framed by her straight hair that went down to her shoulders. Wearing a loose green dress with a T-shirt underneath, she looked like she was on her way out to the garden.

"So you never had a chance to say good-bye to Jessica?" she said.

"No."

"How horrible. It's so backwards. Doctors think that if they take you away and put you in a place where there's nothing familiar, none of your friends are there, you'll suddenly get better. Yet they let you watch TV all day long. Stupid."

"Yeah."

"I hope you don't feel bad, there was nothing you could do. The family has control at this point and from what I know of Jessica's mother she wouldn't have let you see her."

"She was so nice to me one afternoon."

"Yes, Martha is very . . . nice," she said with a grimace. Mol came out of the bathroom wearing a pink flannel nightgown, looking like she was three. Wet computer printouts dangled from her hand and her face was swollen from crying. She walked over to her mother and lay down on the couch with her head in her lap. Amelia ran her fingers through her jet black hair as she cried. I wanted to cry, too, but I couldn't. I could only watch them. How strange, I kept thinking. How beautiful.

Mol sat up, her face full of creases and red splotches. I smiled.

"I look like shit."

"Look at your little face," Amelia said, holding Mol's cheek in her palm. "My watch band made a mark on your forehead."

"I want to kill her parents. I'm not even that mad at her brother," Mol said.

"I know, me too. How could they not know what was going on?" I interjected.

"They know but they don't want to believe it," Amelia said. "People can actually convince themselves something doesn't exist. People do it all the time. She's a sweet girl, too, so creative. Honey, can you get me a beer from the fridge?"

"No, Mom," Mol whined in a child's voice.

"I'll get it," I said, already on my way to the kitchen.

"She's nice. We like her," I heard Amelia say from the other room in a kid's voice just like Mol's. The refrigerator was covered with pictures from a trip to New Mexico. Mol and Amelia stood naked on a giant red rock, laughing their heads off, their similar bodies, happy in the sun. More photos showed Mol and her mom on horses, at the beach, at dinner parties with women and a few men, laughing, food and flowers everywhere. When I came out with the beer they were still cuddled up close. Amelia took my hand and I sat down on the couch, nestled into the circle of her arm. I tried to relax into her body but that kind of touch didn't come natural to me until she touched the back of my ear, then I was gone.

we stayed in the bathroom for over an hour putting on makeup and then taking it off, wanting to get it perfect, as if that could solve something. Mol put concealer over my eyebrows then drew new ones on with eyeliner and blue and purple shadow. She covered over my lips, making them invisible so she could draw them back on in burgundy outlined in black. She did the same to herself.

"Jessica and I used to dress up all the time, then she got kind of tired of it."

"Are you sure it's not too much?"

"Of course it's too much. It's hideous. You look great. Hold still." She held my head steady and painted something high up on

186

my forehead. Whatever she was doing was beyond me. I just had to surrender. She let me look in the mirror and I was fierce, my eyes turning into wings like a superhero. My mouth was both voluptuous and tough. She gave me a dress to wear, black, of course.

"This color doesn't go, I'm too blond."

"You would look great with black hair."

"You think so?"

"I have some dye."

"No way."

"It's temporary."

"But my makeup is already on."

"I'll be careful. Plus, we can redo it."

"It will take too long."

"Pleeeease!" she begged.

I gave in. She guided my head into the sink where she descended on me with hair dye. The nauseating vapors suffocated me in the small space between the sink and Mol's chest hovering over me with all the maternal instinct of a child prepared to chop the hair off her plastic baby doll. After she blow-dried my hair, I looked in the mirror. I looked like a totally different person, my softness giving way to a hard glamour. I couldn't stop staring at myself. Mol took me into Amelia's room to proudly show off her creation.

"Oh my, you dyed your beautiful hair!"

"It's temporary."

"It looks great. You look very European."

"I don't look scary?"

"I think it would be impossible to make you look scary. Black hair and blue lips are actually very stunning on you."

Mol took another hour to finish her makeup. I sat on the toilet and watched her.

"It's nice to not be in my own head for a second," I said. "I could stay in this bathroom all night just chilling out."

"We might be here all night at the speed I'm going." She took a piece of tissue and wiped some makeup from her eye.

"You and your mom, you're so, like, nice to each other."

"Yeah. She doesn't throw hangers when guests are around."

"I can't imagine letting my mom hug me. We hug hello and good-bye, but I never would want her to hold me like your mom does. It would totally freak me out."

we walked into the party with our arms linked together. I was Mol's creation, her Frankenstina. I didn't know who I was supposed to be, looking like that. I would need a few drinks before an actual personality set in.

It was just a house party. The front room was empty except for an eight-year-old watching television who told us everybody was out back. We walked through the house to the garage that was decorated to look like a dungeon. The stereo played music with a slow industrial beat. The air was thick with cigarette smoke even though there were only a few people. Black and red sheets hung from the ceiling, creating different private areas. Plastic bats and spiders were everywhere. A bald mannequin with fake wounds and dripping blood leaned against the wall next to a ten-speed and a lawn mower. It looked like a grade-school kid's idea of a haunted house.

Some people were sitting on a piece of carpet on the floor. A red scarf hung over a lamp shade, giving everyone a romantic or sinister glow, I couldn't tell which. Two of the guys seemed like they were in their twenties. One had bright green hair and tattoos on his muscular arms, the other wore black leather pants. A few preteen girls acted cocky in mall clothes, somebody's little sister and her gaggle of friends. The few goth girls that were there rolled their eyes and smoked. Mol went up to a girl with real vampire teeth and gave her a hug. The girl's arms reached around the back of Mol's head revealing black nails so long they had curled into a circle. Mol motioned for me to follow her. Our small group found a private place behind a hanging red sheet, next to a parked Jeep Cherokee. Mol introduced me to the pale girls, who complimented me on my hair and my dress. I told them my look was all because of Mol. She was a genius. It was strange to be treated with respect by such intimidating girls. I had confidence for a change. It hit me like a drug, making everything seem easier, more fun.

Someone handed me a bottle of whiskey. I took a sip and gave it back but was told that I could keep it. Taking another sip, I handed it to Mol. We all climbed into the Jeep and talked about how bored we were.

"Let's have a séance."

"For who?"

"I don't care. Not a famous person. Let's do a seance for Betty."

"Who's Betty?"

"I don't know. Betty is probably some cleaning lady who lived in Orange County who died sometime in the seventies of a gallstone."

"We can do a séance for my aunt Meg. All I know is she smoked Lucky Strikes, drank four pots of coffee a day, and was obsessed with cocker spaniels."

"My mom has a demon," I said out of nowhere, already drunk. "Can you do exorcisms?"

A short girl with a pointy face said, "What kind of demon, like a transitory one from a house, or like one that comes from her own psychic shit?"

"Our house is fine, it's her own psychic shit."

"What does it feed on?"

That was a good question. Mom had a few addictions. Drugs, alcohol, general drama—but what was the demon really looking for? I thought of her personal-growth workshops and her constant hunger for what she called "transformation."

"It feeds on spirituality," I said. "It feeds on emotions. It feeds on light."

"A light junkie. I hate those people. Oh sorry, that's your mom."

"That's okay. She's being a real bitch right now."

"I bet she is. Light junkies are self-righteous. Many of the new Christians are people who have demons that are light junkies. They're the first ones to blame others because they can't look at their own darkness, or if they do, the demons wither and die. Light junkies have committed horrible atrocities throughout history. They are demons who feed off the Christ spirit because they want to kill him."

The girl took a pendant off of her neck and held it out in front of her.

"What does she look like?"

"Long blond hair. She's got a bump at the top of her nose."

The pendant began to twirl in various directions. Every time it changed, she let out a little grunt.

"There's nothing you can do. The demon wants to feed off you but you can't let it. It's hers and you have to remember that." She let the pendant twirl again. "Uh-huh. It will destroy her. She's almost totally gone now, but you already know that."

I didn't like the way she was talking, it was too ominous. She could have said it in another way. A dark and oily presence of evil was in the car with us. I wanted out. Mol saw me withdraw and she put her hand on my arm, nonverbally letting me know that it was okay for me to go.

mol and i sat together at a small card table set up for tarot readings. I drank the whiskey in big gulps and handed it to Mol who did the same.

"She was trying to put a spell on me or something. That was weird."

"Don't let her freak you out, she's just read a lot of Anne Rice. She's a good psychic."

"Do you believe what she was saying? About my mom?"

"I don't know. She's your mom. Do you believe her?"

I didn't answer. Mol flipped through some tarot cards that were stacked on the table.

"Pick one."

"No, not now."

"What's the matter?"

"I feel dizzy."

"Are you drunk?"

"Yeah. Really drunk."

I lay down on the cement floor as the earth did its spinning thing, and looked up at the cobwebbed rafters. Mol brought over a wastebasket and put it by my head.

"Take it away. I'm not that drunk."

"You sure?"

"Yeah. . . . Mol?"

"Uh-huh?"

"I haven't been a good friend. I've never known what it means to be a good friend. You're good. Teach me how to be a good friend."

She came over and sat next to me, leaned down and kissed me on the mouth. I immediately started thinking too much. I wondered if I was attracted to her. She had a beautiful face, an amazing personality. Did I dismiss her as a potential lover just because she was fat? What did the kiss mean? Kisses have to mean something, right? They're contracts. She rubbed the wrinkle between my eyebrows.

"Just relax. We're friends."

In a place beyond my own noise I met her for the first time.

There was nothing to say. A real friendship lives in the silences. It's a decision you make.

i drank more. I drank with a conscious intent on self-destruction—maybe it was the black hair, maybe it was loss. The more my brain cells died by the thousands, the freer I was from the story of my life. Mol was drunk, too. We wanted to find the girls again, so we stumbled through the garage maze, knocking down the hanging sheets, cracking up laughing. The older boys playing poker and smoking pot looked up at us and waved when we bumped into some cans of paint.

Through a white sheet we could see a space lit by candles. I started giggling and Mol told me to be quiet. I held my breath. The ambient industrial music was loud enough to drown out the sound of our footsteps.

"You look first," Mol said.

There was a space under the hanging sheet about a foot high. I got down on my knees and looked under. Two of Mol's friends were facing each other. They were close to me, I saw a girl's face in the candlelight and the back of the other girl's dress. The girl looked so serious. Her purple hair near the nape of her neck was damp with sweat. She picked up a knife and held it over the flame.

"What's going on?" Mol said.

"Shhhh. Get down here."

Mol kneeled down and put her head to the cement. The girl facing us put the knife to her forearm and made a small cut. Blood rose up in a thin line. She handed the knife to the other girl who I assume did the same. We couldn't see. They put their arms together. I saw the blood drip onto the floor, a perfect red in the candlelight. The girl facing us put her other arm around the neck of her friend and they held on to each other as if for dear life.

"Come," Mol said. She pulled me away.

"Why?"

"We shouldn't watch them."

"What was that about?"

"They're friends. It's weird. Tamara stole her boyfriend just a month ago. I guess they made up."

"Isn't that dangerous?"

"I don't know. I guess it depends."

i threw up for hours while Mol held my head over a bucket. I lay in her lap on the garage floor near a greasy spot where dust gathered, forming a dense sludge. Some of her friends came and hung out with us. I faded in and out of a conversation they were having.

"Mol?"

"What."

"When I was in junior high I had friends who I partied with and I'd throw up and they took care of me and I felt close to them when I was sick. But then they screwed me over and I don't talk to them anymore. I didn't want to throw up, because I want it to be different with us. I love you, Mol."

"Do you need some water?"

"No, Mol. I love you, Mol."

"Shhhhh."

fifteen

mol reached over in sleep and smacked my face, waking me up. We were both on the floor. It took me a moment to remember where I was, that we never left the party. Still drunk, I got up and gulped down a half a carton of orange juice from the refrigerator, then took a shower. To my distress, only some of the black hair dye came out. I put the black dress from the night before back on and walked into the hallway where I met an older woman who was polite yet frazzled as she asked me if I had a way to get home.

"I can walk, thanks," I said, then went to the living room to give Mol a big hug before leaving.

"Don't go. We should go get coffee," Mol said, still half-asleep.

"My mom will be expecting me. It's making me nervous."

"Call her."

"I can't." I hugged her again. Knowing she would drift off into another hour or two of sleep, I walked out into the bright day.

Once home, I noticed Mom's car was in the driveway and I braced myself for whatever might come my way. At first I didn't notice the real-estate sign, Presidio Home Sales, stuck in the lawn like an ugly price tag sticking out of a dress. I thought it must be some mistake. My thinking stopped. I just put one foot in front of the other, into the house of the demon mother. She was sitting in the kitchen in her yellow robe, sipping coffee, a cigarette between her nervous fingers, shaking slightly. She looked like an actor in a commercial for a drug-rehab center. The bags under her eyes seemed unreal. It took her a moment to look up from her coffee and take in the sight of me in my black dress and black hair.

"Oh, Jesus."

"Hi, Mom. I went to a party in L.A. with Samantha," I said, pulling up the name of a friend I'd lost touch with ages ago. "The hair dye's temporary."

"You're a liar!"

Her lips got thin and her eyes looked like an animal's. She picked up the rhinoceros plate from the center of the table and before I could stop her she threw it against the refrigerator. It shattered, some pieces flew across the floor over to the tip of my boot.

"You're a liar!"

"What. What's wrong now? So what's the deal, has anyone moved into my bedroom yet? Has the house sold? Should I check in to a hotel?"

Her body began to quake. She opened up the kitchen drawer where the scissors and tape are kept and took something out and held it in her fist.

"What's this?"

Poking out from Mom's death grasp was a feathery head. Heda. She opened her palm to reveal her little shrinking body still in the pink bathing suit and sandals.

"What is this sickness? Some kind of voodoo? You weren't in L.A. You were here spreading this . . . sickness."

"Jessica and—"

"Of course it was her. You're pathetic. You're a pathetic liar."

"We found the bird and it was a joke. I've been meaning to bury it."

"You look like shit. You look like a drug-addict punk."

"Is there a point to all this?"

Mom stumbled frantically into my room with a simultaneously geriatric and infantile lack of muscle coordination. She looked like she'd been wound up like that for a while. The whole scene had a an unreal quality. I heard her open my drawers. From out in the hallway I could see my clothes being thrown out of my room. She threw objects, too: a clock radio, a lamp, stuffed animals.

"Get out of my house!" she said repeatedly in rhythm with her object-hurling.

"It's not your house anymore, remember? You're selling it. It's not anybody's house!"

"You tramp! You cunt! Who do you think you are, you lying cunt!"

Being that it was a moment of trauma, I left my body and became hyperrational. What would the Child Abuse Hotline tell me to do? Call a relative. Don't engage with a person in a fit of rage. Flee.

"Did you fuck your father's sluts? Did you and your father lick their cunts? You liar. Who was he with? Tell me!"

She'd only gotten this bad once before—when she lost her alimony case. Soon she would figure out that she was yelling at the air and she would come after me and get in my face and demand that I answer her. The imaginary child-abuse counselor was getting very concerned. *What's happening now?* asks the voice on the other end of the phone. *Object-throwing,* I reply. *Get out. Get out now.*

"Tell me who he was with!"

Glass broke. I took it as I my cue. I picked up my backpack, opened the screen door, and ran, my first great athletic triumph.

I ran down the block, turned left, ran another block and turned right, picking the most illogical path so she couldn't find me if she was driving in her car. My lungs burned and last night's alcohol came out of my pores. Running took the place of crying. The exhilarating taste of freedom took the place of loss. I was exempt from pain.

the public library was hot and stuffy. I caught my breath in the maze of aisles, too scared she would come and find me if I sat in the main room. For hours, I hid amid the walls of books, the archaeology section, to be specific. I looked at photographs of ancient relics and drawings of lost cities and my life in that moment seemed like it might have some meaning in the great drama of civilization. Hormones and fear give you that epic feeling. My favorite book was not an ancient one but a contemporary study of West African culture. I was fascinated by a photograph of "a bottle tree." Outside a small house, a tree with no leaves was decorated with bottles of all different colors. The caption beneath it explained that the bottles are used to attract the ancestors so they can offer assistance to the living. I thought of the Pepsi bottle in my backpack and wondered if I was attracted to it for the same reason.

In the poetry section, I found a leather-bound book by Walt Whitman. A certain poem moved me almost to tears. At the same time, I felt a warm gush between my legs. I shoved my hand down my underwear to catch the flow. I looked around to see if anyone was watching, then took my hand out and looked at my blood-covered fingers. I could have wiped my hand off on the particleboard shelving, but in some primal frenzy I found it fitting to wipe it on the ivory page that gave a home to the Walt Whitman poem. I rushed to the bathroom and went into the handicapped stall. I sat hunched over and stared at the blood dripping from me in long strings. The sticky blood touched the surface of the water, transforming into flowers and tendrils that sunk to the bottom in a psychedelic dance, turning the water orange. My hormones rearranged themselves without any help from me—a coup, a siege, an attack.

st. jude's seminary was a safe-enough place to spend the night outside under the stars. Safer than home. Better than an all-night Denny's. It was once a school where boys were trained to be priests but it closed because of various molestation scandals. Now it houses a junior high. From the soccer field you can see the chapel, a gothic stone building that seems out of place among the tennis courts, palm trees, and birds-of-paradise.

It was after dark by the time I arrived. The fog had rolled in from the ocean and blanketed the soccer field. I lay beneath it and watched little particles of wetness move above me with the liquid quality of dry ice. Sleep took me for a half an hour until I became cold and woke up. The fog got thicker, making my clothes damp. It started getting too miserable to think about sleep at all. Romance faded fast from the situation, leaving me lonely and jumpy at the sounds and shadows. I thought of calling Mol, maybe even Lorri, but it was too late at night. I didn't want to bother them. Still, their voices could have changed everything then, reminding me I wasn't as alone as I felt. Getting up, I wandered around the campus and noticed that the door leading into the main hall was open. I went in.

The bathroom was unlocked which was a miracle, as a small concern was turning into a minor emergency. The walls had white tiles from floor to ceiling, very industrial. After I finished dealing with my blood, I sat on the sink counter and leaned against the mirror, my thoughts turning to Jessica. She was probably housed in just such a room with cold tiles and an atmosphere of antiseptic cleanliness. Maybe she was thinking of me.

Being in that frigid bathroom felt like an act of solidarity. I would stay in that bathroom all night as a prayer for Jessica, penance for abandoning her.

Thoughts of her came with intensity and without distraction until her presence in my mind and my heart was complete and total, a possession. The room became saturated with Jessica. Between me and my thoughts of her, there was a third party, something with a personality and an agenda—my love, some stalking thing that eats.

Did she love me? Was I at least her disaster, her last straw? Was she a liar? Was I a true friend or did we just use each other?

i went into the stall again as menstrual cramps wreaked their havoc and drew me inward to the center of my pain. I noticed a safety pin at the hem of my black dress and took it out. I decided to be Jessica then. Not me, but her, comforted by that somehow. Her name would do. *Jessica* on my forearm, the part of the arm that holds. Well, maybe just a *J*. I stared at the soft whiteness of my arm and my imagination danced on the empty plane of my skin. I could almost see images living under the flesh, like my arm was dreaming. Water, volleyball, a soldier, metal, a sleeping bird, a dead bird in my arm.

I pressed the pin against my skin. Cutting myself would change everything. The skin that held the dreams in would break open. Blood would only come in a trickle but something else would flood the room from wall to wall. Dream sludge. Truth and Lies. Nothing that could be made sense of. Jessica, the body dreams. Don't draw on the body, don't make it speak your temporary thoughts.

i couldn't do it, not even for Jessica's sake. Honestly, I was afraid of the pain and my fear made it seem false, a macho attempt at proving myself. The longer I sat there with the pin pressed against my forearm, the sillier I felt. I was embarrassed, even in private.

I went back out into the fog and stood in the cloud that embraced the soccer field until my skin got damp. The wetness magnified the smell of ivy, plum and orange trees. Despite my state, I was glad to be alive then. I've never understood suicide, for myself at least. I thought of Virginia Woolf, how she drowned, gave it all up. A very sad breath simply fell out of her as she began to sink. Her dress clung and billowed as she went down among the leaves and fish. The sun burst down in rays from the surface. Some tortured English writer with sunken eyes. Things floated and swam in and out of her open mouth as her ghost left her body and went into the world, into me. Just like Jessica. And Mom.

sixteen

i waited till class was over to talk to Mr. Tenasky about my paper, or rather, the absence of it. On any other day I would have felt guilty and apologetic but my dress was smelly and covered in grass, I was hungry and homeless through no fault of my own, and I wasn't going to take any shit from anybody, especially Mr. Tenasky. Sam took one look at me and said, "Oooh girl, go home and take a bath."

"So where's your paper?" Mr. Tenasky asked without looking up from his desk.

"I don't have it."

"You don't want to pass this class, then?"

"I couldn't finish it. I got kicked out of my house this weekend. It's hard to finish a paper when you're sleeping in a bush."

"Why are you here, then? You should have notified the school and they would have notified me. How do I know you're not lying?"

My throat got choked up and I couldn't answer him. He kept fiddling with things. His polo shirt was buttoned down, showing his very wrinkly neck. He smelled like chicken.

"I'll let you bring it in next week but you will be automatically downgraded. The best you can do is a B. What's the title of your paper?"

"Images of Madness As a Response to Childhood Trauma in the Writings of Virginia Woolf."

He shook his head slowly from side to side. "That's not the title."

"It's not?"

"You are not writing some *New York Times Literary Supplement* pseudo-biography. This will be much more difficult. You need to write about the text."

"But the text is tied in with her own life."

Mr. Tenasky took his glasses off and looked into my eyes. "Every writer puts his life into his book. His or her book, if you will. Chaucer liked to hike. Shakespeare, Marlowe, and Goethe all have their little ghosts just like Virginia Woolf, and speculating about them is a great way to get tenure at an East Coast women's college but it won't get you a grade in this class. You will stick to the text or you might as well forget about writing the paper altogether because I won't read it. Have you read *To the Lighthouse?*"

"No, I've read *Orlando* and a bit of *The Waves.*"

He sighed heavily and filled a long silence with his exasperation. "Read *To the Lighthouse* and *The Waves* and look at where she talked about water. Forget about Virginia Woolf. Forget the biographies. Look at the texts and tell me about water. Water. Where and why." He scratched his head and softened a little. "If you do three good pages I'll give you a C. You've done well this semester so far. You should talk to the dean and let him know about your situation."

"Thanks."

"Do you have a place to stay tonight?" he said, sincerity transforming his eyes.

"Yes."

"I can get you some numbers if you don't."

"I have a place to stay, thanks."

mom wasn't home. I snuck in through my bedroom window so as to leave no trace of my presence and quickly changed into a new pair of clothes. As I was washing my armpits with a soapy washcloth, I noticed a bad smell. Vomit. Sniffing the washcloth, I gagged and dropped it on the floor, scrubbing myself furiously with soap. Not satisfied, I took a shower. The cloth must have been used to clean up something evil. The smell of it saturated the house. I opened up the medicine cabinet to look for Mom's pills and it was cleaned out. Mom's bed was unmade and there were shards of broken glass in the trash. Looking for further clues, I opened the utility drawer and Heda stared back at me begging for a proper burial. She had lost her magic since being touched by Mom. She had no girlish mischief, no Gothic melancholy. She was just trash. Trash bird. Still, I couldn't throw her in the garbage. I put her in a sandwich baggie, like evidence of some mad child's sick crime.

The phone machine was blinking so I pressed PLAY.

"Hershey Bar, are you there? This is Dad. I need to get a hold of you. Your mom's at St. Vincent's. She's okay. I got a call from Dr. Walker. You need to go over there immediately and fill out some forms. I'd come down but there's a night shoot. Call 687-5489, that's the fourth floor, Mental Health Services. She's okay. I don't know what happened, they didn't tell me anything. Call me. Love you, Hershey Bar. Don't worry about anything. . . ."

"Anna. I have someone who's very interested in the house. She commutes from L.A. and is looking for a vacation cottage. I think we might have something here. Can she come today? I don't have a key. Can you get me a key?"

Dad and the real-estate agent left a few more messages, each of them sounding progressively more annoyed. I called Dad back and left a message on his machine telling him I was alive. I hung up the phone and faced the silence of the house. Pictures went through my mind. Mom on the floor. An ambulance with its lights flashing against the white plaster walls. Mom carried, mouth open, eyes closed. People talking about her as if she wasn't in the room. Did it happen when I was in the bathroom holding a safety pin to my forearm or asleep under a blanket of fog? Urgency blared on an interior loudspeaker in a language I didn't understand. I didn't know how to react. I sat down. Ate a grape. Waited.

I felt Mom as a memory of rain on the grade-school field, a road trip to Nevada, grilled cheese at a diner, strange and meaningless movies that nonetheless carried a mysterious emotional weight. For an instant I could feel what was lost in all of the nonsense and it was horrible to face so I turned away, stopping the pain before it began. I gathered my things—clothes for a week, toothpaste, deodorant, and cash.

dad should have been there. I had to fill out all these forms in a small, fluorescent-lit office. The nurse informed me that if my dad didn't come down and claim custody of me, I would have to be interviewed by a hospital social worker and possibly end up in a temporary foster home. Panicked, I called him on the phone. He was glad to hear from me, but flustered because it was a night shoot and everybody was union.

"How are you, Hershey Bar? How's your mom?"

"Don't call me that and I don't know how Mom is."

"I'm really sorry I couldn't come up. I will, if it's that important to you."

"It's that important to me. You haven't seen Mom lately."

"The last night shoot is tomorrow and then we have—"

"Forget it."

"No. I can be up by Friday."

"That's five days from now. They're giving me a case worker."

"Let me talk to them."

"Do you know why they give you a case worker? It's for people who don't have parents. It's for orphans. I could end up in a foster home."

Dad argued with the nurse over the phone and ended up lying, saying he was coming up the next day when he wasn't. The nurse handed the phone back to me and Dad explained the lie to me in detail. We whispered in code language until he was called away to work on his film. There it was in all its lucidity. The lie. The Invisible Dad. Sneaky. Charming.

The nurse didn't tell me much about Mom. She just said she'd overdosed on some prescription drugs. I sat in a green vinyl chair and waited for visiting hours. Joanna returned from her lunch hour and came over to see me.

"You're back."

"Yeah."

"Who are you here for now? You sure have eccentric friends. I thought my friends were crazy."

"I'm here for my mom."

"Oh," she said, then was quiet. "Jesus, what are you? Designated official sane person?

"I guess so."

She sat down in the chair next to me. "I wish I could smoke in here. Secretaries should be allowed to smoke."

"We could go outside," I offered, desperate for company.

She nodded yes and we walked down the hall together to the orange door that led to the patio. I sat in a plastic lawn chair while she stood and smoked, waiting till the last minute to return to her shift.

"Have you heard from Jessica?" she said.

"No."

"They don't usually let people call out for at least two weeks."

"Oh."

I could smell her perfume even outside. She seemed like she worked long hours and stayed up late at night, yet she still looked really healthy, like a gym person. Even her hair seemed to have muscles.

"Do you work out?" I asked, looking at her strong arms.

"I walk on the beach. I have these two maniac dogs that eat the appliances if I don't walk them every day." She looked at her watch. "It's seven, you can see your mom now if you want."

"Yeah. I know."

"Let me give you my number here. I mean, I'm sure I'll see you again. Do you know anyone else who's likely to go crazy?"

"I might."

"No. You won't. I know you won't."

I took her comment as a fault in my character rather than a compliment. Instead of losing my mind, I have my mind. There's things in my mind I'd like to lose.

"baby. my baby."

She was crying and her arms were under the covers so she couldn't wipe the tears out of her eyes. They kept rolling into her hair and onto the white sheet. Her skin was swollen and pale. I kissed her on her forehead and sat down next to the bed. There were no flowers or cards in the room, just a copy of *US* magazine next to the bedside lamp.

"I'm sorry. I'm so sorry. You need to get away from me, get as far away as you can. I don't understand why I act this way."

"Don't worry. I'm okay."

After babbling on like that for a while, she let out this deep moan that turned into a heavy choking sob. Not knowing what insanity Mom was capable of, I didn't want to be left alone in the room with her. I eyed the doorway for a passing nurse.

"I'm sorry. You're just a child. I'm sorry."

"It's okay, Mom. Really. Just get some rest. It's okay. I'm fine."

She brought her fist to her mouth and bit it as if to stop the endless crying. I couldn't look at her. Something like love entered the air, hot and clammy, covered in salt. I wasn't prepared. She was like a three-year-old lost in the mall and it broke my heart to watch her. I would have put my arms around her if I wasn't afraid of catching something, of being pulled down into her dampness. I turned on the television and watched the news. Her crying didn't stop, just turned into an animal kind of wail. Telling myself I'd stay for ten minutes, I watched the red hand on the clock go around and around in a circle, just like the crying. When it was time, I got up, kissed her on the cheek, and left without thinking twice, leaving her wailing in her bed.

Going down in the elevator, her crying was still in my ears and on my skin. I walked out into the cool air and hoped the crying would rise up off me like steam and disappear into the dark, but the crying sank deeper. It stayed like a song you can't get out of your head.

seventeen

the really desperate homeless kids hang out in front of Macy's. They make woven Deadhead bracelets and sell them for five dollars but it's the cardboard sign that brings in most of the spare change—*Hungry, Please Help.*

Homeless punks hang out at Cafe Sena and get strangers to buy them coffee with tons of cream and sugar. That's what they live on. At night they wander around State Street selling drugs and hitching rides to shows up and down the Coast. That's pretty much what the homeless ravers do, too.

Occasionally, runaway teenagers can be found outside of the Salvation Army. They only go there for the food and never sleep there. A few apartments are available to kids, all-night party stations where if you pass out on the carpet no one will kick you out. Speed is in, it keeps you from falling asleep in dangerous places. Only rich kids do heroin because they have farther to fall so they can enjoy the ride a little longer before they go *splat.* If you're homeless and on heroin, you might as well forget about ever having a life.

These are small details about homelessness I picked up from stoned boys in coffee shops. Runaway boys like to brag. In a town like Santa Barbara, being down-and-out is pretty fashionable. The runaway rich kids hang out with Mexican prostitutes and punks from L.A. on their way to the Bay area. They party every night in Alice Keck Park and are invited backstage at every show. Being a runaway teen is the next-best thing to being in a band.

Outside of Cafe Sena, a girl with a shaved head was selling a coffeemaker and an old Bonnie Raitt album. Two guys with spiked hair stood next to her, smoking. I walked past them two or three times but they never noticed me. Maybe I looked too privileged, too clean. Going in and out of shops all day was making my brain feel greasy. I wanted to sit down with a stranger and talk but I was exuding that sickly loneliness that repels everyone except psychotics and religious fanatics. I went into a used-clothing store to try on a pair of pants and stood for a while in the dressing room, wearing just my underwear. My thighs seemed huge in the mirror. I grabbed a chunk with my fist. If I could just cut off this much I would be perfect, I thought and immediately got hungry for a hamburger. My body closed in on me, got hotter and hotter until there was no space inside me to rest. I just sat there, tried to breathe as anxiety wrapped me in its metal blanket.

things in my bag: a dead bird—Pepsi bottle—a copy of *Poof* and *Bantha Fodder*—Thumper-list downloads—a bottle of aromatherapy oil (Ecstasy)—safety pin—toothpaste—toothbrush—hairbrush—Mol's black dress—St. Catherine's Girls' Camp T-shirt—a pair of jeans—*The Weekly*—*Orlando*, *The Waves*, and *The Biography of Vita Sackville-West*—three spiral notebooks—Chemistry textbook—Power Bar wrappers—Virgin Mary pendant—a mix tape—pens—lots of sand.

at the library, a woman wearing a gigantic pink dress, carting around a suitcase with wheels, was taking record albums from the shelf. She removed the disks and put them back in different sleeves. She did this methodically and with great joy until she got through the whole top shelf of the classical section, stopping a few seconds before a library volunteer came over with a cartful of books.

She began walking out, then paused to look at me. I was startled. I had spent the whole day being pretty much invisible. The smell of the street wafted toward me from her filthy clothes.

"The days go by like rabbits!" she said in a triumphant proclamation. She walked off mumbling other inaudible things. I got up and walked down the stairs and stood reading *Vanity Fair* by the magazine racks, indulging in the fake escape of fashion photographs and the smell of perfume ads. I was reading a long article about a fashion designer's girlfriend who hurled herself off a roof when I saw Lorri over by the checkout stand—right there, when I needed her most and didn't even know it.

She was wearing jeans and a tight black T-shirt. Her long hair had been trimmed. It hung down just past her shoulders. She was cleaner than me, saner. I felt small but came up from behind anyway and touched her lightly on the shoulder. She turned around, happy to see me.

"Hey!"

"I was standing by the magazines and I looked over and there you were."

"How are you? Are you okay?"

"Yes. Are you?" I said, sounding a little sarcastic. I hate when people ask if I'm okay. It always feels like a power thing. "How's volleyball?"

"We beat La Jolla. Why'd you quit?"

"Are you kidding? I had to quit. I sucked. Come on. You knew how much I sucked."

"You were getting better."

"I was not." I got shy standing next to her. In her presence, I felt something chaotic and noisy beating against my skin from

213

deep inside me. She must have sensed that I was about to dig my-self into some conversational abyss by wallowing in self-pity, so she volunteered first.

"This semester's been hell. I had to get a job at Häagen-Dazs to pay for the damages to the Lexus. My dad has the money to pay for it but he has this thing with responsibility so I have volleyball practice then I have to work. This is my first weekend off. Who was that girl you were kissing at the party?"

That was how she said it. As if it was normal.

"You saw us?"

"Everyone saw you."

"Oh."

"Who was she?"

"Are you doing anything now?" I asked, trying to change the subject.

"No."

"Want to walk with me somewhere?"

"Where?"

"I don't know," I said, lying.

"We can go for a hike," she offered.

"Great. Yeah. Nature. Her name was Jessica."

"The girl?"

"Yes. The girl I kissed."

eighteen

sometimes you can like someone so much that you
want to pretend nothing in your life happened before you met
them. You say nothing about the past because you want the person to erase you and remake you into something completely new.
Jessica was that kind of person for me. Lorri, on the other hand,
made me want to talk about everything. I wanted to start with Jessica, to conjure up her memory and offer it to her as a way of saying, *This is something I love, see this and you will know a secret place in me that
I can't describe with words.* I told her everything about Jessica as we
drove on Mountain Drive with the passenger seat down. I watched
the tops of trees fly by against the cloudless blue sky, enjoying a
child's view of the world from a car. When I started to repeat myself I went on to stories of childhood accidents, the time I stepped
on a sprinkler, the time I fell on a nail and crucified my palm.
When I was with Lorri, my whole life was in the space between
us. Everything except Mom. She stayed in an iron box in my head.
Sirens went off if I touched it.

"Back to Jessica. The bird. What did you do with the bird?"
Lorri asked.

Lorri was fascinated by Jessica. She had seen her around

campus and had always wondered what kind of person she was. When she saw that I was hanging out with her, her curiosity just increased.

"I still have the bird."

"Where?"

"In my backpack. It's kind of gross, I know."

"Do you want to bury it or something?"

"Can we?"

"We can do it on the mountain."

We drove up a dirt road that ended in a small clearing with a few parked cars. A No Trespassing sign was posted on a cattle guard. A path overgrown with grass wound its way through a forest of oak trees bordered by a small creek. We heard the sound of running water when we got out of the car. As we walked up the hill, I held Heda in her little bag and talked about Matrix and Harmonics. I was about to explain the Emotional Roller Coaster Game when I stopped myself midsentence. All afternoon I had been telling Lorri my most tacky stories, making myself out to be a fool. What was she thinking of me? I had to shut up.

We got to the creek lined with huge ferns. Rain was not scarce that season, water rushed over the sandstone boulders, making a sound that was strong and clean.

"What's that smell?" I asked.

"Sulfur from the hot springs."

The barely used trail started to narrow. The bushes grew more dense and soon we were crawling through a kind of rabbit tunnel completely covered by foliage. The sun found its way through the leaves, dozens of golden swords. The trail ended in a clearing the size of a small bedroom. The grass was new, rain-drenched and edible. I pulled a sprig out of its rooted shaft and chewed on the soft base.

"I've never been here," I said.

"I like to come here and imagine it's my bedroom."

"Whenever my mom took me shopping as a kid I always

snuck off to the dressing room and imagined what it would be like to live in one."

"I liked bathrooms at restaurants."

"Absolutely. The ones with the antique couches."

"And ceramic ashtrays that you can steal."

We were quiet for a while, our attention on Heda. Lorri had already begun to dig. The black damp dirt smelled strong. Small roots crackled under her fingers. It didn't need to be all that deep. I took Heda out of the bag. She was a little bit squished and the Barbie clothes were dank from being in the moist bag so long. I expected Lorri to recoil and say something sarcastic but she didn't. In fact, something inside her opened up. I could feel her watching me.

I held Heda in my hand and placed her in her grave.

"What's the story of your life, Heda?" I said.

I would have said more but something about Lorri commanded quietness, something in her muscle and bone, no excess. I covered Heda up and we stared at the pile of disturbed dirt. Falling. A little lost.

I thought my being quiet might allow Lorri the space to talk but she didn't. She lay back on a soft mound of grass and closed her eyes. I studied her face. Small nose, eyebrows a happy brushstroke. She had a strong chin. Peach fuzz. Little-kid mouth. Greek or maybe Russian. Her face taught me things that had nothing to do with me. Beauty for its own sake. Compared to her, my sunny American face was generic, almost boring. She was so much more beautiful than I was. I liked that. It made me forget myself, at least the surface.

Resting side by side, we looked up at the sky through the branches and I felt with absolute certainty that Jessica was going to be okay. Our ritual had everything to do with it. The sun moved past a large leaf that was casting a shadow and the light shone hard in my eyes, hypnotizing me, making me sleepy.

Breathing and dozing, we lay there for a long time, maybe

more than an hour. I calculated reasons to move an inch closer. Asleep and touching slightly, one of us would wake and then the other. We watched each other sleep, thinking things.

She put her arm over me like it was the easiest thing in the world. It was just her arm but her skin, her smell, everything was right there. A wave of desire went through me, revealed through my breath. She was breathing that way, too, fast and heavy. Floating in that feeling for a while, I reached up and entwined my fingers in hers, then I couldn't move at all.

We pretended we were sleeping. I lay there and waited for the heat to come around again and when it did I gave her hand a squeeze. She squeezed my hand back then we went inside ourselves to hide from what was happening. With my eyes half open I could see her mouth nestled into my shoulder, a thousand miles away.

we woke up when all our sun had gone and we felt a chill. Dazed, we walked back down the path, joking about the keg party a week before, not touching on what had just happened.

"It was the stupidest thing. I had like, six beers that night. I was totally drunk but I drove fine. I go to drop my friend off at her house and I open the door and—*thwam!* This car comes by and literally takes the door off."

"Scary—it could have been your hand."

"I know. So I had to call my dad to get insurance information for this lady who's totally freaking out because she just hit this Lexus and she's got like a 1980 Pontiac or something." She reached over and touched my forehead, brushing something away. "You had a leaf on you."

"I always thought of you as this good-girl kind of person," I said.

"It's the teeth. I have good teeth."

"Right. So we both had big nights. We both kind of . . . crashed."

"I guess so."

When Lorri talked, it was usually about her family. Her dad, her brother, her mom. She talked about how she felt pressured by them. When she spoke, it was to work something out, to get real advice. She didn't talk to entertain or fill the silences like most people I knew.

By the time we got down to the bottom of the winding road it was already dark. My stomach got nervous when I thought of my mom waiting for me, angry at the kitchen table. When I remembered that Mom wasn't at home, but in the hospital, the unease moved to my heart and stayed there. In silence, we listened to a song we liked on the radio. Lorri missed the turnoff that would have taken me to my house. I didn't ask where we were going, as if the wrong words could be dangerous, with the power to break a fragile spell. She drove down a long driveway to what I assumed was her house.

It was a large estate of nondescript style, probably built in the seventies, judging from the large windows, sliding glass doors, and use of diagonal lines. It seemed like the property covered a lot of acres though I couldn't tell in the dark. The trees were dense and I could hear coyotes. We walked to the well-lit foyer and Lorri opened the door with two different keys. The entrance hall led into a sunken living room with plush carpet. The color scheme was white-on-white with oceanic overtones of green and blue. The sliding glass doors gave a view of a gigantic black-bottomed swimming pool surrounded by statues of chubby child-angels spouting water out of vases. It was impossible to take my eyes off them. They invaded the living room like a wet dream of some pedophilic interior designer. I was completely seduced and wanted to go for a swim immediately. The sheer excess of the house outweighed the basic fact that it was badly designed. I loved it.

"How gorgeous, can we go swimming?"

"The pool hasn't been cleaned for months."

"I don't care."

"Are you doing anything tonight?"

"No."

"You can stay over if you want. We'll have a picnic out on the lawn or something."

"Great. That would be great."

We walked down a few halogen lamp–lit corners and arrived in the kitchen where her brother sat at a glass table sorting small white pills.

"God, Jimmy, I have guests. What if I was Dad?"

"He's in Sacramento. Want one?"

"What are they?" I said.

"Roofers."

"Gross," Lorri said with disgust. "Whatever happened to the innocent days of crack?"

"Hey, it's cheap."

Jimmy looked about twenty pounds underweight. His boniness was exaggerated by his baggy pants and oversize hooded sweatshirt. His face was long and pale, dotted with acne. Some of the pimples on his temples had little whiteheads and I wondered why on God's earth he didn't pop them.

Lorri suggested that we put together a picnic. She left me to forage in the refrigerator for something for us to eat while she went down to the basement to get some wine. I felt Jimmy looking at me but I couldn't think of anything to say.

"Do you ever sell Ecstasy?" I offered, sounding like a little girl trying to be cool.

"Maybe," he said, with a hint of flirtation, saying nothing else so as to leave me off-balance.

I was glad I didn't have a teenage brother. They're like wild animals you hear outside the tent in the middle of the night, always on the edges of things.

"You should come," he said.

"Where?"

"Universe II."

"We're just going to hang out here, I guess. I didn't have such a good time at the last Universe."

"Whatever."

"The music seemed okay."

Jimmy stood up and put the bag of pills in his jacket pocket and held out his hand for me to shake, a gesture taken from television.

"Later," he said. "I gotta bail."

i cradled sun-dried tomatoes, capers, goat cheese, and French bread precariously in my arms and walked out to the lawn by the swimming pool where Lorri met me with a blanket she stole from her parents' room. We held it taut by each end and spread it out on the grass. I arranged the food on top of it. She forgot the wine glasses then said we didn't need any. We lay on our backs looking up at the stars, not eating or drinking anything for a while.

The night was warm, no difference in temperature between my skin and the air. The black-bottomed pool glowed with a supernatural light, like a superhero's doorway to a middle world. We took the cork out and drank the wine straight from the bottle. Lorri looked like a princess. She spoke like one, talking about things that mattered as if she had a right.

"Sometimes I think my brother's going to die. I watch him leave the house and I try to make a mental picture of what he looks like 'cause it might be the last time I'll ever see him again. Then I think my doing that is what keeps him alive. Sometimes I hear him leaving and I'll be like, 'Hey, Jimmy, didn't you forget your jacket?' or something, just so I can get a good look at him. I feel like that keeps him safe now. Do you do anything like that?"

"I used to think Jessica kept me safe. Before that it was houses. Still is."

"Houses?"

"I visit certain houses around town that I like. Houses are like people. Some make you happy just to be around them, you don't even need anything from them. They just need to exist."

Getting drunk allowed us to talk in slow half-sentences full of meaning.

"If you were a house what kind would you be?" I asked.

"I don't know." She itched her nose and turned to lay on her stomach.

"You'd be a Cape Cod built not far from the ocean, near a soccer field. Old wooden floors. East-facing windows in the breakfast nook."

"You would be a sailboat."

"No, I wouldn't."

"Yes, you would, if I'm an east-facing breakfast nook, you're a sailboat."

"I wouldn't be that. I'd be my house. The one I live in now."

I got sad in an unexpected wave. That part of my life was over. I felt it to be true for the first time. Totally over.

The night had an exaggerated scent and heat. Graduations and wedding parties were always on nights like that. Nights with catering, a band doing B-52s covers, all the kids gulping down half-full champagne glasses left on tables. The air touches you, goes inside and pulls you out. Things begin and end.

It was one of those nights where you might expect relatives to arrive from out of town but in the glow of the pool light, it was just Lorri. The air smelled of chlorine and night jasmine. Not touching her was painful. I couldn't read her body language as she lay on her stomach with her arms crisscrossed, her hand grasping the wine bottle. I didn't know how to get in.

"I feel so comfortable around you," she said. "I don't feel that way around many people. Most of the time it's like I have to put on a show."

"It's because I tell all my most embarrassing stories to you. You're comfortable because you think, 'Wow, she's such a geek, I could never surpass her geekiness,' and that knowledge calms you, puts you at ease."

"You are so funny. You are not a geek. I am a geek."

"You are not. You are like Princess Grace or something. I mean, anyone around you would feel like a mess. That's not what I'm trying to say. You're so gentle, when I'm around you I feel how there's this obnoxiousness in me. I'm not making any sense. I talk too much. I'm drunk."

She didn't answer and seemed a little irritated. I accepted then that I was a total failure at the art of seduction. I would have to live a life of celibacy, perhaps become a goddess worshiper on a Greek island somewhere, wear sandals and read science fiction, have a house full of cats.

I just looked at her, letting that be enough. Her back, the way her T-shirt crinkled up near the waist, and her butt curved up like a cat ready to pounce on a fly. Her strong arms not thinking about themselves.

Drunk and on to the second bottle, I started scheming a way to kiss her without having to ask. Just lean over. Find a bug. Reach for the wine bottle. A moment cleared and the time was right. Her eyes were closed.

"Lorri?"

She didn't answer.

"Hey, Lorri, are you sleeping?"

strange, the way sleep can be such a loss, an abandonment. I stared at her face, looking for signs of life. Not discovering any, I stood up to find I was drunker than I thought.

223

My hands were hot and I relaxed into the night air like a body sinks into the bed before sleeping. I considered going for a swim but ended up kneeling by the black water, tripping out on the way things reflected in the lit depths. Shades of gray tried to find the shadows around the bright, almost golden, pool light. A black-bottomed pool, a good idea, like a river or a lake but safer.

All day I had been concerned about Mom, never once did I stop thinking of her. I went on with things, not knowing what else to do. Her mind was in pieces like broken glass stuck in me and my job was to pick out the shards and put them back together. I was lazy. I didn't even try. I had to do something just to go on, though. Worrying about her was breaking me. Some kind of a deal or a pact would have to be made regarding what part of her pain I would carry and what part I would have to leave behind.

The code: Mom's favorite dress was a blue floral print. I knew that because she wore it to Mastery II. She liked salmon-smelt eggs and lemon ice cream. She wanted to be a wife. Being a wife meant she could enter into a story as old as time, a story strong enough to hold her up while she did the things the world cared nothing about, like picking flowers and making clay bowls, things the world laughs at unless you're a wife. She wanted an ounce of dignity. She wanted goat cheese and naps at two o'clock. She wanted to be absolved of ever having to be strong. Because she wasn't strong, she imagined herself to be a spirit without a body, like an angel or a ghost. She demanded the privileges such creatures get, like not having to deal with anything at all. To be carried.

that night, as part of a deal, I agreed to carry Mom up to a certain point. After all, it wasn't exactly her fault. People had made her promises, that she would have a home and a life that would unfold in a logical narrative but it had all fallen apart, largely because of her own decisions. Still, she gave me life. Despite everything, I feel I owe her for that, not with my whole life but with a part, a math equation I have to figure out in my own head. My own unique debt.

After leaving the poolside, I wandered through the house like a thief. Lorri's house was sexy, but not because it was beautiful. In fact, the house was truly ugly. It was sexy because it wanted to be something. The house was a panicked middle-aged woman wearing too much perfume, armed with a large checkbook. You wanted to feel sexy in the house just to ease the sadness that oozed through the drywall. The house was so artless, sex was the only thing that could give it life, like pornography.

The entertainment center was huge—there must have been over a thousand CDs, lots of classical titles and status CDs like Ella Fitzgerald compilations and *The Best of Leonard Cohen*, even Michael Jackson's recent album. Most of the art in the house was abstract, nothing that could be made sense of as if they liked it that way. The confusion of mishmash substituted for true taste. These people wanted to be liked.

Needing air, I went outside. The Santa Ana winds were rustling the leaves and the coyotes were up to something I didn't want to know about. They moaned and shrieked and barked. Something was being killed or raped. I stood over Lorri, who was sleeping on the picnic blanket, and waited for her to wake. She didn't, so I continued walking down a small path that led to a barn. A ripe smell permeated the air as I got closer. Standing in the corral, still and ominous, was a brown horse. A lost relative. A long-awaited answer.

Drunkenly stumbling forward, I put my arm around the horse's neck, just another part of the night's dream. It didn't pull away or bite. It smelled of musk and sweat. I let my pain flow into its skin and pulled back to look in its eyes to see if it minded. It didn't. The horse just looked back at me like it didn't even know what I'd done to it. If it only knew the heaviness I wished upon it, the weight I tried to place upon its back, it wouldn't have looked at me the way it did. With such kindness.

I petted her nose and looked into her clean eyes then sat down against the fence and watched her, not sure how she felt about unexpected nighttime guests. She looked back at me, occasionally blowing air through her lips and scratching a hoof on the ground. My skin was hot with everything that had been held in, now surfacing.

My mom. My mom. My . . .

A big body in the warm air. A creature wiped clean of excess thought, pure muscle, movement, and scent. Near the horse, I felt safe enough to cry until my bones got washed with salt. I fell asleep just feet away from her. Close.

"hey," she whispered, waking me.

"Is it morning?" I knew it wasn't; it was still dark. Just something to say.

"I drank too much."

"Me too."

I sat up. My face was swollen with wine and crying.

"What's the matter?"

I almost said *Nothing* out of habit, but stopped myself. A confession began. I told her about my mother, where it seemed everything began and where it had ended. A hospital room. A horse corral. All along a crazy voice in me, surprised that such things could even matter or have the power to hurt so much.

When a house is blown up, the drywall separates from the frame with almost no pressure at all. Something in my skin felt like that, coming loose and falling. Falling. The feeling of being alone for the first time ever is falling. Not knowing if you've been prepared to survive, to continue feeling, to love—is falling.

She unwrapped the death grip I had on myself, placing my hands at my sides. I smiled but I couldn't look at her.

226

"I know. I know about your mom."

"How do you know?"

"I just heard. Around school and stuff."

I got defensive for no good reason. She ran her fingers through my hair and I let it go. Desire returned, this time with a thousand wings. A celestial jolt. A fast intake of breath.

She moved closer till she was facing me and we held on lightly, making room for the heat that swept around our bodies. I pulled my head back and our cheeks touched. The smoothness of it was overwhelming, I moved against her face, first softly then with an intense friction that was made wet with my tears.

"I'm glad you're here," she whispered in my ear.

I touched her back, releasing little pockets of desire that went from her body to mine. She reached up with a shaky hand and touched my mouth with her finger, parting my lips. My tongue touched the electric tip and slid down till her finger was all the way inside my mouth. She made a sound and pulled me toward her own lips and I rested there, feeling her breath. I could see her mouth half open against mine and the way our breath took us deeper in. It was almost too much. We couldn't even move.

The coyotes stopped howling and the roosters started crowing. We kissed for hours, wrapped around each other in the dirt, sweaty, lost in the heady, religious world of deep sex. Still clothed, I only touched her breasts. When I saw the light turn silver I wondered if I should have done more.

"What are you thinking?" she asked.

"Nothing."

"No, what? You're thinking about something."

"Can we go to your room?"

i stood and watched her fluff up pillows, move sheets around and arrange irrelevant objects on her table. My

227

body felt separate from myself yet more inhabited than ever before, as if lit by something that had nothing to do with me, like I was in service to it. She lay down finally, and I climbed in bed next to her and held on loosely, kissing. The perfectness of her body erased any touch that had ever come before, both good and bad touch, even ocean water upon my skin was forgotten as her body fit around me. A destination. A way of seeing the world.

I didn't have much to say. In fact, I was a little self-conscious about it. She would say this sentence every now and then, *What are you thinking?* and I would have a glitch trying to trace back my thoughts to where they dissolved into sensation. *What are you thinking?* I'd say, throwing the question back to her and Lorri, always more coordinated than I, would have an answer. *I like the way your back feels. You seem familiar. This feels so normal, like, more normal than anything. Your mouth smells good.* She said the things I was thinking and could have said if I had the ability to speak. I could have said, *Yes, your mouth smells like a grassy place where a deer was sleeping, or maybe, like rain.*

Under the covers, those unspoken laws of stop and go. Wait. What? Just wait. Go now. I reached under her shirt and touched her breasts, very sweaty. Not innocent second-base breasts, but hours and hours of kissing breasts, sex-organ breasts, hysterical at the nipples, and touching them. Her head went back and sounds came that I tried to memorize. She did the same to me, though my breasts were more shy, especially the left one which she gave special attention, wanted to give a name to. An hour or more of breasts. Morning already, everyone into the land of coffee and toothbrushes, but not us.

Our clothes were off in the flicker of an inspired idea. Shy. Backstepping into kissing again. Her knee moving up in between my legs. I felt how wet I was then. Moved my knee up into where her wet hair had turned cold, bereft of contact. The knee, a comfort at last. *What are you thinking? No! Don't ask me that now. You feel good. So do you.*

A delay during more kissing, biting lips, bumping teeth. Drama. Holograms of seeing her at different ages, a cliff, an overlook where a kind of past pain becomes a shared erotic secret. You can see in. Then, trivial histories in ear-licking.

You move on because you might as well. Everything else that has been done before has exceeded the taboos of what inevitably comes next so that the next thing comes uncrowded with meaning, just raw with sensation. I reached, feeling in between her legs, fell in, exploring a not-so-simple terrain of depths and swollen surfaces. Just like me, but still, the other. She held on to my head, clenching my hair a little bit and we were pretty serious then, no fooling around. Maybe it was her athleticism or a certain maleness, but when she came around to do the same to me she quite simply, with two, maybe three fingers, fucked my brains out, all seriousness dissolving until, laughing, I had to stop her because it was almost too much.

There was a place then where we could have stopped, proud of our brave achievements. We even held on to each other sweetly like children, thinking we could get some sleep as the room was getting warmer with midmorning. Sleep was a total illusion, however, and I just kept touching her with my fingers, lazily, until things began to build into a kind of story that was working its way to an end. Wanted to go there with my mouth but thought that might get our minds spinning too much. There are things that I could keep, that I made a conscious decision to remember. We are allowed to save only a few things from a burning house. She shivered in her thighs then apologized. Oh God. Oh God, she said, her head arched back when she came. When I made her. Taking everything. Through the jasmine, the salt pools, the floodlights on the football field. Everything.

I was too shaken to want anything in return. The commerce aspect, the "you do me because I did you" element was unthinkable in my state of transcendent reverence of her amazing body, her whole amazing person. She walked around her room in a robe and I lay in bed in my T-shirt. One moment slipped into another moment in a way that was glaringly senseless and funny; we looked at each other and laughed, getting the joke.

"Now what do we do?" she said.

I shrugged, without words for a change. The Future had disappeared.

nineteen

"can you come by tonight?" Lorri said, dropping me off to meet Mol for our coffee date at Zuma's.

"Yes, I'll call you after I'm done. I should visit my mom, too. I'll call."

She kissed me. I pulled myself away from the orb of us and went into the cafe. Mol was waiting at a table alone. Her long hair was up in French braids and she wore dark plum lipstick, very regal. I didn't know I'd be so happy to see her.

"How's homelessness?

"Fine," I said. I chose not to tell her about Lorri, thinking it might bother her. We were such new friends. Still, it was hard to hide my altered state. Luckily she had a topic of her own to obsess about.

A friend had gotten her a job at a high-end pet-grooming salon. She was being trained to cut nails. All kinds of dogs came in there, big and small, with temperaments ranging from Little Orphan Annie to Genghis Khan. She showed me a scratch mark on her hand from a chihuahua, but that wasn't the main scandal.

"So my friend brushes dog teeth. First she injects them with a sedative, Valium and something unpronounceable. When the dog is out cold, she cleans its teeth. Simple enough. So the day's over and she has the job of closing up the office and she calls me over to the bathroom and she's got this syringe. She's holding it up and she says, 'Mol, this is great stuff. There's nothing better. You wanna go home on a cloud?' "

"Oh my God."

"I know. 'Oh my God' totally. I hate needles but I'm playing it cool because I can't believe what I'm seeing. I want to see how far she'll go. So she sits on the toilet and injects herself with this like, pooch sedative. Her eyes get glassy."

"Shut up."

"They do! I swear!"

"So what did you do?"

"I said I had to finish a paper, maybe some other time. I opened the door and I like, ran."

"Are you going to go back there?"

"I don't think so. I mean, there are some dogs there that you like, never see on the street. For a good reason, too. They're like baby-eating dogs, dogs that were like, marines that were in like, Vietnam."

"Dogs don't live more than fifteen years."

"These dogs did. They made a deal with Satan. And their owners are like these little old diabetic men."

"I missed you, Mol."

"I miss you, too. Where'd you go to?"

She told the pet-grooming story two more times, a little bit different with each retelling. I was starting to wander off into Sex World.

"Have you been rug-munching?"

"What?"

"You have this dazed look in your eyes."

I blushed uncontrollably.

"What did you do?"

"Wow. You caught me."

"What did you do?"

"Last night I slept over at Lorri's house, this girl who was on my volleyball team before I quit."

"Did you do it?"

"Yeah. I guess so."

Mol drilled me on every detail. I filled her in, being careful not to say anything that might affect our new friendship. I didn't know her well enough to tell if she could get jealous. I'd always suspected she had a crush on me.

"Hmmm. It's funny. I didn't want to tell you for some reason," I said.

"Why?"

"I don't know."

"I'm probably the only friend you have and you don't want to tell me that you got laid. What is that shit?" I thought she was mad at me and I got really scared. Mol's not the kind of person you want as an enemy. "I'm not jealous of you, if that's what you think. I mean, yes I'm jealous that you got laid but I'm not jealous that it was you. You know what I mean? Do you think your getting laid is going to hurt my feelings or something?"

"I wasn't sure."

She exhaled and tapped her fingers on the table, shaking her head back and forth. Busted. The sensation of falling started again, the feeling that I knew nothing about anything and maybe never would. I started crying. It was right there on the surface.

"I'm your friend. I'm happy for you, you little shit. Why are you crying?"

"You kissed me that night, I thought . . . I just . . ."

"As a friend, Skye. No tongue. Get it?"

"I'm so sorry."

"Whatever. It's not that big a deal. Do you need a tissue? God, now I feel bad."

"No, really . . ."

"You're not exactly my type." She paused and looked at the

233

wall, still angry. "You've never had a real friend before, have you?" she said, all the wisdom in the world in her eyes making me feel two inches tall. She handed me a napkin.

"No."

"I can tell."

"Can we go outside? I don't like to cry in public places."

mol softened up on our walk. Maybe she felt bad about going off on me.

"I think Jessica's schizophrenic," Mol said. "She was over at my house one night and she just started babbling stuff for no reason. I'm like, 'You want some pizza?' She's all, 'I want the moon, I want shopping carts, stop the noise, bring me a basketball.' "

"Really? She did the same to me. Sort of."

"Yeah. She doesn't make sense at all sometimes. I asked my mom about it but my mom loves Jessica so much, she doesn't want to think she's schizophrenic, she just says she's creative."

On our way to nowhere in particular, we turned up a path and entered the patio of a furniture store that was transformed into an extravagant garden of irises, birds-of-paradise, and other garish flowers. A St. Francis fountain made a home for blooming water lilies. I put my hands in the water.

"That girl who was at the party, the one who talked about my mom being a light junkie? Is she like, a Satanist?"

"It depends what you call a Satanist. No one's really a Satanist anymore. Like, people just want to make a point. Like her, for instance. Her mom is Navajo and sometimes she says she's a Satanist just to get back at the people that converted her family to Christianity but she's totally just this innocent witch-girl who burns incense and carries crystals around in a little pouch."

Mol took an eyeliner out of her purse and reapplied, without use of a mirror.

"I just thought it was kind of interesting what she said."

"She freaked you out. She said something to you and the next thing I know you were throwing up in a trash can."

"She was right, though. About that light-junkie thing. I guess it just scared me."

"She's a little pushy. I mean, most witches abide by the law that you shouldn't volunteer information unless someone asks for it. I think she does it to get attention."

"It was okay. I was out-of-it. Normally it wouldn't have bothered me."

I wanted to talk more about it with Mol but the ideas were so new I didn't trust my sentences to come out fully formed.

"Hey, Mol, can I ask you a favor?"

"Sure."

"I have to stop by and see my mom. In the hospital."

"Your mom's sick?"

"It's a long story. A mental thing. It's not really a big deal. It happened once before," I said, trying to downplay the urgency of the situation.

"Why didn't you tell me before?"

"I don't know. It all kind of happened really fast."

Her curiosity rose to the surface, needing to be fed but I didn't want to talk about it. Words wrapped around the facts seemed dangerous. Everything was going to be fine.

"I was in L.A. when she checked in. I shouldn't have gone away. She wasn't okay when I left."

"Are you blaming yourself?"

"No, it's just I had a bad feeling about going to L.A., not just because of Mom but because of Jessica, too."

"You can't build your whole life around insane people, Skye."

"I know. But I had a feeling, you know."

Goldfish nibbled at the tips of my fingers in the murky water. I reached up and ran my wet fingers through my hair, touching my face. A breeze came, turning the water cold and waking me up again to the hum of my fear.

"We should go."

I stood and started walking. Mol walked beside me, her eyebrows crinkled together, concerned. Her kneesocks had fallen down and hung bloblike around her ankles, revealing her bulbous white calves that had a very gung-ho attitude about life. They cheered me up, took my mind off things.

"We had this hideous cat come into the vet," Mol said, seeming to sense my need for distraction. "It had this bad case of acne on its chin."

"I didn't know cats had acne."

"They do. We had to put it to sleep to pop everything. Pus was spurting everywhere. It squirted all over my shirt."

"Disgusting. That's so gross."

"There were black chunks. White chunks."

"Shut up."

"Mostly just this pink goo."

"Stop!"

"I think it's still under my nails."

Her jesterlike attempt at entertaining me fell flat as we approached the hospital grounds. My stomach turned to acid in one intake of paranoid breath. The sliding doors opened for us and we navigated around wheelchairs and the elderly with canes, first to the bathroom where I sat in a handicapped stall, doubled over with minor intestinal anxiety while Mol reapplied eyeliner in the antiseptic light. After washing pond water off my face with tap water and antiseptic soap, we went back into the maze of shiny hallways where nurses in white nylons walked up and down pushing carts, projecting a necessary though disturbing ambivalence. Tasks everywhere. The utter absence of comfort. Mol was a good song in my head to ward off the bad, that and Lorri's touch still under my skin holding me up.

We entered the Acute ward, aware of the impostor status our dress projected, caught a few glances. Fear smashed me. I took hold of Mol's hand.

Joanna was working that day. She greeted us by the linen closet.

"Skye. I was wondering when you were coming." She hugged me. I fell into her perfume, hair gel, and sweat, barely surfacing, her goodness already dislodging loose bolts and hinges in me till I could have cried, falling apart in a youth-crisis moment, inviting intrusions by doctors and hospital social workers. I tried to hold myself together despite the fact that I wanted to give up then, to let anything else but me take over.

"This is Mol. One of Jessica's friends," I said in a voice, shaky and disembodied.

They shook hands.

"Come to the nurses' station. I have something for you."

Mol and I followed her to the office of half-eaten donuts, instant coffee, and paperwork stacked high like a disaster.

"How can you work in this light?" Mol said.

"It's bad, isn't it? I hear this kind of light depletes vitamin B-12. I take B-12 shots every week. Do either of you want a B-12 shot?"

"Why does everybody want to give me shots?" Mol said.

"Don't get paranoid, Mol," I said, following their banter just barely, my nervousness mounting.

"I like being paranoid. Paranoia is one of my assets. That and my generic self-loathing."

"Oh, I almost forgot, I got this for you." Joanna reached into a drawer and pulled out a child's toy, a plastic blue dog the size of a tennis ball. It was old and dirty; she squeezed it and it let out a squeaky sound. She noticed the blank expression on my face.

"Isn't it pathetic? I found it on my way to work, lying in a field."

"And you immediately thought of me, right?" I took it. It smelled like catsup.

"I thought a well-developed sick sense of humor might be something you could benefit from right now."

237

Mol became inspired. "You could like, do all kinds of abusive things to it. You could drown it in yogurt and set it out in the hot sun and call it Stinky all the time to its face."

"No! Don't do that to Stinky!" Joanna defended. "Stinky needs to be loved!"

I looked at the blue toy with no opinion either way. It looked back at me blankly with painted cartoon eyes. Mol and Joanna's intentions weren't harmful, maybe even loving, but as a salve, they missed the wound of my heart so drastically that it was like I'd been hit. A hot flash made its way through my broken pieces made less numb by Lorri's touch, and I cried then.

"What's wrong?"

"I don't know."

Joanna hugged me. Mol touched my shoulder with a comrade-like distance. Whatever support I had, whatever luck, didn't matter in that moment. When it came to me and my mom, I was alone. For the first time in my life, I had to gather real courage.

"Do I just go to her room or what?"

Like bad news working its way around a room, all joking ended and Joanna took on a businesslike air.

"You need to check in with the doctor, I'll ring for him. We'll be right out here if you need us."

The doctor came walking down the hall energetically. I was expecting a demon doctor, something along the lines of Dr. Hayward and I was surprised to find he was very normal, not sinister and cagey like the underfunded New Age practitioners in my mom's circles. He was younger than I thought he'd be. He put his arm around my shoulder and guided me into a small waiting room.

He asked me how I was doing. I made sure to mention my dad, to let on that I had a guardian so he wouldn't put me in a foster home or anything. To my relief, he took my lie at face value and went on to the more serious topic of Mom's condition. A possible suicide attempt, though most likely it was just a call for help.

Ingestion of drugs that might have caused permanent damage. Tests would have to be done. His clinical attitude was a relief. I was not the problem, just the guest to a problem.

By the time he guided me to the door, I'd already skipped the tracks on my own ability to make meaning of anything. I was just going through motions, thinking about Lorri, pretending everything was normal, like a trip to the dentist. The doctor closed the door behind me and I was faced with my aloneness and Mom sleeping in a hospital bed, the evening light shining upon her body through the window like some elite addition to an already expensive package. Her blond hair on the sheets looked small, like she had the head of a puppy or a canary.

Next to the bed on the nightstand was a recently accumulated array of greeting cards by her New Age friends—angels, galaxies, and Native American shaman images adorned with single rhinestones, small crystals, smudge sticks beneath them. Light-junkie stuff, I thought. Get rid of it. Bring in the *Daily News* with its black-and-white dim realities, toxic with fresh ink. Even I knew enough to realize the cheesy cards were bought at the last minute at the health-food store. No massive amethysts or expensive hand-made warlock-wands for Mom. No one in those workshops really cared about her, not enough to watch over her like a real friend. Not like I was watching her.

The fact she was asleep and that it was dusk, added an atmosphere of importance to the situation and I found myself unable to match up to it. I couldn't feel anything. It was hard to really see her, like there was a veil in front of my eyes that had been there a long time. Her mouth was like Grandma's. Her eyes had changed just in the last year. A battle was being fought through her face between who she imagined herself to be and the person her soul demanded that she become. She was losing. All she was doing was gathering little thingamajigs, cheap theories, anything to seduce this thing called the light to come save her. This thing called the light she paid for with cash, Mastercard, and check, paid for with her own belief system she had sold in order to embrace it. One last bet. Just in case.

There are tragedies. Pieces of ourselves can become irretrievable. There are thresholds we cross that mark a place of no turning back.

She stirred. I gathered everything inside me and went up close to her.

"Mom?"

"Honey," she said, drowsy.

"Do you need anything? Are you thirsty?"

"No. Did you see the beautiful altar?" she slurred. I assumed she was referring to the mess of cards on her nightstand.

"I did, Mom. It's amazing."

"They're going to do a soul retrieval for me at six o'clock tomorrow. Can you come?" She barely got her words out, like she was talking in a dream.

"Yeah, Mom. I can come. Do you need anything?"

"I need some sage. Brian said I should have some sage."

"Okay, Mom."

She drifted off a little, silent, thank God. I looked at her lying there with a mixture of horror and relief. Relief, because she wasn't vengeful or in hysterics. Horror, because, well, she'd horrified me for a long time, for reasons I couldn't name. Maybe just because she was my mom, something in the thighs, the stomach, the jaw, the possibilities of sameness, of backstepping into a decade that wasn't meant for me. The loss of future. Of me ending up like her.

I reached into my bag and felt around for the cool round glass of the Pepsi bottle. I pulled it out and held it up to the light, searching for the opalescent rainbows. There was no ficus tree in the hospital room to hang the bottle off of to make my own bottle tree for Mom, so I just put it down next to the cards on her nightstand. Maybe the pieces of Mom out floating around, lost to the world, might get attracted to the bottle and come for a visit. Might even stay awhile.

The light through the window was getting darker so I went out into the hall, closing the door behind me, finding the fluorescent glare of the hallway almost comforting. I leaned against the white wall and slid down it till I was sitting on the cold floor, my knees to my chest. Started crying. Shaking. A long time passed where I didn't think, just felt the loss of something. Joanna and Mol came walking toward me from the nurses' station.

"What's the matter?"

I nodded my head from side to side.

"Are you okay?"

"Why don't you come outside for a minute?"

"I can't. I have to go back in."

"No, you don't," Mol said. "Your mom's crazy right now, you—"

"She's not crazy, she's just—"

"Skye, this is an Acute mental ward. She's not in here for past-life-regression therapy."

"Shut up, Mol," I said, not knowing why I was being so rude.

"Whatever."

Joanna touched Mol on the elbow, calming her, then kneeled down and put her hand on my shoulder.

"Come outside. Your mom needs to rest."

They walked me to the elevator, one on each side of me, like escorts. We went up to the roof, got out, and stood on the gravel that gave off a synthetic kind of heat, a plastic smell. I walked to the edge to look at the view. Joanna walked close behind me as if she was afraid I'd jump or something. After she saw I was just looking, she walked back across the square expanse to where Mol was standing and bummed a cigarette from her. They smoked without talking. A match struck. A small flame barked. Inhale. Exhale. Feet shuffling on gravel. Wind through the sad trees. I

looked at the ocean in the distance and the tops of familiar buildings, glad to feel empty for even just a minute, undeniably lost in
the beginning of everything. A stone was swallowed that day.
One of those things that never goes away. I turned, leaned against
the railing, and watched Joanna and Mol smoke. They looked
ridiculous and adorable, Mol holding her cigarette like a man and
Joanna like a woman in an old movie, the smoke blown out and at-
tacked by the wind, never getting a chance to form complete sentences.